T.A.P. Woodard

Balance

Cover design by www.mintink.co.uk

Published by T.A.P. Woodard 2018

Copyright © T.A.P. Woodard 2018

The moral right of T.A.P. Woodard to be identified as the author of this work has been asserted by him in accordance with the Copyright, Designs and Patents Act 1988

All rights reserved. No part of this publication may be reproduced, stored in a retrieval system, or transmitted, in any form or by any means, without the prior permission in writing of the publisher.

This is a work of fiction. Names, characters, places and incidents either are products of the author's imagination or are used fictitiously. Any resemblance to actual events or locales or persons, living or dead, is entirely coincidental.

ISBN-13: 978-1981423736

ISBN-10: 1981423737

For those on the journey…

Prologue   Cyprus - The Fissure

The gang mounted the last rise almost as one, skidding their bikes to a dusty halt at the edge of the sheer cliff. As far as the eye could see the blue Mediterranean stretched away, dazzling in the hot sun, almost too painful to look at for more than a few seconds at a time. At their feet the hard rock face fell away in a drop of dizzying proportions to the foamy sea at its base, the impact making them reel back from their initial euphoric rush to the lip.

As usual, Jerome was the first to recover and take the initiative, stepping forward once more and opening his arms out wide. He balanced precariously, his bike discarded carelessly behind him. His head was thrown back as if in an ancient ritual: an acceptance of nature's grandiose design and the frailty of their own temporary existence on earth. The others followed suit, once they had regained their courage. Shutting away their fear of heights, they joined Jerome on the cliff edge, in a sort of primeval group celebration. There was no one else in sight for miles around. Just the five of them, perched on a Cypriot cliff top, with only the sun, sea and hard rocky landscape to witness the moment.

As he had led, he was the first to break away. Jerome signalled the time had passed and stepped back to pick up his rusty bike. They all rode the same machines, low slung single crossbar types with only one brake, operated by pedalling backwards. Handed down from military family to family, as their postings came to an end and the next people arrived. Ideal for side skids. With a foot down, you could let the bike slide away from you along the numerous dirt tracks that traversed the military base on the peninsula.

The others pulled their bikes up off the sandy floor and meandered down from the cliff after Jerome. The boys wore shorts and colourful short sleeved shirts, tan ankle socks and bundu boots. The two girls, lightweight summer frocks and sandals. All were deeply tanned, the result of constant exposure to the brutal Mediterranean sun and a general tuning out of their mothers' daily exhortations to apply sun cream. Even Michael bore streaks of muddy, bleached highlights in his thick, dark hair.

A hundred yards or so below the cliff sat the fissure they all considered to be their spiritual home. Arriving first, Jerome dropped his bike once again and moved to the edge. The fissure was a narrow gap in the small sandy plateau, just below the cliff top. It ran for some thirty feet or so in length and its width was similar to the height of Jennifer, the smallest of the group. The children were fascinated by its appearance. It was like an ugly sneer on a cruel, crooked mouth. Most of all, it was the jet black bottomless interior that fired their imaginations. The fissure was the danger point, where they could prove who could hold their balance the longest, and, unlike the cliff top, this dare had the heightened thrill of the unknown chasm below.

They had run together as a gang over the last few months. In the Summer Term lessons on the Base finished at midday. Their fathers worked out on the airfield, or abroad, flying sorties across the Mediterranean and beyond. The mothers, with an endless two-month summer holiday ahead of them entertaining kids, gladly let them loose onto the peninsula on weekday afternoons, with sandwiches and bottles of squash. As long as they stayed away from the airfield and firing ranges, they could pretty much roam wherever they chose.

On the eastern side of the peninsula lay the bundu – the rocky, wild, uninhabited scrubland that ran for a couple of miles in length. It was crisscrossed with tracks created over the ages by wild animals, and, over the last few decades, by military brats such as themselves, creating a perfect playground of hard rock and dusty tracks leading up to the spectacular coastline. It was their usual routine to meet up at one or other's houses down in the Officers'

Quarters, and then head off for the afternoon up to the bundu, away from prying adult eyes.

Jerome was their acknowledged leader. Tall, with a mop of unruly brown hair fringed over his eyes and shaved high at the back, army style, by the camp barber, he dominated the gang and brooked no challenge. The others were in awe of Jerome and it wasn't past him to use his fists unsparingly, where he felt his position threatened. His brother Michael was unmistakably his sibling – although he was short, pimply, – even at nine – as if all of the beauty genes in the family had been used up in the procreation of Jerome. He was a runt by any standard, but his brother demonstrated a fiercely protective stance around his younger brother and would intervene at the slightest threat or challenge to his wellbeing. The youngest, Jennifer – daughter of one of the Base's doctors – was a quiet, unassuming girl who said little. She was one of those individuals who always managed to fit naturally into the background of a group. Never moaning, or contradicting the others, always keeping up with the rest of the gang on their incessant cross-country courses, despite her petite physique.

And then there was Olivia. Olivia was the sole reason Bartholomew continued to hang around with the others. At ten years old, he was in love for the very first time. Not a physical longing, not even a glimpse of how physical love can grab a person and make them mad for nothing else. Just an idolatrous love of her beauty, her stature and nature. Olivia was twelve, green eyed and tawny haired, long limbed and somehow complete in Bartholomew's mind. Beautiful and easy-going and the one in the gang who kept them all together, soothed the bickering, patched up the differences.

Bartholomew would have cut away earlier from the constant excursions each day out onto the peninsula. He would have preferred spending part of the afternoon at home, head buried in a book, but the lure of Olivia kept him out on the tracks. He'd mistakenly made his feelings too public at one stage: that the constant roving was too much, they needed more downtime at the beach, or kicking around in the back garden. Not unexpectedly, this had drawn particularly harsh words from Jerome. Scorning Bartholomew in front of the others, that he wasn't committed to the gang, he didn't really belong. He had been careful thereafter to keep his thoughts to himself.

At the fissure, they had now all dropped their bikes and moved into position around the edge to play the dare. The balance game, which provided the usual climax to each afternoon's excursion. The gang was urged on by Jerome, who usually won the dare and seemed particularly keen that day to start. Quickly, but gingerly, they moved closer to the edge and slowly turned to face outwards, with their backs to the dark, forbidding crack. In the usual order, they shuffled closer together. At last, they stood ready to take the final step backwards and begin. Who could balance the longest on the edge, without having to fling themselves forward to safety, down onto the safe, sandy ground. They stood along one side, in line, half an arm's length between them: Jerome, Olivia, Michael, Bartholomew and Jennifer.

Jerome counted... one, two, three... and they were off. Each balancing, with just the balls of their feet on the side of the fissure. Staring forwards, arms out, concentrating as hard as they could on maintaining their central equilibrium. When, later, Bartholomew tried to recall the muddle of the next few seconds, he struggled to make any real sense of the sequence of events. All he could remember was breathing deeply, to steady his poise. Then, abruptly, the sudden explosive ear-piercing crack overhead, followed a split second later by another and another, totally deafening him and forcing his attention upwards. He lost his balance. His wind-milling arms, he believed, collided with Michael's, who may or may not have tried to grab his arm. He wasn't sure. Finally, he was able to pull himself back from the brink, and pitch forward onto the ground in a sweating, jumbled heap.

It was then that the commotion above was replaced by another, more sinister, and terrifyingly human sound. An intense, hysterical howl of grief, deep from within someone's core. Bartholomew rolled over on his back and looked over to the fissure, still dazed and confused. Jennifer sat on her haunches at the edge, her hands over her face, screaming and screaming one name over and over again, so that it echoed all around, bouncing off the barren landscape. Jerome and Olivia stood like stone statues, rigid in shock, their faces ashen, staring down into the black void, unable to utter a single word. As for Michael, he was nowhere to be seen…

Chapter 1 The Call

He awoke in a cold sweat, raggedly sprawled across the double bed under the large sash window. Cascading relief flooded his burgeoning conscious state, as he groggily came to. The same old dream, he mused disconsolately, grateful for the morning light that crept in through the tatty blinds. Welcome the day, another night past. He was safe in his own bed, not teetering on the edge of the fissure. The ghosts of thirty years past.

He stared up at the central cornice rose in the cracked and tired ceiling and recalled now what had so fortuitously broken his paranoiac nightmare. His smart phone beeped again on the bedside table. The display told him Kennedy had texted him three times since six o'clock this morning. It was now eight-thirty.

"Need to speak to you urgently," the message brusquely informed him. "Got an assignment. Starts tomorrow. Call me."

No sign off as usual. Lovely, muttered Bartholomew to himself, before deciding not to waste another ounce of thought on something he could never change.

He swung his legs off the bed, stood up and immediately winced. These boxers will never do, he moaned to himself for the umpteenth time, as they cruelly scissored his tackle. He clutched his abdomen as a nauseous wave spread rapidly up from his groin. A good start to the day he grimaced wryly.

Accidental self-inflicted harm over, with boxers and nature's design now correctly re-arranged, he looked at his reflection in the long bathroom mirror. Over forty years old. Dark curly hair, still reasonably thick. Stomach just about flat (God knows how), but definitely a forty plus face. Deeply wrinkled already. Skin a bit pasty. Life taking its toll, he sighed, and then laughing at himself, deciding that was more than enough critical self-reflection for one day.

He dressed and then paused in the small hallway from where all the rooms led in the first floor, two-bedroom flat, wanly surveying his own private domain Apart from a sagging sofa and scuffed black leather armchair, the only other item in the living room was his iPod, set in a cheap mini speaker system on the floor under the big bay window. That, his smart phone, bed and a few clothes were all the permanent lifetime possessions he had here of any note. He wondered what exactly it was all supposed to mean. There was, however, nothing more than a fuzzy blankness to his reasoning that morning, so he decided wisely to leave it at that.

As was his habit, and to provide a quick antidote to the three quarters of a bottle of mid-range Bordeaux he'd consumed the previous evening, he assembled his favourite solo breakfast: Italian coffee, freshly percolated through a battered espresso pot; two rashers of smoked Old English bacon, lightly grilled, and an egg, poached to perfection and pierced across its yellow centre, so that the runny yolk flowed like a sea of joy over the accompanying thickly buttered slice of toasted ciabatta. A touch of salt over the egg and a drop of Lea & Perrins to finish it off. All wolfed down in a couple of minutes – no one around to tell him to mind his table manners.

Pulling on an old, dark grey battered overcoat, he slammed the front door, descended the internal stairs two at a time and exited the building into the cold December morning. Turning left, and at a brisk pace, he reached Earl's Court Tube Station in a little under four minutes. From where he took the District line to South Kensington. To Kennedy's home patch.

In the rich, warm, coffee infused atmosphere of Raulo's Brasserie, he spotted Kennedy at the back. In her usual spot, seated at the last table before the swing doors of the bustling kitchen. Raulo's was a second tier establishment, as far as the wealthy inhabitants of South Ken were concerned. Not one of the obvious mainstream landmark eateries appearing in the tourist guides, or regularly critiqued in *The Sunday Times*. Raulo's fare was just as good, the décor and staff just as persuasively chic, but there were no plebs, no tourists to intrude into the clientele's private ambience. Which suited the regulars perfectly, and made it just the right sort of locale for Kennedy to choose as her private place of business. She could be seen by current and potential clients, but they would know she would always highly value their privacy.

JoJo Kennedy. Ms Silky Smooth. From her handmade pinstripe designer suit, manicured hands, short jet black, glossily groomed hair and round tortoiseshell glasses, you'd never have guessed at a hard Liverpudlian upbringing. Nor by her accent. Richly enunciated, projecting that particular confident aura of a top drawer, southern English (but never specifically named) private girls' school. A million miles away from the tough state school environment, where Kennedy had grittily combated – a few hard knocks, given and taken – and dared to dream of a better life.

"Look at you!" she tut-tutted, as Bartholomew slumped down untidily into the seat opposite and nodded tiredly to José, the cranky old waiter, for an espresso.

"You've been up all night drinking again, alone in that sad flat of yours, haven't you? Contemplating how wonderful your extensive antique furniture and art collection is, the envy of the great and good of Earl's Court. Ruminating on all the glorious successes you've enjoyed over the last few years, as a master of the universe. All the mergers and acquisitions you've personally pulled off, the…"

"Come on Kennedy!" Bartholomew cut over his grinning boss. "Give me a break. You've had me up since six this morning. Early starts take their toll."

She was a real piece of work. Sometimes, he found himself wondering whether or not he found her attractive. In a handsome sort of way. If that's your type, he mentally debated, finally concluding, probably not. The body of a man. There were no curves on Kennedy. And hard as nails, no doubting that. Other than her true origins, he knew nothing of her personal life, of a partner or lover, or other. She seemed to work all hours and brooked no conversation in that direction. The only other piece of information he had was that she lived in Bayswater, and he knew exactly where. He'd found out by chance, on one of the first jobs he'd carried out for the agency, it being in close vicinity to the property he'd been engaged on. And what a way to find out, he recalled, picturing the scene that had confronted him as he'd sauntered up Kennedy's street on a balmy afternoon, in late September last year.

He'd been returning from his wine merchant after a bit of lazy lunchtime tasting. After finalising arrangements for a number of cases to be delivered to the Earl's Court flat, he had decided to take a few sample bottles back to the house-sitting job in Bayswater. Just to be sure, he justified to himself, he'd got his selection right. As he'd turned the key, and began to push open the door to the client's white stucco fronted town house with his knee, he'd heard a woman cry out from the Hyde Park end of the street.

Well that doesn't sound very good, he decided. After retrieving a bottle of the 2009 Fronsac, he popped the Wine Merchant's branded carrier bag down in the hallway and pulled the heavy front door to. As he loped swiftly down the street, he caught his first view of what all the trouble was about. Two swarthy, heavily stubbled men with torsos like Mike Tyson in his prime were trying to persuade a woman into a sleek, black Audi A6. Thing was, she was having none of it and as he got closer, he understood why. It was Kennedy. Kennedy, whom he had quickly come to learn would never be coerced into anything against her will, was refusing to budge. And, after taking a closer look at the two gorillas - once he'd got over his surprise that the woman involved in the fracas was actually his new boss – he had to wholeheartedly agree with her.

Someone had once told him that in moments of crisis charm could be just as an effective weapon as other suitable means: such as in this case, a water cannon, or a baseball bat. He hadn't really thought about it any further: just sauntered up to Kennedy, fine wine in one hand, and after slipping the other firmly into the small of her arched back, had kissed her astonished mouth hard like a true lothario, for a good thirty seconds.

The gorillas were taken aback too. On Bartholomew's breathless: "God! darling, I've missed you so much" – once he'd broken the prolonged stage and screen kiss - they seemed unable to deal with the situation any further. It was as if all their menace had somehow been neutered by the fervent outpouring of love. Bartholomew turned, still tightly holding onto Kennedy, not really sure of his next move - other than maybe to waste a good bottle of claret by cracking it over their thick skulls – however the duo had already silently merged into the black saloon, which then pulled rapidly away.

He guessed she would have hated the idea he'd helped her in such a way. That she'd had to rely on him to get her out of a mess. But he could still recall the way she had touched her mouth with her fingers, where he had kissed her, and held him with a look that spoke as much about uncertainty, as it did of pique, at his outrageous act.

Bartholomew had never asked Kennedy who the men were or why they had wanted to drag her into the Audi. Instinct told him her response was likely to be frosty in the extreme. It gave him some leverage though, and, he sensed, something else in his relationship with Kennedy. Something he couldn't quite put his finger on.

The agency was Kennedy. Or to put it bluntly, The Kennedy Agency was all Kennedy's. She was the sole owner, driver, client liaison, strategist, and, as far as Bartholomew was concerned, far and away the major beneficiary. The discreet, wealthy UK-based client was her speciality. The type that owned multiple, major residential properties and, as typical of their social or monetary elite, spent a limited amount of the year in each.

Many employed live-in staff, but not all, for a variety of reasons usually known only to themselves. A number of them needed a bespoke service that could quickly place trusted staff into these hidden gems and babysit the property. From a couple of days to more than a year, if that was what was required. Kennedy could also arrange security too; in some cases an absolute necessity. For many though, discretion and a low profile were key. Therefore, the solo temporary house-sitter fitted the bill exactly.

Kennedy, Bartholomew grudgingly admitted, had it sussed to a tee. She had cleverly expanded her market by word of mouth alone, via a no-nonsense reputation for trustworthiness throughout the vaulted world of the super-rich. When she told clients "Just leave it to me" she meant exactly that. Leave it to me Mr and Mrs Too-Much-Money-To-Know-What-To-Do-With- It. You can jet off to wherever it is you want to go, and your property will be safe in my hands. At a truly reflective price, of course, Bartholomew judged by the heavy gold Cartier watch and dazzling rocks adorning Kennedy's sinewy wrist and fingers.

Clever client management wasn't Kennedy's only forte. Her second great knack was selecting exactly the right profile of house-sitter. Oh yes, Bartholomew grimaced, she was a real picker on that front too. He had only ever met a couple of other employees, but it was enough to make him not want to repeat the experience. The word loner sprang easily to mind. The type of person who was happy on their own, mature, handy around the place. Ok, pretty robust too, but with no strings attached, footloose, mobile. Probably suffering from commitment phobia too, no doubt, he continued to ruminate. No, he thought; quickly, move on. Christ, what was it with the introspection this morning?

José broke through his reverie by slamming an espresso down on the table mat in front of him.

"Bet you're much kinder to all the rich boys and girls around here, José. Really helps on the tipping front too, no doubt," said Bartholomew.

"Yes, sir, Mr Bartholomew," José retorted over his shoulder, already six feet away, barging through the swing doors. "You right there. You got no money. I not waste my energy."

Kennedy slowly scrutinised Bartholomew across the table, her sharp green eyes glinting through the wacky professor spectacles. He stared back. Bizarrely, he almost enjoyed the duel.

"Enough!" she snapped, crisply commanded in that no-nonsense tone of hers. "Down to business. Here's the brief."

"Hang on a minute, Kennedy. Slow down. Who said I'm available? I've got my nose into something else at this moment. I'm not sure if I'm…"

Kennedy's left hand slapped down on the table like the crack of a bull whip. Bartholomew, cut off in mid flow, shifted uneasily in his seat. Violence generally made him hesitant.

"Cut the crap, Bartholomew. I know you haven't worked for at least a month. That means you're probably hunkered down here in London in that barren fleapit of yours, and good claret and a fixation on fine food are expensive habits. You may have your flat, but, from what I can see, you have no other visible means of income at the moment than what's in my grant. So no bullshit, please."

"You are a man," she continued, hesitating at this point, questioningly raising her finely shaped eyebrows. "You are a man," she eventually resumed, "ideally suited to this assignment and you are bloody well going to do it. Besides, you owe me big time after Mountfort Crescent. I'd never heard of a chocolate fondue before last August and trust me, I never, ever, want to again."

At this point Bartholomew knew he had nowhere to turn. He probably would have accepted the assignment in any event. She was right. He needed the money. It was just Kennedy's assumptive tone that put him back in the old school mode. Digging back against all those authoritative, demanding bastards, who always wanted it their own way.

And there was the chocolate fondue. With the hedge fund manager's daughter. Now, that really hadn't been his fault. He had been told it was a standard solo job. He'd be the only one in the house. It was Kennedy's failure to tell him that the owner's eldest, unmarried, late thirty-something daughter was in town. The one famous for being extremely picky… when it came to the opposite sex. Super vixen princess. Rottweiler number one. Man hater. Disaster striking, however, upon her discovery, one dark evening in the seductively-lit depths of the basement kitchen, of the heavenly, multiple delights of molten Swiss chocolate, turning her into an altogether different animal.

He almost blushed at the memory of it. Kennedy had managed to bail him out the next day, following Bartholomew' desperate SOS call – promptly actioned for her own sake, not his, of that much he was sure. Replacing him with a pug-faced matronly type – who would have been odds-on selection for the England Six Nations front row – she had somehow managed to keep a lid on the whole affair, and, most importantly, well away from the client. But with a typical Kennedy twist, she had pinned the blame squarely on Bartholomew's shoulders.

"Ok, tell me," he slumped back resignedly in his chair, draining the last drop of the bitter espresso.

Kennedy ran her fingers quickly through her hair, adjusted her glasses and, with a thinly disguised triumphant tweak of pursed lips, launched into the brief.

"It's a rural job. Minor country house set in about one hundred acres. Near a small market town called Brilcrister. Little country get-away for the client, about an hour and a half south-west on the Waterloo line. I understand ten odd bedrooms, usual range of ground floor living accommodation, drawing room, morning room, study – roomy – you get the picture. House is set in the middle of the estate, not visible from the road. Most of the land pasture, grazing, or whatever you call it. Good amount of woodland too. He likes pottering around in the woods with his twelve bore apparently. Hmm…" she paused momentarily. "Woe betide any unwary rodents."

"Who does?" interjected Bartholomew. It was Kennedy's wont at the brief to give you the minimum amount of client information possible. He'd learnt from previous experience to get in there quickly, to see if he could ease any useful tit bits out of his principal.

No such luck this time. "You don't need to know the detail," she continued, dismissively. "Just that he's called Mr Eves. You'll be his sole representative at the house. Any enquiries though, questions, requests for contact with the client from anyone else – other than local people providing the usual services and so on – then tell them to call me direct. My usual mobile number."

"Alright then, how long is the assignment?"

"Anything up to a couple of months. Not entirely sure at the moment. The client usually spends this time of year at the property, but he's away abroad on urgent business, with no current return date. I'll obviously keep you posted. Report to me daily initially, but after that we don't need to speak so regularly. Call me though, if anything unusual comes up. Otherwise, once a week will do."

"What do you mean unusual?" He shifted in his seat, something niggling at the back of his mind.

"Bartholomew, it's just a turn of phrase" Kennedy replied, looking at him almost indulgently, seemingly ready to forgive him for what she perceived to be just another silly Bartholomew comment. He felt her scrutinise him once more, as if debating with herself about something which, for the life of him, he couldn't fathom. "Don't worry your sorry little head. Just get down there by tomorrow evening and do the usual. Check the property daily, keep it locked up and secure, make sure the oil tank doesn't run low and so on. And absolutely no visitors."

Handing over a chunky A4 manila envelope, Kennedy continued: "Here's the address and directions. Get a taxi from the station and a Mrs Goode will meet you at the house. Do a thorough handover and then you're on your own. And Bartholomew… just three more things."

"Oh… I'm all ears," replied Bartholomew, raising his eyebrows and then giving Kennedy what he considered his most roguish grin.

"One: your usual terms apply. Normal day rate and any necessary, and I mean only really necessary, expenses. No negotiation."

After a moment's pause, Bartholomew grudgingly indicated agreement with a small nod of his head.

"Two: you are not to live in the main house. It has a one bedroom flat at the rear. That's yours. No sleeping in or occupation of the main building itself – just caretaking. Understood?"

Bartholomew nodded again slowly.

"And thirdly, Barty…"

Unusually for Kennedy; he sensed some procrastination.

"I… umm… I… want some of your curry balls."

Bartholomew slowly exhaled. Gathering himself together, he rose to his feet. Leaning over the table and looking directly down at her, with the most put upon face as he could muster, he replied:

"Kennedy, for the last time – it's Bartholomew, not Barty. And they are curry puffs, not curry balls. You can make them yourself. It's easy – even for a novice like you. So listen up."

"You roast a couple of chicken breasts. Boil and mash a large potato. Shred the chicken, mix in the potato and some tikka masala paste. Add a good dollop of mango chutney. Home-made fig chutney is even better, but that's probably a bridge too far for the likes of you."

"Roll out some puff pastry and use a fluted pastry cutter to make as many little rounds as you can. Then run your wetted, dainty finger around the edges. Fill with the curry mix, bring the edges together and then pinch to seal. Use the handle of a teaspoon to crimp the edge."

"Bake until the pastry turns golden and serve warm with a dip of crème fraiche garnished with sprig of coriander. A whole Indian meal in one, delicious mouthful. Goodbye, Kennedy. I'll make sure I check in with you when I get there."

He exited the brasserie as fast as he could dart between the tables. He heard her mutter behind him, "The espresso, I suppose I could stretch to putting it on your expenses."

***

He had one of the other dreams that night - not where Jerome pursues him relentlessly around the fissure with grasping hands, as Michael's screams fade into the greedy depths - no, it was one from school, in cold, inhospitable Portsmouth: where down through the tennis courts and out onto the ramp beyond - with chest heaving, lungs burning and legs like lead – all he can hear is Solville's steady pounding behind and his murderous, venomous chant.

He hits the foot of the ramp and the black night that envelopes the playing fields beyond. Instinctively, he veers right, staggers on for another twenty metres or so and then cuts back left. He crouches down by the great retaining wall almost weeping at the lack of oxygen and his own naked fear. Solville is crashing around out in front, somewhere on the playing fields, still calling and threatening. He moves quickly left, further along the base of the wall, desperate to keep the noise of his own movements down to the absolute minimum.

Surely Solville is out of earshot, he reasons desperately, as he reaches the end of the wall and clambers up onto the bank above. Scrabbling across the mossy incline he heads back around to the far side of the tatty Sixth Form Block. With his breathing now just about under control, a tiny glimmer of hope surfaces that he might just make it back to the dormitory and relative safety. There is one last hurdle however: the access past the WC Block. It is the only way to reach the protection of the main building. Arriving at the lit entrance, he just goes for it, racing across the slippery black tarmac, safe haven a mere forty metres ahead.

It is not good enough though. Out of the far end of the WC block steps White, smiling triumphantly with arms outstretched.

"So nice of you to join us at last, Bartholomew. Please, come into our splendid office," White chuckles malevolently. "I see you've been out jogging with Solville. So clever of you to warm up before your little nautical outing."

19

He whirls around only to be confronted by a hulking, sniggering Solville, the sweat glistening across his Neanderthal forehead.

"Knew you'd cut left all the time, fuck face. Think I'm stupid or something? Now for your little treat!" He feels his arm being locked into a hydraulic pincer grip, as Solville drags him into the WC block.

He listens with numb terror as White, standing by the urinals, hands in the pocket of his long greatcoat, announces: "This is where you begin your journey, Bartholomew. Where you finally understand that whatever I say goes. Whatever I say…"

Nodding to Solville to hold him tight, White saunters along the row of cubicles. At the entrance to each, he peers over his long, thin nose, tut tutting intermittently and shaking his head before moving on. Until finally, he reaches the second to last cubicle.

"Ah…" he sighs. "Here we are."

With a grandiose, theatrical, sweeping gesture of unfurling arm, hand and fingers, White looks back at Bartholomew and declares:

"Sir, prepare to meet your king!"

Savagely grasped by the hair and with an arm jacked up behind him, he cannot stop Solville ramming him into the confined space and forcing him down onto his knees. He stares at the gruesome display before him, eyes bulging in horror. The filthy bowl is full to the brim with brackish, putrid water and off white swirls of loo paper. In the middle, floating, like a piece of wicked art work by a half-mad pre-Great War German expressionist, is a huge, blackened monster turd.

"Here you go Barty boy!" he barely registers Solville laughing from above: "Time to meet the Royals!"

His head is forced down deep into the muck, before he has a chance of taking even the shortest of breaths. With eyes and mouth clamped shut, as tightly as he can, he just holds on. The water is freezing. He tries with all his might to block out the slimy sensation of the loo paper slowly wrapping itself around his face. Wrenching violently against Solville's iron grip, he struggles in vain to raise his head, but to no avail.

It is then that he feels the edge of the floating beast brush his face. He can hold his breath no longer. Involuntarily, his mouth opens. His mind screaming, he begins to drown. Slowly blacking out, sucking copious volumes of rancid water and the slimy paper, deeper and deeper, into his rapidly filling lungs…

Chapter 2   The Eye

Waterloo Station engendered mixed emotions for Bartholomew. He trudged slowly across the vast concourse, searching the electronic arrivals and departures board for the Brilcrister train. A slightly shabby middle-aged man, in a grey, well-tailored but past-its-best thirties-style overcoat. Carrying a battered green Gladstone bag.

Was this, he wondered, how he would have visualised himself, when as a thirteen year-old schoolboy he'd ridden the train into London? I very much doubt it, he thought morosely. Life ahead at that age had seemed to be so full of endless possibilities, a myriad of opportunities with countless intoxicating horizons. Not the narrow confines of how the journey actually pans out. The decision points which define the eventual path you tread. The mistakes. The inability at times. The languish…

Ah… bollocks, he swore, finally chastising himself, perspective re-surfacing and making him almost laugh out loud. If he'd been a schoolboy today he'd be thinking nothing of the sort. He'd have been Jason Bourne. In the Bourne Ultimatum. The chase scene through Waterloo Station. Imagining himself dashing through the bustling crowds, hiding behind unaware pedestrians, ducking down behind shelving in the concourse shops. With one eye on the CCTV cameras that he knew were tracking him, and the other on the naïve *Guardian* Journalist. The one you knew was going to get shot in the end. Because he didn't listen to me, Jason Bourne, aka Bartholomew, spotty schoolboy from Portsmouth. Now, I'm up in the service tunnels above the station itself, with the sinister East European hit man sniffing along behind, right on my tail, creeping up the metal staircase…

"Sir, excuse me, sir. Do you want the 12:20 to Brilcrister?"

The deep Caribbean baritone burst the bubble of his day dream. The ticket inspector looked at him with a kind, concerned frown, as if he might have one of those poor aimless folk on his hands; one of those the Mental Health Authorities seem to turf out onto the streets these days, as if all their patients' problems had instantly ceased to exist.

"If you do, you have about one minute to come through the barrier here and board the train. Your ticket, sir. Please?"

Presenting his fare and sheepishly thanking the inspector, Bartholomew, finally purposeful, marched down the long platform, under the imperious steel and glazed roof, and opened the door to the train.

He was just about to place his foot on the running board and enter, when suddenly a body boldly bustled past him and swept up into the carriage. All he got was a rushed thank you over the shoulder and a rapidly disappearing view of an expensive knee length, fur-lined hooded beige parka, over high-heeled suede boots. And a particular whiff of perfume. Something about the contact struck a chord, but now was not the time, he thought, as whistles blew and he bundled himself into the carriage just as the train began to ease gently out of the terminus heading south-west.

He sat back in the second class seat of the virtually empty carriage and watched the reversal of society's desire to live cheek by jowl with one another slide past. Packed inner-city terraces gave way to suburban semis and in turn to sprawling villages, then sporadic hamlets, and finally to the open countryside. The cloying, grey blanketed sky cast a one tone pallid stamp across the constantly changing vista. It reminded him of coming home once from a holiday in South Africa, in February. Of leaving huge, open endless space, dazzling light and a panoramic kaleidoscope. To arriving at Heathrow. From Technicolor to black and white.

Resisting the urge to buy a sandwich from the buffet car only to spend the next ten minutes cursing the limp, tasteless offering, he crossed his arms, closed his eyes, and napped. It seemed no time at all before the train manager announced their imminent arrival at Brilcrister.

He grabbed his bag and gazed out at the station as the train slowly came to a halt. As one would expect, the usual Victorian architectural design; high ceilinged waiting rooms and steel framed glass covered platforms. He'd googled Brilcrister that morning. It seemed a typical market town of around twenty-five thousand people, serving quite a large hinterland of villages and hamlets. Nothing of any particular interest, if the truth be told. There might be a good deli or two. One could always hope.

He stepped down from the train and, as he headed for the exit, caught sight of beige parka again, ahead of him, the only other person to alight. Rapidly heading out through the barrier, still with the furry hood shrouding the face.

Passing through the ticket hall, he stuck his head out of the double entrance doors into the car park, looking for an available taxi. At the far end, he caught a momentary flash of a large black vehicle turning out onto the main road, before it was quickly lost to view. Otherwise, there wasn't a car in sight apart from a rusty old Lada, parked skew-whiff over in the corner. He thought he could just about make out a figure in the front seat. Moving back into the ticket hall, he approached the bespectacled lady sitting behind the glass barrier, her head buried in a computer.

"Afternoon," he politely greeted her with a pleasant grin, only to receive a grunt from the other side, but no other visual sign of acknowledgment.

"Umm… I'm after a taxi. Are there any around here, or is there one I could call?"

"What's the matter with Cyclops?" came back the marginally irritated reply.

"Ehhh…Who? Look, I'm just after a taxi."

"Cyclops is a taxi. Outside, over on the far side. Lada. Easy to spot. No other taxis here until past four, when the first rush-hour people start coming through. It's either Cyclops, or wait."

Resigned to the situation, Bartholomew backtracked out of the hall and crossed the car park. Halting by the driver's door of the ancient vehicle, he knocked on the window. After a lengthy pause, the glass was grudgingly rolled down a couple of inches. All Bartholomew could make out through the gap was a flat tweed cap, pulled down low over a bearded face.

"Yes?" bearded face gruffly barked.

"I need a taxi to Haddlewell, which I think is about six miles up the valley from here. I actually want to get to a place called Minsham Court, a little out of Haddlewell. You available?"

"Of course I know where Haddlewell is! What do you think I am? I'm a taxi driver. Don't spend all my time dozing in car parks, you know. Get in."

Strongly resisting the urge to tell the old bugger where to go, leaving him to his grumpy reverie, Bartholomew hopped into the back. Now was not the time or place for getting cussy with moody old locals. He needed to get up to the house.

The Lada pulled out of the station in a haze of blue smoke and a couple of clunky gear changes. The car stank of damp towels, and something else rather unpleasant that Bartholomew could not quite place.

As they pulled onto the main road heading north out of town, he got his first good look at Cyclops in the rear-view mirror. The name was not entirely accurate. His driver had two eyes, not one. It was just that one was at least twice the size of the other, and much closer to the bridge of his nose. Giving the impression he was really only looking out of the one large viewing portal, while the other satellite eye faithfully followed its bigger brother's gaze around. Bartholomew wondered what it must have been like at the DVLC driving test all those years ago. Imagine it, Cyclops arriving in the Test Centre… and the inspector's reaction. Now, that would have been an eye-opener…

"What you doing out this way, then?" growled the bearded big eye, as he negotiated a tight corner.

Tearing himself away from further mind-boggling speculation of the potential hazards of a big eyed world and deciding that a bit of information given away might glean a little local gossip in return, Bartholomew took an open approach.

"I'm here for about a month. I'm a professional house-sitter. My London agency has assigned me to manage Minsham Court whilst the owner is away. D'you know it?"

"Yep," Cyclops chuckled. "I know everywhere round here. Owned by a bloke called Eves, if I'm right?"

The huge, inquisitive eye registered Bartholomew's slight nod of confirmation in the rear view mirror.

"He's not around much, from what I've seen. Don't think he comes down that regularly and when he does he keeps a low profile. Looks to me like he's the type happier in a city."

Big eye studied Bartholomew knowingly in the mirror again, as if already placing him in the same category.

"Wouldn't be seen dead in an old banger like mine anyway! Plenty of bigger fish in the sea around here though, than your man Mr Eves. Lots of big houses, all the way up through the valley. Good shooting country. Very popular with the London set at weekends. Wankers in my view, by the way. The lot of them!"

Bartholomew watched the countryside slide by through the filthy windows and let Cyclops ramble on, little of it of any further value.

After another ten minutes, the car crawled past a sign announcing the village of Haddlewell. They soon entered the outskirts. As it was the middle of the afternoon, Haddlewell, like the Station he'd just left, was a bit of a ghost town. A few cars, mainly 4x4s, parked up along the single street of brick-built terrace houses and a village Spar on the corner. At the far end, a thatched pub straddled the village green. Its sign, depicting an enormous white shire horse straining away in front of an ancient plough, swung loosely in the wind.

"Welcome to the metropolis of Haddlewell!" announced Cyclops sarcastically. "Now on to your ancestral home, sir!"

"Ho ho!" retorted Bartholomew, equally waspishly, although amused by the taxi man's particular brand of humour. The Lada climbed a narrow road bordered by thick hedgerows out of the village and up over the brow of a low hill. In the distance, he caught sight of a large stately home on the right of the meadowed and wooded valley, which spread out ahead for a good couple of miles.

As they reached the middle of the next dip, Cyclops, barely slowing the car, abruptly swerved right in between a pair of formidable brick pillars and glossy black gates. Left open, Bartholomew wondered, for his own arrival? He'd have been surprised if this was a regular arrangement, to leave them ajar. As they flashed past the gates, he was just about able to make out the sign for Minsham Court.

"For God's sake slow down, Cyclops!" he snapped, holding onto to the back of the front passenger seat for dear life. "I don't want to get wrapped around a tree before we even get to the house."

With his driver muttering something rudely inaudible and reluctantly de-accelerating, he was able to get a better look at his surroundings. He had to admit, the trees which guarded the drive like over-sized sentries were pretty impressive. The road snaked on between the huge, gnarled old monsters. It was as if the trunks and exposed sinewy roots were slowly gobbling up the gravelled access way. Forcing it to twist and turn, whilst the crossing boughs overhead formed a morbid, gloomy canopy, adding to the general aura of suffocation.

A moment later, they were beyond the dense tree line, sweeping around to the right and past some iron railings. Bartholomew briefly glimpsed manicured lawns on either side, dotted with rhododendron bushes and a couple of the standard Greco statues you'd expect. Then suddenly, in an arched spray of stone chippings, they ground to a halt outside the entrance to the house itself.

"We're here," Cyclops announced unnecessarily.

Raising his eyebrows once more, Bartholomew got out, paid the taxi driver, and reluctantly accepted a grimy business card. In case he ever needed his services again, chortled Cyclops.

Slim chance, judged Bartholomew, though not unkindly, as, bag in hand, he watched the car erratically skid away back down the drive. Well, he thought, here we finally are. He turned around slowly and looked up to take in his first full view of the house, just as the front door was wrenched violently open.

Chapter 3 The Lumpy Bed

"About effing time! I was told you'd be here by midday at the latest!"

A short, squat, spikey-haired woman in jeans, padded jacket and with a voice from deepest Yorkshire rushed down the steps from the front door. Taken aback by the unwelcome onslaught, Bartholomew dropped his bag and held up his hands.

"Hey, don't shoot me, I'm just the hired help told to be here at some point today. You must be Mrs Goode. I'm Bartholomew, from The Kennedy Agency. How'd you do?"

"How'd you bloody well do too, whatever your fancy name is. I was told I'd be out of here by one o'clock. Not late effing afternoon. Get your bag. I'll show you the ropes and then I'm off. If it's too quick for you, then that's your bloody fault for dawdling, no doubt, on your way down here."

With that, she turned on her heel and marched back up the steps, into the house.

Jesus, thought Bartholomew, looking up at the grey edifice of Minsham Court. What was it with people today? But another, more pressing thought had surfaced at the back of his mind. He'd dealt with many angry and difficult people in his line of work. Both the rich and their underlings could be extremely ill-mannered, in equal measure. He'd learnt mainly to let it go over his head. No, what worried him was not the anger. She was extremely pissed off that was for sure. But it was another emotion that got his worry antenna going. What he found much more disconcerting was the fear he saw in her face.

Bag in hand once more, he mounted the steps and followed her inside. A large hall made up most of the ground floor, its vast floor decked in black and white chequer. A huge fireplace dominated one side of the room, where a couple of high back armchairs and a Persian rug were positioned around the leather upholstered fender, framing the enormous hearth. As Bartholomew scurried after the rapidly pacing woman, he quickly glanced around. All the main rooms seemed to lead off the central hallway, whilst a grand staircase, set against the far end of the hall, swept down from either side of the upper floor, to then join and descend centrally.

It was towards the foot of the staircase that Mrs Goode scuttled, now barking over her shoulder:

"Come on, hurry up! You needn't look around now. I've got all the instructions documented in the back here. Mr Eves likes all the windows shut in the main house, heating on, hall lit in the evening and, of course, the security alarm permanently activated!"

As she neared the foot of the staircase, Mrs Goode suddenly veered right and disappeared round to the side. Following quickly, Bartholomew realised the space below the stairs was walled in, with an inset access door. Passing through, he found himself in what looked like a utility cum boot room.

Mrs Goode was already across the other side, gesturing urgently for him to follow her through yet another door. The utility room had a sash window and a second, partly glazed entrance. Through it, he could just about see the side of some outbuildings, before she pulled him none too gently in behind her through the far door.

"Close it," she instructed him sharply, as he realised he was now in his new home. The caretaker's flat.

He shut the door and they stood facing each other across an old, oak scrub top kitchen table, like a couple of sparring partners ready for the next round. She seemed though, by her less rigid body language, to have relaxed a little now they were in the sanctuary of the flat.

"Ok, take a seat Bartholomew," she brusquely directed.

She sat down herself, looking now more like the professional housekeeper he assumed her to be. On the table in front of her was a blue ring binder.

"In here is everything you need. Details of all the suppliers servicing the house, rota of cleaners, the contract gardeners, local doctor, etc. How to work the electronic gates with the mobile clicker and the intercom system. Central heating instructions, and so on."

"Strangely," she added sarcastically, "most of the mobile networks seem to work round here too! I'm sure the agency have already informed you that the bills are dealt with via the accountant, so you don't need to get involved in any money transactions. On the pin board over there, on the wall, is a plan of the house. Security alarm details, codes and contact numbers, in the event of a problem, are all here in the folder too. Basically, the ground and upper floors of the main house are alarmed. Not the utility room, or this flat." She glanced up at him searchingly before continuing:

"The alarm control panel itself is in the utility room we've just come through. This flat is all yours. It's reasonably warm and cosy, nodding her head over to the ancient but serviceable looking, dark blue Aga.

"There are some provisions in the larder and fridge, enough for tonight, until you can stock up yourself. Lastly, the rack over there by the door has all the house keys. They are individually labelled. One set of keys is for the white pickup in the barn. It's yours for the duration. Insurance is all covered under the house group policy."

With that, she rose to her feet and simply announced: "Right, I'm off then," before heading for the door.

Bartholomew, somewhat bemused, and with a fixed, pleading look, lightly grabbed her arm as she passed.

"Heh, hang on a minute – could you help a bit more?. What about some background on this assignment? You know, any tips, useful local contacts, pitfalls to watch out for, a proper tour of the place…"

"Take your hand off me!" she shot back, roughly pulling her arm away and giving him the scared look, the one that got his antenna going again.

"Come on," he pleaded, trying his utmost to remain polite. "Give me a break. You must have been here for a while as housekeeper for Mr Eves and…"

"What? Look, just let me go and get on with what you've got to do." She reached the door and stepped outside, fingertips still on the handle. "One more thing you need to know. The main gates open automatically when you approach from the inside, and then close after you exit."

With that she slammed the door and a moment later he heard an engine roar and tyres screeching off down the drive.

Bartholomew stood by the kitchen table and listened to the noise of the car dwindling in the distance. Suddenly it was deathly quiet. He stood quite still for a couple of minutes and listened to the natural sounds of the house. He'd have to get used to it. To get to know the place's own particular rhythm.

He dwelt for a while longer on his impression of Mrs Goode. God knows what her problem was. It was as if she couldn't get out of the place fast enough. Maybe, it was just because his loosely arranged arrival had clashed with her own particular travel plans. But odd for a housekeeper, who knew the property well and must have felt a parting sense of responsibility, or at least have had some sort of residual care for the place, concern that it would be looked after once she had moved on. Rather than just the bare essential two-minute administrative briefing he'd received.

Oh well, he decided, best forget about it. He looked around the kitchen once more. It was a reasonable size, yet cosy. He was really pleased about the Aga. It was the best thing that had happened to him all day. At least he could cook. Leading off the kitchen, he discovered a compact sitting room, with another welcome bonus – a diddy, glass-fronted wood burner. Plus, a sofa and an ancient, brown leather armchair. An inspection of the rest of the flat revealed a basic bathroom and, lastly, a bedroom with a small double bed and the usual flimsy wardrobe provided for staff. Plain, uninspiring, but entirely functional he had to acknowledge.

After unpacking his bag and setting his iPod and speakers up in the kitchen, he decided to look over the ground floor of the house, just as darkness was swiftly descending outside.

He searched through the ring binder for the codes to the security alarm and memorised them. Flicking on the hall light switch, set next to the door under the stairs in the utility room, he re-entered the main hall.

From what he could see, the place was in extremely good condition. Light, cream colour-washed oak panelling clad the walls of the hall, creating a soft contemporary feel. A couple of sparkling chandeliers hung above, illuminating the vast fireplace to the right, sited between two large doors. There was, however, little evidence of any personal belongings or clues as to the owner's identity anywhere in sight.

Bartholomew conducted a quick recce of the two rooms either side of the fireplace. Nearest the front door was a vast drawing room. Another marble topped fireplace, backing onto the same wall as its neighbour in the hall, dominated the room. A lot of art was hung throughout. Modernist stuff, he noted. Art was not his forte but it was obvious Mr Eves had expensive taste. Persian rugs, art deco chaise longues and smart table lamps made up the rest of the furnishings. Again though, no personal items.

From the drawing room he was able to access the next room. It was a library, with grand piano and a huge desk, leather topped with an elegant brass inkwell, set in one corner. Made for some VIP no doubt, judging by its enormous grandeur. Do powerful people always have to have oversized desks for all that paperwork, he asked himself? Wasn't it a virtual world now, full of discreet electronic payments made through anonymous shell companies in the Cayman Islands? He guessed visual evidence of wealth and power was still just as important now, when you invited your power bankers or venture capital buddies round.

On the piano he at last found an item with a human link: an elegantly framed photo of a lean faced, silver haired man in his fifties. Mr Eves? he wondered. Certainly he looked the part. Patrician, capable of fitting the perceived image of the master of Minsham Court. You never know though, he laughed dryly to himself, all of a sudden thinking Jeeves and Wooster. It could just be a very good looking butler.

The other side of the hall revealed, as he had guessed, a huge state of the art kitchen. Beautifully arranged. Typically though, he pontificated – without a scrap of character. All shiny granite worktops, top of the range eye-line cupboards and drawer fittings, Bosch ice-dispensing fridge and swanky central island. Spotless, the latest vogue and looking like it had never been used. Basically, he despaired, bloody soulless. He wanted to spill some cooking fat, scar a few surfaces, leave a bunch of mouldy bananas and potato peelings in an untidy, leaking Co-op bag atop of the posturing granite.

And, look at that, he thought, sadly shaking his head. Although there was a large, professional gas cooker and hob at the far end of the room, in pride of place opposite the central island was a brand, spanking new, 4-oven cream coloured Aga. Pristine, with not a scratch blemishing its lovely lines. He grudgingly admired it, as he leant back against the shiny towel rail and warmed his bottom. I really know my place in life, he chuckled derisively - allocated to the old, battered 2-oven journeyman in the spartan flat out back.

Bartholomew stuck his head around the two remaining doors, as yet un-explored, to get a picture in his head of the task in hand. These revealed another sitting room, or what he supposed might have been called the Morning Room, and, lastly, a grand dining room, with long table and antique chairs surrounded by more modern wall-hung art. Enough he decided. He'd have a more thorough check tomorrow, including upstairs and over the rest of the estate too. He closed all the doors onto the hallway, retreated back through to the utility room and activated the alarm. With a small sigh of relief, he heard it beep three times as specified in the ring binder, and then silence resumed.

Back in the flat, before he settled down, he had one last official task for the day. He retrieved his smart phone from his back pocket and scrolled up Kennedy's name. Pressing the call button, he wondered where she'd be. Holding court at Raulo's, or perhaps, snuggled up in front of a warm fire in that smart Bayswater town house of hers.

She answered on the second ring, with her usual dulcet, 'Benenden School' style delivery;

"Good evening. The Kennedy Agency."

"Kennedy, it's Bartholomew," he announced.

Immediately her tone altered, from accommodating to demanding.

"Yes?" And when he didn't immediately respond, "Well go on then, tell me. What have you got to report?"

Strongly resisting the urge to sharply bite back that a please would be nice, he took a deep breath and briefly confirmed he'd arrived and a handover had taken place. The property was alarmed and secure and, from what he could see from his quick tour so far, all looked to be in order.

"Ok, good."

He thought he could detect a little relief in her voice, not just the standard professional interest.

"Just continue on as normal and follow the house management instructions to the letter," she hastily continued. "Make sure you call me tomorrow. That's it. I've got to go now, so…"

"Kennedy," Bartholomew interjected – in his best subservient employee tone – but getting to the real reason why he had wanted to speak to her.

"Mrs Goode the housekeeper. I can't say she hasn't provided me with what I need to do the job, but, frankly, she gave me about as much time as you would a double glazing salesman. It's just a little bit odd that's all. I'd have thought that in her employer's best interests, she'd have bent over backwards to make sure the agency had a really thorough briefing. Any idea why?"

After what seemed like a peculiarly long pause, Kennedy replied, in a flat, even, voice:

"Look, Bartholomew, it's turned out Mrs Goode wasn't really suited to this assignment. So I agreed to her release. And, if you recall, I did tell you that you were the man for the job."

"What?" he shot back. "You mean, she wasn't the housekeeper – she's actually one of yours? Why didn't you…"

"Bartholomew," Kennedy venomously cut over him. "I've already told you. This is your assignment. You owe me. Stop looking for issues. Get on with it. Do your job, earn your money like a good boy and check in as agreed"

He opened his mouth to object, but the line had already gone dead.

For Christ's sake, he cursed, shaking his head in frustration and tossing the phone down onto the kitchen table. He sat there for a few minutes longer, trying to regain his calm. Why did Kennedy always have that uncanny ability to get under his skin? And, to boot, what the hell was going on here?

Kennedy, Mrs Goode. Miserable sods the pair of them, he bitterly cussed. Right, enough. Let's park it for tonight.

As in other times of discontent, he turned his mind to something altogether far more motivational. The larder. He opened the door and was surprised to find the shelves reasonably well stocked, with a number of the basics: tins, spices, flour, sugar, oils and so on. Pretty quickly he'd forgotten about the frustrations of the day and began to plan what he could conjure up from Mrs Goode's leftovers.

The fridge revealed a carton of milk, some lettuce ends, and, to his delight, a block of Parmesan cheese. Plus a half bottle of Chilean Sauvignon Blanc. Kerching! Things were definitely looking up.

Metaphorically jumping for joy, he forged ahead, and within five minutes was well into the assembly. Cutting the end off a not quite stale loaf of bread, he quickly made croutons. A dousing of olive oil and a little sea salt and into the Aga they went.

Next, he crushed a clove of garlic and half a tin of drained anchovy fillets in a bowl, with some Parmesan shavings, white wine vinegar, and a good dollop of mayo from a jar someone had tried to secrete at the back of the larder. He waited for the croutons to toast whilst flicking through his iPod collection. Eventually, after choosing a bit of Arctic Monkeys (to suit his up-yours attitude to everyone else that evening), he laid the table for one. Always partake with a little ceremony, was his mantra. No sense in going to all that effort just to scoff it down like you were standing outside a football ground.

Soon, the croutons emerged from the Aga, filling the kitchen with a heavenly roasted olive oil aroma. Now in serious culinary anticipation, Bartholomew flipped lettuce leaves into a bowl with the rest of the ingredients and most of the croutons. With a tablespoon, he gradually mixed it all in. Then, dolling it out carefully onto a plate, he scattered the remaining croutons on top and finished it all off with a few more Parmesan shavings.

He sat at the table and poured himself a large glass of the Sauvignon Blanc. Silently toasting the chef of a small gentleman's dining club in Marylebone, he took a sip of the white wine before taking his first forked mouthful of the salad. He closed his eyes and cast his mind back to another life...

He had been Mr Man about town. A thrusting, all too sure of himself London property developer. That is a developer with some hard-nosed South African backers pushing him along. It had seemed at the time as if everything he touched turned to gold - all the riches he wanted were there like low hanging fruit, just waiting to be plucked. St John's Wood, Maida Vale and Hampstead had been his playground and between Bartholomew and half a dozen other young property bucks, they'd made a killing out of flat conversions off the back of the inevitable tide of re-gentrification.

For once his backers had turned their noses up at a prospective deal he had in the offing – a large terraced house, located well within what was considered to be the good end of Maida Vale, unmodernised and ripe for conversion at a very attractive margin. They had though, made a point of suggesting some alternative sources of finance and legal services he could utilise. In hindsight, it was obviously the juncture at which alarm bells should have rung out loud: but when you are invincible and all too easily swayed by a sense of your own self-importance, prudence was not necessarily a virtue.

So he'd found himself inviting to lunch one of those faceless finance bods, necessary in such circumstances. Who'd also turned out to be the most incredibly boring individual he'd ever had the misfortune to share a table with. Bartholomew had desperately scoured the menu to find the quickest thing he thought the kitchen could throw together, so he could exit in the shortest timeframe possible.

He'd decided on a Caesar Salad, a first for him. He'd vaguely listened to Mr Finance twerp droning on, then, as he took his first taste of the salad, he recollected how his eyes had closed as a wave of beatific, heavenly joy suffused his taste buds. Finance twerp, still banging on about interest rates and milestone phasing, or whatever, had never the slightest inkling he was sitting opposite a man silently having the gastronomic equivalent of an orgasm.

This isn't too bad either, he surmised, as he wolfed down the last shreds of lettuce and creamy shavings on the plate. Not a patch on what he'd had that day in Marylebone though. Now that had been superbly constructed. Traditionally, with eggs, lemon juice, Worcester sauce and so on. But this had been pretty good for a scratch job, he concluded. He downed the last of the Sauvignon Blanc and decided to call it a night. After all, he'd prefer to end the day with a fond culinary recollection – rather than one of a catastrophic property venture which had very nearly destroyed him.

Locking up and taking a final glance at the security alarm panel in the utility room, he flicked all the lights off. As habit decreed, he stood stock still in the darkness of the kitchen and listened to the sounds around him. Nothing unusual, he decided, after a couple of minutes. Just the wind in the trees along the drive, and a couple of creaking timbers, no doubt from the outbuildings.

Sweet dreams tonight, he prayed. No nightmares. He entered the bedroom and took the last few steps at a run, leaping and twisting in the air, so as to arrive back first on the bed, hoping for comfy oblivion.

He landed with a yelp. The bed was as hard and lumpy as a Rajasthani Thar Desert camel. He clamped his lips tight, closed his eyes and tried as hard as he could not to think another, evil, thought.

Chapter 4   The Dusty Map

He was jerked bolt upright in bed by a fearful screeching. Still partly disorientated, he clumsily donned jeans, fleece and his scuffed brown suede dealer boots before heading out into the kitchen. Only seven-thirty, he moaned, looking at his phone, now realising it wasn't a stray cow gone mad in the yard but the main entrance gates' intercom blaring on and off.

"Yes! Can I help?" he barked at the wall mounted unit, after depressing the red talk button.

"Hello," fired back an engaging, female voice in a rich Highland brogue. "I've a parcel for Mrs Goode. If you let me in, I'll bring it up the drive for you?"

"Ok, here you go," Bartholomew replied in a more conciliatory tone, pressing the entry button, disarmed by the breezy official friendliness. He unlocked the back door, filled the coffee pot (one of the few items he'd brought with him from Earl's Court) and waited for his visitor.

A minute later a Royal Mail van pulled into the yard. A thin, dark-haired woman in her late fifties, clad head to toe in matching red waterproofs and carrying a parcel, bounded out of the vehicle and headed purposely for the back door.

"Hello there, again," she greeted him cheerily, smiling broadly right up to the door.

Blimey, thought Bartholomew. First really pleasant person I've met in 48 hours.

"Hi there," he replied warmly, returning the smile. "Fancy a cup of coffee?"

"Oooh, go on then. Suppose I can take a wee break." She laughed and placed the parcel on the table. "I'm Sheila your friendly postie, if you hadn't already guessed!"

"Bartholomew," he replied, grinning again and shaking her gloved hand.

"Whatever happened to Mrs Goode, if you don't mind me asking? Not that I'm going to be deliriously upset if she's departed for distant shores, I have to say! She hardly bothered to talk to me, but when she did deign to pass a word it was usually a moan. I think she found the place creepy or something. You her replacement?"

"Yes, that's right. She left yesterday," he replied, catching her eye and raising his eyebrows knowingly. "Apparently the job didn't suit her. The agency dispatched me down here instead. Tell me: was there ever a permanent housekeeper here?"

"Oh yes, for many years. A couple actually – Peter and Jo Riss. They left just under a year ago, very soon after the estate changed hands and the new owner, Mr Eves, came in. It seems he prefers to deal only with agencies such as yours. Place used to have all permanent staff – housekeeper, gardener, groundsman and so on – but now it's all contracted out. The upkeep of the gardens and grounds, as you may know already, is carried out by a South African firm. Keep it local I say!"

Bartholomew nodded sagely; he'd seen all the details in the ring binder. Most likely it kept it all anonymous for the elusive Mr Eves. And strategic too. It maintained gossip to a minimum.

"So, did Mrs Goode ever tell you what it was she didn't like about the job?" he gently enquired further.

"No, not really. Not that she'd share with me. I've never known there to be problems here at Minsham. Not in the house that is."

"Here you go," he said, placing a steaming mug of freshly ground Italian coffee in front of her.

"Oooh thanks. Mmm, delicious," she enthused, sipping carefully from the hot mug.

"So," she resumed, "how long you down here for then?"

"Oh, not sure at present," he returned, deliberately keeping it vague but still friendly like. "It's a bit open ended actually, but initially for about a month? I live in London most of the year, so I'm not unhappy about getting a bit of fresh air for a while. What about you? Talking about keeping it local…"

"Yes, yes, I know." She laughed heartily, throwing her head back. I haven't actually lived in Scotland for nearly forty years. Came down to this neck of the woods for a job, after leaving school, and ended up marrying a local plumber for my sins. Still am married to him, luckily! I've worked for the Royal Mail for the last twenty."

"So you're based out of Brilcrister?"

"Oh aye. That's where I live too. My patch is all rural though, north of Brilcrister, running up to Haddlewell and the valley here, stopping at Evensthorpe."

"Evensthorpe? Where's that?" he asked.

"Carry on along the valley road for another couple of miles, going away from Haddlewell, and you're in Evensthorpe. Pretty quiet this time of year. A lot of the cottages are second homes. Should get busier around Christmas though!"

God! It's Christmas next week, he suddenly realised. He hadn't given it a thought. Oh well, not exactly his favourite time of year. So what would you call it then? Bartholomew Scrooge goes to Minsham Court? No, definitely not. That really sounded far too much like a really bad charity shop DVD.

"Ahmm," he resumed, breaking his own inane reverie. "I suppose you get to meet all the great and the good. In the locality, that is."

"Aye, 'fraid I don't get as much exercise as I would like. Basically, it's all up and down the valley in my Postman Pat van, back and forth along the drives to the big houses and farms. There are a good six or seven of them between Haddlewell and Evensthorpe, including this one here. The largest is just up the valley, same side of the road as you. Rissborough Hall. Owned by Mr Gerald Rissborough. Big noise in the county here."

"Crikey!" she suddenly exclaimed, snatching a glance at her watch. "Got to dash. Talking too much, as usual. Can't keep the public waiting for their morning mail! I'm off. Thanks for the coffee and see you soon no doubt."

"It's a pleasure, and good to meet you," he replied. Quickly grabbing a biro from a jam jar on the table top, he crossed out the Minsham address and scribbled Kennedy's name and Raulo's, South Kensington, London on the parcel for Mrs Goode.

"Here, d'you mind. You better take this back. One thing is for certain. Mrs Goode won't be here any time soon to pick it up."

Watching her drive off, he finished his coffee and thought about next steps. He de-activated the alarm in the utility room and made a quick cursory check of the ground floor. Satisfied all seemed to be in order, he mounted the stairs up the left hand sweep to the first floor level. He stood looking down a long corridor, interspersed with artificial palm fronded plants planted in classically styled urns. Hmm… a bit uninspiringly corporate, he decided.

On further inspection, the corridor on the other side led to exactly the same arrangement. The panelled bedroom doors were all shut He paused a while longer, looking down the cold silent corridor – and thought: bollocks, what I actually really need right now is some fresh air and a bit of a trip out.

Retracing his steps back into the flat, he pulled on his old grey overcoat and grabbed his wallet, phone and the keys to the pickup. With a twinge of conscience, he quickly took an exterior circuitry tour of the main house, glancing up and down as he followed the gravelled path around the outside to make sure all the sash windows were closed on the upper floor. With everything looking as it should, he walked back into the yard and for the first time since his arrival, made a close inspection of the outbuildings.

They formed a loose, square arrangement at the rear of the main house and flat. An open-sided tile-roofed barn formed one side. It was empty, apart from a large heap of split logs in the corner ready for the wood burner. A dozen vacant, but brand spanking new loose boxes were sited at the far end. Hmm, he thought, someone's planning an equine expansion, that's for sure.

Finally, he turned his attention to the last outbuilding. He pulled open the double doors to what was a traditionally arranged barn, with open space below and a mezzanine above for hay. There awaited his trusty chariot.

The white pickup must have been nearly twenty years old. Generous of Mr Eves, he jibbed to himself, to kit his staff out so luxuriously. Actually, on closer inspection, he rather liked it. The cab was clean and tidy and in the open back was a large, lockable, watertight box for provisions. Started up first time too. A good omen, he hoped. He reversed out, cranked up the engine and headed out down the drive.

Bartholomew steered the pickup from side to side, weaving down the gravelled drive beneath the menacing tree canopy overhead. Bloody hell, he laughed to himself cornily, looking up at the crazy foliage above, this really is all a bit du Maurier – 'Last night I dreamt I went to Manderley'.

He reached the main entrance. The glossy, black wrought iron gates opened on cue and he swept through, halting momentarily on the other side to confirm their automatic closure.

He was down the road and passing though Haddlewell before he knew it. He was still getting used to the clutch and grimacing occasionally as he mistimed the gears, the engine emitting a horrible grinding noise.

After a while, he had mastered the co-ordination of his new means of transport and breezily trolleyed along the main road in the direction of Brilcrister. This is the life, he thought, and for the first time really acknowledged to himself how badly he had needed to get out of London. Out of the Earl's Court flat and the spiral of inactivity, the obsessive eating, drinking and… yes – he forced himself to face it, the thing that scared him the most – his general sense of apathy. Kennedy for all her shit was right. He needed this job. The alternative did not bear thinking about.

Black introspection thankfully put on hold, he entered the outskirts of Brilcrister and began to search for a place to park. It was the usual town layout. A charming, historic High Street and quaint little side roads juxtaposed with an ugly 1970s modern shopping precinct. The far end of the High Street opened out onto a market square, with a tired statue and fountain, the latter centrally sited, chipped and scarred, pathetically spewing out a dribble of brackish water.

He pulled the truck up in one of the last spaces available and jumped out. One half of the square was taken up by a bustling street market and he headed into the mêlée of shoppers, eagerly purchasing the cut-price veg, cheese and meat on display. Bartholomew quickly worked his way around the stalls, thoroughly enjoying himself. The veg and cheese were good value and he was soon cheerily weighed down with a couple of full plastic carrier bags, after vying with the grannies and local restaurateurs, elbows freely used by all, to secure the choicest produce.

He stored the bags in the lock up box in the pickup and went to look for a butcher. Market meat was for suckers, he reminded himself. Don't ever waste your time on bargains, when it comes to really decent meat or fish. He'd learnt by bitter experience. With the advent of the supermarkets en masse, there always has to be a classy, independent butcher in town. Sure enough, up an adjacent cobbled alleyway, he discovered Edgars. Ten minutes later, and pleasingly bogged down again with a heavy bagful of carnivorous swag, he stowed it away in the pickup box along with the rest of his booty.

In the same alleyway he'd spotted a funky little deli, with a couple of cast iron tables and chairs plonked down outside under a ragged stripy awning. A wonderful smell of freshly baked bread and ground coffee washed over him as he sauntered in. About to order the easy latte choice, he clocked a range of colourful flavourings on a glass shelf above the bar. Go on. Try something new. Why not, he thought. He ordered a hazelnut milkshake, chuckling away nostalgically at his choice. The first sip was marvellous. Simply, bloody, marvellous. Wimpy. Circa 1978. Not so new after all.

He strolled around for a while, soaking up the county town charm of the older backstreets, delaying the moment that he ought to be heading back to Minsham Court to take up his sentinel duties once more. He was just about to call it a day, when he eyeballed a scruffy looking bookshop at the end of a long, non-descript terrace, near the point where the old architecture met the new modern shopping precinct. It must have had some luck, he judged, studying the worn façade and grey matt paint peeling off in great swathes from the thin window frames. Looked like it had missed bulldoze oblivion – in the name of progressive town planning – by a whisker.

Bartholomew could just about make the name out above the door: *Casper's*. The 'r' and the 's' hung forward in a paint curling arch, divorcing slowly from the remainder of the lettering through decades of neglect. He pushed his way in through the door, which swung open surprisingly easily, tripping off a small entrance bell. He had actually expected to have to put his shoulder into it to budge it open, wondering, not unkindly, if the shop ever enjoyed much trade.

Inside he quickly realised he was mistaken. Chortling to himself, he had to say it – nakedly, unashamedly: never judge a book by its cover. Certainly not. The bookshop was vast, its thin frontage belying the cavernous space within. It had aisles and aisles of floor to ceiling book casing, branching off either side of a thin, threadbare carpeted access way to the rear. Sitting behind a cluttered counter at the back was, as one might expect to find (he continued to chortle), a bald, elderly, bespectacled shop assistant. As if straight out of Dickens, jotting down numbers in a pocket notebook with the yellow stub of a pencil.

Plenty of customers too. Bartholomew counted at least a dozen, perusing the extensive book shelving. Not all local either, by the look of them. Perhaps it wasn't just down to luck that *Casper's* had dodged the bulldozers. It would probably have caused a local outrage if they had tried to pull this place down all those years ago.

Mass marches with banners up and down Brilcrister High Street. Petitions to Downing Street too, no doubt.

"Ehmm, can I help you – sir?" enquired the elderly assistant, sizing him up and down, the question still lingering in his eye as to whether Bartholomew truly deserved this form of address.

"Yes, thanks. Hello. Busy place you've got here."

"Indeed," replied the assistant. "That's because we specialise only in quality books. Either second or third editions, in the main. Sometimes first, if we're lucky."

"As you can see," he continued, dramatically gesturing around, "it draws in a wide audience. Local, regional *and international*," he intoned, proudly emphasising the latter. "Thankfully," he haughtily added, "it's not all about internet purchasing for our customers. They like to come in and actually get the *feel* and the *smell* of the books."

As he said this, he rubbed the wrinkly tips of his thumb and index finger together under his thin aquiline nose, from which sprouted two enormous rampant bushes of curly white nasal hair. Bartholomew looked on, slightly alarmed, as the assistant inhaled deeply and tilted his head back, with his eyes closed tight, as if on some higher intellectual plain.

"Ah, yes I see," Bartholomew interjected quickly. "Well, great to see your business is thriving here. Ahm… moving swiftly on – I do need a bit of reading matter to while away the hours. But more importantly, I'm after an Ordnance Survey map. Of the Haddlewell area. Or, to be exact, the Haddlewell-Evensthorpe locality. Do you have that sort of thing?"

Irritated to have been broken out of his peculiar trance, the elderly assistant scrutinised Bartholomew with swiftly narrowing eyes and hissed,

"You're not a surveyor are you? *We don't like* surveyors in *Casper's*. We think they're all council spies. Planning our demise to make way for more grotesque money grabbing development. Just like that beastly shopping precinct next door!"

"Whoa, look," Bartholomew answered, taken aback, backing off slightly, holding his palms up in front of him to calm the man down. Suppressing the urge to remove himself as rapidly as possible from this neurotic oddball, he replied,

"I'm not a surveyor! Honestly. Believe me. I'm just a regular citizen, who happens to want a map. Can you tell me in which aisle I can find one?"

"On the right, third aisle in from the front," murmured the assistant airily, eyes now down, head already buried back in the notebook, as if Bartholomew was just a distant memory.

Bemused and shaking his head, Bartholomew retraced his steps towards the front of the shop. It took him a couple of minutes to find the particular bookshelf he wanted.

Casper's did stock a good range of Ordnance Survey maps. Filling two whole sections of dusty book shelving. But not a single edition printed after 1980. In pristine condition though. He bet oddball up at the counter had got a real bargain-basement price for this lot. With some further searching, he found exactly the map series he was looking for. Minsham Court was named too; he could see it in tiny lettering just off the Haddlewell-Evensthorpe road.

A map's a map, he supposed. Surely the locality can't have changed that much in the ensuing three decades – could it? After a further peruse along the adjacent aisles, he selected a couple of novels too and paid for them along with the map at the counter. Thankfully, his close friend from earlier on must have been on his coffee break, as this time the till was manned by a more rational human being. That is, a twenty something hippy who seemed to be able to say: Hello. Is that everything? That will be £17.49 and thank you very much. All perfectly affably. With a small sense of relief at the resumption of standard discourse, Bartholomew gathered his goods and wandered out of the shop.

Fifteen minutes later, he was back in the pickup after buying a case of *Saint-Julien* – a *Chateau Lagrange 2003* – from the wine merchant on the corner of the market square. Some things you just can't stint on, the trencherman in him reasoned, wincing a little though at the thought that, on his current day rate, one day's house-sitting would hardly cover a couple of bottles of the stuff.

It was only when he was passing back through the outskirts of Brilcrister that he realised he'd forgotten to purchase milk or the Italian ground coffee. Haddlewell soon appeared over the horizon, and he vaguely recalled Cyclops yesterday muttering on about how important it was to support the local Spar in the village.

Pulling up near the Plough Inn, alongside a low chain-link fence bordering the green, he hopped out and headed off across the grassy common. The Spar was the usual village convenience store, offering newspapers and boxes of near-mouldy fruit in an open area at the front, and a wide aisle with display shelving either side to the rear. Milk was easy to locate in the glass-fronted fridge at the back, but the Italian coffee was going to be a long shot, gauging by the generally limited selection on display.

"Looking for something special?" said a soft, honeyed voice behind him as he bent down to check the bottom shelf in the vain hope of finding any sort of ground coffee at all. He straightened up and turned around.

What is it all about, when you meet someone you are attracted to for the first time? he asked himself. As opposed to someone with whom you just want to interact. Everything takes on such a different shape. Your body language. What you say. How you react. The speed of your reactions.

Like in this instance. For a good ten seconds he was unable to respond at all. For Christ's sake, he chastised himself finally, stop acting like a randy, tongue-tied teenager and say something.

"You alright?" she laughed at him, a little of a local accent coming through. He guessed this wasn't the first time she'd had an awkward, middle-aged, dumbstruck, drooling man making a fool of himself in front of her.

And it wasn't surprising either, when he took it all in. Dark, wavy, bobbed hair framed a gorgeously freckled face, cheeky but sensuous month and smoky blue eyes. It took all his willpower not to take a peek at the rest of her too. Judging by the packaging under her sweatshirt, she was either a serious investor in silicone, or just about the luckiest girl alive.

"Yeah, Italian ground coffee actually. It's a bit specialist I know, but one has to keep one's standards up," he replied, now not able to stop himself from grinning at her cheekily.

"Oooh, listen to you, Mr Sophisticated," she teased, still laughing at him with that damned lovely mouth of hers. Turning on her heel and heading back to the counter, she informed him over her shoulder, "You're right though. Spar basic ground variety is all we stock. But I can put some on order for you."

Her walk up the aisle confirmed all his suspicions; that the rest of her was just as spectacular as the front view. The tightly-clad jeaned rear and long legs were downright criminal.

"Thanks. Just the milk then, please." He stood facing her across the counter, neither of them willing to break the eye contact.

"You're the new caretaker at Minsham Court, aren't you?" she carried on. "I'm Roxy, by the way. Help out here occasionally to give the owner a break. Most of the time, though, I exercise the thoroughbreds over at Gallion's stud."

He didn't doubt it, reluctantly – and not altogether successfully – trying to blot out the image in his mind of sleek, toned bodywork.

"Hi, I'm Bartholomew. Very nice to meet you." He continued to hold her gaze with a long appreciate smile. To be frank, he couldn't have stopped it if he'd tried. "News travels fast around here." He wondered where the gossip had come from. Sheila the postwoman, perhaps?

"Yes, that's me. The house-sitter actually. Just arrived yesterday. Lovely part of the world. And, I have to say, all the better for meeting you," he laughed, smiling again. "But I mustn't hold you up. I'm sure we'll bump into each other again."

"Oh, we will. Don't you worry," she smiled knowingly, her blue eyes not wavering an inch from his own. He couldn't but help feel a tiny flutter in his stomach, deep inside. Enough to make him decide it really was time to get the hell out of there and back to Minsham Court.

"We do a van delivery service twice a week. I'll put your coffee down on the list. We'll bring you a couple of pints of milk too."

"No, honestly. I manage fine on my own. Used to it. Please, I wouldn't want to put you to the bother," he replied, with his best spaniel eyes.

"No, I insist. Got to keep our customers happy. You never know, you might get lucky and have me on the delivery rota that day."

She was laughing at him again and, before he could say another word, skipped quickly back to the rear of the shop.

He reflected on the interaction with the shop assistant as he climbed into the pick-up, revved the engine and headed out up the hill towards the Haddlewell valley. All he'd wanted on this gig was a bit of peace and quiet. Still, as he tried to justify it, he supposed it kept him in the land of the living. A bit of bonding with the locals cannot be a bad thing. The local lines open.

In less than five minutes he was back in the flat unpacking his purchases. The map he left until last. Unfolding it carefully, he flattened the starchy paper out and stuck it up on the old cork notice board by the back door, with some multi coloured pins someone had left there for calling cards. He could now clearly see the full profile of the terrain. There was Brilcrister, with its secondary and tertiary roads, spreading out like a spider's web from the centre. He ran his finger along one of the lines and found Haddlewell. He could see the valley he was in, sweeping up from Haddlewell, with the road carving it into two. As Sheila had mentioned, there were three or four farms over on the left hand side of the road as you headed up towards Evensthorpe. The one just before Evensthorpe was named Gallion's. Presumably the stud. Hmm, he thought. Moving quickly on, he studied the ground the other side of the road. There was Minsham Court again, the house surrounded by open land and fenced paddocks. Directly to the north, a wide belt of woodland ran for some way, before breaking out again into open pasture. And there, just beyond, was Rissborough Hall. Yes, it was clearly the largest estate of note in the area, according to the map. It must have been the sandstone coloured stately pile he'd spotted on the way up here with Cyclops.

It was only much later, whist reading in bed, side light on and a glass of the *Saint-Julien* beside him, that he wondered whether he should have checked in with Kennedy. Not able to face another confrontational spat, he decided to leave it. No news was good news after all. Eventually, he switched the light off and slept.

***

He thought it was the Rose Tremain novel. A Letter to Sister Benedicta. One of the two he'd picked up in Casper's. Her second novel, from 1978, and oddly disturbing in parts. Everyone was very depressed and sleeping with somebody they shouldn't be sleeping with, including a brother and sister. Clever book, which set him off. This time, though, the dream wasn't about Jerome or the one where he was slowly drowning in putrid water. This was a slow mechanical banging noise, from somewhere just always out of reach, right on the edge of his consciousness it seemed. When he thought he was about to identify what it was, out in the blackness beyond, the noise cleverly faded and moved further away.

He sat up abruptly in the darkness. Shit. It wasn't anything to do with Rose Tremain. Or a dream. It was a noise outside. He decided to leave the light off and grabbed his mobile from the side table to check the time under the bedclothes. Half past two in the morning. What the hell is that, he worried, hearing the slow knocking noise again. Almost as if someone, or something, was banging a hard object against a metal surface. But it was moving around, closer to the house for a while and then moving further away, as before.

Oh God, he groaned; this is all I need. Taking stock, still on the bed, he wondered, his nerves twanging, what he could use for a weapon if he needed one. Finally, he told himself: stop dramatizing, get your clothes on and go out and find out what the hell's going on. Clumsily struggling into his jeans and top, he eventually managed to locate his boots near the door. He crept out towards the kitchen, and in his heightened state of trepidation couldn't quite manage to clench his buttocks tightly enough together. As he stepped through the door, he was unable to suppress the most enormous, ripping fart. Bloody hell, he thought, his nerves making him giggle almost helplessly - and setting off another couple of high pitched squeaks - if that doesn't alert them to the fact someone is awake, then God knows what will.

In the darkness of the kitchen, he managed to calm down a little. He stood and thought for a moment. Recalling earlier seeing a large plastic torch on top of a cupboard near the Aga, he reached up in the pitch black and groped around the cupboard door, before finding the edge of the top. Feeling around gingerly, his fingertips eventually brushed against the hard, plastic tube handle. Bringing it down, he pressed the switch, and a powerful beam shot out across the kitchen floor.

First things first, he decided, grimly. Opening the door to the utility/boot room, he flashed the beam onto the security alarm panel on the far side of the room, as he approached. All seemed to be in order. De-activating the alarm, he moved into the hall and slowly commenced a tour of the ground floor of the main house. Not sure whether to switch all the lights on or to rely on the torch; for some reason he couldn't quite fathom, he decided on the latter. The rooms were all as before, emptily silent. He couldn't see a thing out of place, or a window that wasn't shut tight. His inspection of the first floor revealed exactly the same unchanged state of affairs as down below.

Descending once more, he retreated into the utility room and re-activated the alarm. Ok, he steeled himself, now for the tricky bit. Let's take a look outside. Shoving his mobile into the back of his jeans pocket, he donned the overcoat and unlocked the back door.

Grabbing the torch once more, he stepped outside onto the gravel. The grey cloud cover, from earlier in the day, clearly hadn't moved on. It was absolutely pitch black, until, as he took a couple of steps forward, a security light above the back door to the flat burst on, illuminating the outbuildings in its glare.

Still unable to see anything out of order, he moved around the side of the house to the front drive. Keeping close to the edge of the building, he flicked the torch up and down, over the windows on both floors, and then back out and across the sweeping lawns. The rhododendrons loomed out of the dark like a herd of ghostly mammoths, swaying gently in the chilly night wind. He walked silently on, past the front door and then on beyond to the far side.

Eventually ending up where he had started by the back door to the flat, he suddenly realised the obvious. The noise had ceased. In fact, so lost had he been in his focus on checking the house over, that now, thinking back, he couldn't recall hearing it at all since he'd exited the kitchen. Heartened somewhat by the knowledge that whatever had been out there had now hopefully gone, he took a tour around the outbuildings.

Arriving back at the corner of the open barn, he halted by a covered lean-to sheltering the re-cycling bins. He noticed that one of the bins – the only iron one amongst the other plastic variety – lay on its side, the lid a few feet beyond. Could this have been knocking somehow, against the rear of the corrugated ironclad side of the barn? Placing the torch on the ground, he bent down to pick it up. As his hand reached for the upturned bin, something shot out from underneath and scurried across his arm. It gave him an almighty fright and with a loud yelp, he leapt in the air, losing his balance as he did so, and with arms and legs flailing, landed heavily in a heap, flat on his back.

Gasping and wheezing, he rolled onto his side and stood up, dusting old strands of straw and muck off his trousers and coat. It was a bloody cat, he cursed, having had just about enough excitement for one night. Blasted mog must have knocked the bin over, and consequently, it had been jarring against the barn by the force of the wind. He righted the bin, fixed on the lid and jammed it firmly up underneath the lean-to, before marching back around to the kitchen door. The cheeky creature had even the nerve to be waiting for him by the entrance to the flat. It was as black as coal, with one white paw, sitting there cleaning itself without a care in the world. Bloody thing. He ought to give it the toe of his boot.

Re-gaining some sense of self-equilibrium, he gave it a saucer of milk instead. Leaving the cat outside on the door step, he brewed a hot cup of cocoa, heavily laced with sugar, and took himself back off to bed. He lay on the lumpy mattress, allowing the heat and richness of the cocoa to gently lull him off to sleep, whilst wondering: yes, a cat can knock a bin over, but how did it manage to orchestrate such a range of noise too?

Chapter 5   The Shadow

After his night excursion, he was dead to the world until nearly ten o'clock the next morning. Arising groggily, he stood in the kitchen, rubbing his bleary eyes before drinking a couple of strong cups of the Italian blended coffee as he peered out through the kitchen window. The weather hadn't much improved either. No rain but still deeply overcast, with a chilly wind coming in from the east.

Two boiled eggs and a couple of slices of buttered toasted ciabatta later, he felt somewhat re-energised. Wiping the last of the egg yolk off the plate with an end piece of toast, he munched with satisfaction as he took another look at the Ordnance Survey map on the wall. Last night was a joke. He had felt like a prisoner in the house, not really sure of what was out there or how anybody or anything could actually get near the building. He'd considered reporting the incident to the police in the night, but had prevaricated, knowing he didn't really have anything concrete to say to them. What… that he'd heard a knocking noise from somewhere outside, which came and went, and when he discovered a bin lid had blown off behind the barn it stopped altogether? No, a waste of time, he concluded. What he ought to do was to have a good recce of the grounds. Walk the boundary, check the fencing. See if there was an obvious way someone could easily access the estate, unobtrusively.

He had a look in the ring binder. The South African maintenance team were due this afternoon. He'd talk to them to see if he could glean anything useful. Pulling on his overcoat, he wandered into the utility-cum-boot room and cast his eye around. Amongst a jumble of wellies by the door to the rear, he managed to find a neoprene-lined, French branded pair. A perfect fit. On a rack above, he spotted a well-made but slightly battered, brown felt fedora. Trying it on, he was surprised again to find how it snugly moulded to his head. Crikey, he laughed, unless these belonged to the handsome butler whose picture stood on the grand piano, he and Mr Eves must be dead ringers.

As he moved back into the flat, another item caught his eye: a long hazel staff with a fork at its head. Grabbing it and trying it out for size, he decided to take it too. Yes, quite the sage, he declared to himself, part jokingly part – he had to admit – narcissistically, as he caught his reflection in the kitchen window.

He set off southwards, skirting the outbuildings and heading off across the first paddock. Two fields later, under the dark threatening sky, he arrived at what appeared to be the estate boundary. Six-foot-high timber staking and pig netting ran directly left and right. One direction led towards the Haddlewell /Evensthorpe road, the other over the brow of a little hill. The fence matched with what he could recall of the likely boundary line on the Ordnance Survey map, so he set off in the direction heading away from the main road. Passing over the small hill and along the edge of a number of further paddocks, the fencing then struck left, heading up towards the vast belt of woodland north of Minsham Court itself. He paused on a piece of higher ground, which provided a perfect view down onto the house. From this vantage point, Bartholomew could see all the detailing of the tiled roof, the colonnaded parapets and, beyond, the sweep of gravelled drive, weaving off towards the estate entrance before disappearing underneath the canopied avenue of trees.

On reaching the line of the wood, it confirmed to him that the fence and netting continued on into the trees. All in pretty good condition too. It would present a difficult but not impossible climb for an intruder, although, so far he could see, there were no obvious signs of forced entry. About turning, he re-traced his steps to his starting point and then carried on further, until he finally reached the road. The boundary here was all traditional brick estate walling, which was easily eight feet high. A small belt of trees ran along the inner edge of the wall. As he meandered through the low level ash, he could see the top of the wall had a jagged brick edge. Installed many years ago, presumably to deter those members of the public actually curious enough to try to climb the wall and see what lay within.

Finally, he reached the front gates and seeing that the wall continued on up into the large belt of trees, he decided to strike back towards the house and then head north into the central section of the wood. There was something about the walk through the shrouded avenue, though, that sent a shiver down his spine, set his teeth on edge. The constant gloom didn't help either. All in all, it created a forbidding, threatening atmosphere, the feel of which he couldn't quite shake off. He wondered, tetchily, whether it was all just in his own mind, still in overdrive after the tribulations of the night before.

Grateful to reach the end of the drive, he turned left in front of the house and after crossing more paddocks, all immaculately maintained, he arrived once more at the fringe of belted woodland.

He was startled immediately by a burst of wildlife, shattering the stillness. He'd spooked a couple of flighty pigeons. They jinked around above, rapidly putting some height and distance between themselves and their unexpected interloper.

Pushing on in through a fringe of scrub and bush, he stepped out onto the floor proper of the wood. It was mainly populated by oak, beech and ash, and, although not formally planted, it was clearly managed on a regular basis. At the point he had entered there was no discernible footpath, so prodding ahead of him with the staff, he set off in a rough northerly direction, away from the house.

After some five minutes, the trees thinned out and ahead he began to make out a clearing, where a greater amount of light was able to penetrate from above. It had started to rain quite heavily. Bartholomew stepped cautiously into the edge of the open space, pulling up the collar of his overcoat to combat the increasing chill and ramming the fedora further down on his head. The clearing was actually a sizeable bowl, roughly thirty to forty metres in diameter, fringed on all sides by the trees. It was pretty deep too. The sides were steep, but assailable. Deciding on a closer inspection, he scrambled down to the bottom, before coming to an untidy halt in the scraggy, grass-covered centre.

Must be an old minor quarry site he decided, slowly turning in a full circle as he inspected the pit from under the brim of his sodden, dripping hat. On the far side there was a faint outline of a track. More likely made by foxes or deer than human traffic, he surmised.

The rain continued to fall hard, masking most of the other natural sounds in the wood. He had a sense, though, of not being alone; more by instinct than the actual evidence of something specific. It could be anything, from a rabbit to a deer he speculated, suddenly feeling even more chilly, and now, almost ridiculously, a little isolated. Stop getting spooked, he chastised himself. It's just nature. Moving on, he clambered up the slippery incline opposite, grateful for the small toe-holds in the rutted path, until he reached the fringe of surrounding trees once more.

No, let's face it. He now had to acknowledge the fact – there was a 'presence' out there. Over in the trees from where he had entered the old pit. He had definitely heard the movement of something quite large behind the immediate row of ash that lined the lip of the quarry. That's not a rabbit, he decided; alarmed enough to strike off quickly again, anxious not to get himself any further wound up.

A couple of minutes later, he found himself on the edge of an established pathway heading north. The rain hadn't ceased but it was more of a drizzle now, rather than the heavy drenching of earlier on. The clouds above, skitting along furiously, were at least of the brighter variety, albeit still a mundane, desultory grey.

As he followed the path, he heard a careful crackling of undergrowth over to his left. A quick flash, deep in the gloom of the wood, was all he caught of a movement of shadow. He now walked swiftly on eager to reach the end of the wood as quickly as possible. As he began to break into a stumbling, undignified jog, a swish of branches again to the left gave him another glimpse. This time it was enough to catch the briefest image of a lithe figure, clad head to foot in the heaviest black, before it glided once more into cover.

"Hey!" he shouted, relieved it was not a wild beast, but indignant now he knew he was being stalked by some sort of sinister onlooker. "Why don't you show yourself? Suppose you think it's funny? Pretty big of you to hang out there in the trees trying to frighten the life out of me!"

He got no answer. Just a little more snapping underfoot, but no further sighting. And then, silence once more. Bartholomew slowed his pace and put a hand to his chest to find his heartbeat racing along furiously, embarrassed now at his own fright. Bloody weirdo, he cursed. Finally, having calmed down somewhat, he wandered on, eyes and ears keenly alert, until a few moments later he reached the edge of the wood.

Down a gradual incline and grandly laid out before him was a huge stately home, its façade the colour of sandstone. It was centred within its own landscaped deer park, dotted with the customary ancient oaks ringed by cast iron fencing. It sat squat and heavy on the landscape, with a wing at either end. These were dwarfed by the vast colonnaded middle block, with sweeping entrance steps each side leading up to the imposing double entrance doors.

This must be Rissborough Hall in all its glory, Bartholomew realised. But it wasn't the building, or its impression of power and prestige that held his attention, as he stood quietly at the edge of the treeline. Nor the majesty of the landscape. It was the little black dot far in the distance that caught his eye. The one that moved incessantly, like a worker ant, across field after field. Until finally it was lost to view in the distance, where he guessed the final hedgerow met the line of the Haddlewell-Evensthorpe road.

Chapter 6   The Dare

The rest of the day passed uneventfully. After ruefully watching the shadowy figure move out of sight over the horizon, Bartholomew had headed off right. Keeping discreetly to the inside edge of the tree line, he reached another established footpath which appeared to run parallel to the one where he'd seen the shadow. It headed south through the trees, and, as he'd guessed, eventually brought him back to the set of neat paddocks overlooking Minsham Court.

Descending towards the house, he'd spotted the South African maintenance people, weeding industriously along the main drive. A battered old blue Land Rover Defender was parked up nearby. A tall, blond, balding Afrikaans man in his thirties, called Jan, introduced himself and his wife, Jeanette. Jan was gruff, pragmatic and didn't beat about the bush. No, they hadn't seen anything untoward on their twice weekly visits. Yes, the estate fencing and walling to their knowledge was sound. But, if an intruder was determined and agile enough, then, in his view, the boundary could easily be breached.

A sanguine perspective, thought Bartholomew, shaped no doubt by many years of living in his mother country. Deciding he wouldn't get much more change out of these hardened outdoor professionals, he'd thanked them both and returned to the flat.

Later, he sat at the kitchen table, with a scalding hot cup of tea. With the light rapidly descending outside, he speculated about the identity of his companion in the woods. Just an honest runner, who'd inadvertently strayed onto private land, and, on being surprised by Bartholomew, had fled into the trees? Or, some kind of voyeur who got their kicks from dressing up in SAS style gear and terrifying vulnerable ramblers? God knows, he thought, although the nagging feeling remained that something was not quite right. He'd had a sense of being observed. Not, of accidently bumping into someone.

Putting it out of his mind he did his rounds of the house, turned the security alarm system on, and, after happily quaffing half a bottle of the claret to assist with his determination to think only positive thoughts, he went to bed. For the first time in a long while, he enjoyed a long, uninterrupted and dream-free night's sleep.

Even Kennedy was vaguely pleasant to him, when he phoned to give her his report at nine the next morning. He wasn't going to mention the episode in the wood the previous afternoon. He knew she'd just call him a wus and lecture him about an over-active imagination. So, with no issues to hassle her with, it led to a brief, amiable, and business-like conversation.

Mid-morning, he was interrupted by the gate buzzer, just as he was mashing some smoked mackerel fillets in the bottom of a mixing bowl in preparation for a tasty lunch for one. He greeted Sheila through the intercom and carried on with the assembly of the fishcakes, whilst he waited for her to arrive at the kitchen door.

To the mackerel he added a few tinned anchovies, a couple of messily sliced hard-boiled eggs and some mashed potato. Finishing it off with a couple of teaspoons of horseradish sauce, some chopped parsley and seasoning. He then fashioned the fishcake mix into circular patties, dusted them with a little flour and popped them into a hot frying pan.

Sheila caught him wiping his hands on a grimy apron, before urgently jiggling the fishcakes around the pan to stop them sticking to the bottom.

"My... look at you, the proper little cook. Hard at it in his Master Chef kitchen!" she chortled.

"I don't quite think so," Bartholomew laughed back. "More like amateur gourmet struggles in the servant's quarters!"

"Oh well. Smells bloody marvellous, that's all I can say. Planning a grand dinner party, are we?" she continued to tease.

"No. Just like to keep myself in the style to which I'm accustomed," he grinned. Besides, not much else to do round here when the weather's like this."

"Yeah," Sheila concurred. "Lucky I'm not on foot and it's all delivery by van. It's been terrible up and down the valley for the last 24 hours. Let's hope it stops before Christmas!"

Oh God, thought Bartholomew. The Christmas reminder once again. Crikey. It's only in four days' time. Unusually for him, he felt a stab of regret as he listened to Sheila expand on the jolly festive arrangements she had planned with her husband and close relatives. Part of him shied away from the thought of all that close intermingling and personal dependency. Part of him too thought of his parents, who he hadn't spent a Christmas with in many a long year.

Shaking himself out of his reflection, he got busy once more and made them both a cup of coffee whilst continuing to listen to Sheila rambling on about this and that, chipping in with the occasional quip to make her laugh. As he leant against the Aga, flipping the fishcakes over to give them a crisp, browned finish, the intercom blared out once more.

"Bloody hell!" he grumbled, which temporarily put a halt to Sheila's monologue. Depressing the red button, he barked at the white grilled box: "Yes! Can I help you?"

"Hello there, Bartholomew," came back the soft, velvety reply. "It's Roxy from the Spar. I have your deliveries for you. If you open the gates, I can bring them up to the house."

He felt his pulse quicken a little, and, for some unfathomable reason, a rush of guilt like a naughty school boy.

"Of course. Sorry," he said, in a voice that was a lot more conciliatory than he'd intended to sound. He pressed the button once more. "They should open now. Drive round to the back of the main house. You'll see the flat. Come on in."

"Ooo," cooed Sheila, smirking at him from the kitchen table. "See you've got yourself sorted out pretty quickly. Never seen a newcomer to the area get such prompt home delivery from the Spar before!"

"Oh, stop it!" he said, dissembling. "I told Roxy I didn't want a home service. I'm quite capable of picking up my own groceries. But she wouldn't take no for an answer."

"Well, you could always turn her away," she shot back, raising her eyebrows mockingly. With the smirk still touching the corners of her mouth, she thanked him for the coffee and headed briskly off through the door, just as a small Spar van pulled into the yard.

He was thankful Sheila had got back into her own van and was already down the drive before Roxy entered the kitchen. As, no doubt, she would have laughed again at the look on his face. In Roxy bounded, with a carton of milk and a bag of ground coffee, to lean one firm slender hip against the kitchen table.

"Got it!" she announced triumphantly, holding the coffee aloft. "Exactly the one you specified."

He congratulated her with his heartiest smile as she looked up at him with those big blue eyes. "Delivered in person too. Now, that's what I call service."

He couldn't actually remember naming the particular brand, let alone the regional variety. But, hey ho, he thought to himself, who cares when the scenery in his kitchen had been so gloriously uplifted.

She was dressed again in those spray-on jeans with tight, calf length leather boots and a jockey style windcheater. On any other woman it would have looked like every-day, equine country attire. On Roxy, she could have been modelling for a Cartier-sponsored polo match, of the type you used to see covered in *Harper's & Queen*.

He turned back to the Aga to check the fishcakes once more. It helped to keep his vision otherwise corralled.

"Mmm, that smells wonderful!" she crowed, moving up to stand right next to him. He just about managed to mask a gulp as he felt her toned thigh brush against his.

Even the aroma of the cooking couldn't quite diffuse the warm, perfumed, wholesome scent emanating from her, overwhelming his senses. She stared down at the frying pan.

"My, didn't take you for a cook, Mr Caretaker. Hidden talents, I see. You ought to show me what else you have in your repertoire.

He was torn between shaking his head at another of the basic innuendos Roxy seemed to trade in, or just playing along further. It was all a little bit surreal, but as she appeared to enjoy the roguish approach, he thought: why disappoint her?

"Yes, maybe I ought to. Although I'm not really the entertaining type of cook, Roxy, I'm sure I could rustle up something to guarantee your full attention..." He had to admit though, to feeling himself wince at the banal response, and the cringe worthy smile he had fashioned to accompany it.

"Really" she purred, turning to face him now, lips pouting outrageously.

Suddenly losing the nerve to proceed any further, he asked: "By the way, what do I owe you for the deliveries? You must have a lot of other houses on your round to get on to."

"Oh," she said, retreating back to the kitchen table, with what was now edging on a sulky expression. "I kept you until last so as to give you my fullest attention, seeing as you are our newest customer!"

"Well, I'm very flattered, he smiled broadly, trying to re-assure her. "But as I explained in the Spar, I really am pretty self-sufficient. I'm going to be a long way from the most lucrative customer you've ever had. Just don't want to get your hopes up too much."

He carried on flipping the fish cakes for a while. Finally, he turned around from the Aga to see if he could gently ease her off back to the Spar. To his surprise however, he found he was now alone in the kitchen.

"Roxy! Where the hell have you gone?" he called, peering out through the kitchen window into the yard. It was completely empty, apart from the Spar van.

Bloody hell – he realised she must have gone into the house. Bartholomew quickly darted through into the utility room, just in time to see Roxy trying to turn the handle of the door leading into the Great Hall.

"Stop, for God's sake!" he shouted. "You'll set the alarm off and we'll have half the County Constabulary up here in no time. It's all alarmed, you fool. Get back into the kitchen. No one's allowed in there, it's out of bounds."

"Sorry," she demurred, grinning like a Cheshire cat. "Thought I'd just have a quick peek around whilst you were Ramsey'ing out there. No harm intended. Never been inside Minsham before. I just wanted to have a look, to see how the other half live."

"Well, no one's allowed in there. C'mon, into the kitchen now." He brusquely shepherded her back to the table. "Sit there quietly while I rescue the fishcakes. Don't move an inch."

"Whatever you say, Mr Bartholomew." She sat with her long legs crossed, fingers steepled under her shapely chin and watched him again with those smoky blue eyes.

Setting the fishcakes atop some kitchen paper on a plate, he shoved the frying pan in the sink and joined her at the table.

"Look, I'm sorry. I didn't mean to be sharp with you."

"You're very law abiding aren't you?" she remarked, a provocative smirk now playing at the corners of her mouth.

"It's just that the house is definitely off limits. In here is fine, but the main building you need to keep out of. Owner's orders."

"Oh, alright. If you say so," she popped back at him, now a little frosty.

"You know something," she continued, staring hard at him. "First impressions are usually correct in my experience. In your case, though, I think maybe I got it wrong. I thought you were the strong type – and a little bit cheeky too – which I like. Now, I think you're actually a little hemmed in… if the truth be told," she added, rather mockingly.

She stood up, giving him a full view of her shapely thighs and the apex of her crotch outlined in the tight jeans.

"I was going to see if you fancied doing something together, but I think I've changed my mind." With that, she turned on her heel and headed out through the door.

He followed her out of the entrance, and could not help but watch the way her bottom moved within the tight denim material as she sauntered over to the van. Mesmerised, a pathetic voice he didn't really feel fully in control of spouted:

"I think you've got it wrong, Roxy. You're sounding a bit too serious all of a sudden. Look, why don't we hitch up sometime at the village pub for a drink?"

She turned on her heel and looked back at Bartholomew with something approaching a sneer.

"Hitch up at the pub for a drink? You're having a laugh! Why would I want to meet you for a drink, when every other plumber's mate, jockey or rugger bugger within a twenty mile radius would stand me any amount of drinks at the pub at just a click of my fingers?"

Turning away, she was laughing at him now, her humour resurfacing as quickly as it had deserted her a moment before. Slightly scary, he thought. She opened the door to the van and put one long, shapely leg inside, before turning back to look at him challengingly.

"You want to take me out? Ok, I'll go out with you, Bartholomew. On one condition. You wine and dine me right here at Minsham Court. I want the full works. Not in the grotty staff flat. In the main house. Drinks in the Hall, dinner in the grand dining room and then, we'll see… Bartholomew."

"Look, Roxy, I've already explained. The house is out of bounds. Ok, we don't have to go to a pub. What about a local brasserie or…"

"Forget it, Bartholomew!" she shot back. "I've told you. I've got plenty of other men desperate to take me out to the pub, brasserie or whatever! You want an evening with me? Then it's Minsham Court or nothing at all. See if you can dare to break the rules for once. Owner's rules. Ha! Didn't anyone ever tell you? Rules are there to be broken!"

"Bye bye, Bartholomew." With that, she slammed the van door firmly shut, turned the ignition and accelerated rapidly off down the drive.

He returned to the kitchen, shaking his head. What on earth had made him ask the question, for Christ's sake? – knowing exactly why. Forget it. Out of sight, out of mind. The Spar was definitely off limits from now on. He'd ask her to leave any deliveries by the front gate, if she ever turned up again with that siren voice of hers wailing though the intercom.

Good. Decision made. It was only when he crossed the kitchen to the sink to wash up the cooking utensils, though, that he saw the yellow post-it stuck to the chipped vase on the table. Roxy, it said.

Scribbled quickly, next to a doodle of a pair of long legs and a mobile phone number, highlighted in bold type.

Chapter 7   The Bang

It was some time later after he'd polished off the fish cakes and washed up that he decided to conduct a tour of the house. He ought to earn his bread, so to speak, and with Kennedy it was always best to have as much up-to-date information as possible to report on – in case she made a second surprise call of the day, just to keep him on his toes.

Perhaps it was the effect of the lunch, his bloodstream trying to cope with it all, for he felt soporific and heavy as he de-activated the alarm and opened the door to the hall. Vigorously scratching his stubbly chin and scuffing his hand through his hair a couple of times to try and snap himself out of his post prandial stupor, Bartholomew gazed at the space, taking in the grand fireplaces and experiencing, yet again, the slightly aesthetic feel of the building. Somehow, it felt a little more public than it ought to, not quite institutional – no, that wasn't an accurate description – but neither did it have the real feel of a private home, or at least someone's treasured country get-away.

He sauntered across the polished floor. To shake himself out of his languor, and for a laugh, he was almost tempted to take a quick short run up and see how far he could skid across the shiny black and white chequer surface in his rubber soled boots. Reminding himself sternly, to try and act like the professional house-sitter he was supposed to be, he nobly resisted the puerile urge to frolic and carried on with the inspection before coming to a halt near the door of the drawing room.

An abrupt realisation rooted him there to the spot with a sharp intake of breath – comedy now about as far from mind as his desire to listen was acute. He was sure he had heard some sort of resonation, although he could not discern whether it was from inside the building or out. A resonation that was at odds with the usual creaks or groans of the place, the hubbub the wind made when it got up across the various facades of the building - sounds that he had become familiar with since his arrival on the estate.

A couple of short strides took him to the entrance of the room. He was acutely aware he could feel the hair standing up on the back of his neck. He couldn't quite put his finger on it but he was certain there was a presence out there - not in the room itself, but nearby. He could feel it. Stark – and not particularly helpful – recall brought to mind Mrs Goode and the fear etched across her face, deepening his sense of isolation: of being one individual alone in a sizable country house, set within an enclosed one hundred acres. Or maybe not so alone, he fretted. He wondered whether Mrs Goode had stood here too, in this exact spot, hearing the same ambiguous muffled sounds, feeling about as scared and rattled as he did now.

Swivelling around a fraction at a time, he surveyed the room in detail. Everything looked the same as on his last inspection: Not an item out of place, nor anything newly added, or indeed missing – as far as he could tell. After a further minute of observation, coupled with intense listening, he realised that all he *could* actually hear was silence. He cajoled himself to get a grip of his tightening nerves. Gradually, by breathing deeply and shaking out his shoulders, he began to relax a little and feel the tension ebb away.

He laughed inwardly for being a fool and wandered over to the piano. And there it was: the photo had been moved. The good-looking butler, or was it Mr Eves, so elegantly captured in the smart frame was now a good two feet from where it had stood before, atop the dark, gleaming veneer of the lid. In the moment his attention was drawn directly to the photo frame itself, a fearful scraping noise emanated from the far window of the room, involuntarily triggering an evil shiver down his spine. And, as he looked up – or was it his imagination… did he catch a split-second glimpse of a long slender finger, just as it finished raking it's ear piercing, torturous progress across the external glazing?

Overcoming his initial shock, Bartholomew leapt to life. Fuelled now by sheer indignation, he dashed back out into the hall. Sprinting towards the utility room, he inadvertently achieved an impressive rendition of the skid he had contemplated earlier: only just about managing to collect his feet from under him as he reached the under-the-stairs utility room door.

He passed through to the kitchen in a flash and wrenched open the back door before scampering around the side of the house to reach the drawing room window. Holding a hand to his chest to quell his pounding heart, he looked around frantically - but there was nothing to be seen. All he could see was what one would expect: a peaceful, ordered vista of landscaped estate grounds. Finally, as he walked around the entire house perimeter, his breathing more even now, he had only one thought. Whether it was connected or not, or just plain intuition, he just couldn't remove the image from his mind of the lithe figure in the woods, decked out in black, stealthy as sin, and always one step ahead of him.

After carefully checking and re-checking all the ground floor windows latches and looking for evidence of further disturbance along the gravel paths that circumvented the main building – and finding absolutely none – Bartholomew retreated to the flat. Any hope that the making of a recuperative cup of tea and sticking his head in his book, sprawled out on the leather armchair in the sitting room, might ease his mind, proved useless. It was impossible to ignore the equally pressing emotions of frustration and paranoia that had seemed to dog him since the outset of the assignment at Minsham Court.

Giving up and tossing the book aside, in the shortening afternoon light he walked out again, north across the paddocks and up into the woods. Wrapped up tightly in his overcoat with the fedora pulled down over his eyes, he stomped along the footpath that ran past the pit as the sky blackened overhead, promising rain once more. Morosely, he kicked the leaves out of his way as he headed through the trees, in the direction of Rissborough Hall.

Reaching the far side of the wood, he halted in the same place as before, with the panorama of Rissborough laid out before him. He wasn't quite sure what kept making him stop at that particular point, other than for the obvious view. Something about it seemed to niggle at the back of his mind, which he couldn't quite grasp. Shaking his head at his own foibles, he followed the circuitous route he had forged yesterday, skirting the edge of the wood, before heading south again, back in the direction of Minsham Court.

Dark skies, rustling leaves, creaking boughs and the wind picking up sharply all created a rather sinister, threatening atmosphere, as he strode out hard to try and reach the house before the heavens opened. All the elements conspired to create a great amount of noise in the build up to the storm, yet there was one thing he was certain of: he had his trusty shadow back once more. Always out of sight, intangible. But definitely there. It was like having your own guardian angel, he cynically mused. Or stalker.

He tightened his grip on the hazel staff he'd brought along for the walk. If it came to it, he determined grimly, it would provide enough of a weapon to give someone an almighty crack across the kneecaps. Reaching the point where the trees began to thin and the paddocks became visible, he finally halted and turned back to look into the dark depths of the wood. He resisted calling out again to challenge his watcher. Don't give them the satisfaction, he decided. As the skies opened and the rain began to hammer down in earnest, his only consolation was that he would be back in the warmth of his flat long before his shadow could hope to reach their own, particular sanctuary.

He should have known the dream-free period of sleep of the previous night wouldn't be repeated. As Bartholomew sat in the kitchen in the evening gloom, enduring the din of pounding rain outside, he had a premonition of even greater difficulties ahead, of an impending crisis. Although, he told himself once more, he really had no idea how this would manifest. It was probably the claret, he mentally joked, thinking it over. Who says a daily wallop of bloody good wine doesn't play tricks with your mind, even though it might not result in a bad hangover?

***

That night he dreamt he was floating in a swimming pool, on his back. Vaguely wiggling his fingers and toes to keep himself just afloat. He wasn't sure exactly where he was, although above him he could just about make out a beige coloured, corrugated roof. The water was very warm, lapping his body in a languid velvety caress. The school pool, perhaps?

He could hear whispering nearby. Whispering and tittering laughter. The heightened laughter of people anticipating some entertainment, or an act which is going to provide them with a great deal of satisfaction. He wanted to move, to roll over on his stomach and swim urgently to the other end of the pool, out of sight, into the deep shadows. Something held him, though, freezing his limbs in a star-shaped formation in the water, so that the voices began to draw closer and closer, the tone of their laughter becoming ever more evil, ever more threatening and blood tingling.

He knew what it was now that held him in this iron-like grip. It was fear itself. He recognised one of the voices too and, Pavlovian like, the fear now descended into terror, deep within his core. It was Solville, his glistening, brutish face just coming into view along the edge of the pool. And when there was Solville, of course there was White. Like a caricature of a couple of leering hyenas, licking their lips in anticipation of a very tasty offering.

He looked on helplessly, as if observing the scene from another place altogether. Solville picked up a heavy rubber training brick and swung it round his head, roaring hilariously. From amongst the other paraphernalia scattered poolside, White grabbed a plastic paddle that lay on top of a battered canoe. Slowly, he began to rap the paddle edge hard on the slippery tiled floor.

"In his face, in his face, in his face!" White chanted in time to the crack of the paddle, his eyes flashing furiously, a maniacal expression fixed on his thin, cruel lips. Both the chanting and the crack of the paddle increased in tempo, until Solville could hold himself back no longer. With one long, rapid lunge of his arm, he launched the rubber missile directly across the pool. The hard black brick traversed across the water in an arch. As if in slow motion, Bartholomew watched it coming in towards his soft, open face. White howled with glee in the distance, with the paddle ringing out on the poolside: crack, crack, crack...

No. This is for real, he realised. The duvet was wet with sweat. He freed his legs from the tangle and sat up on the side of the bed, listening intently.

Nothing, though. Just silence. God, he moaned, looking about at the wreckage of bedclothes. Clearly a night off from the dreams meant an extra fruity one the next time round. His bitter laugh summed up the situation. Graveyard humour was the only way to deal with the night terror, he knew from long experience.

Crack! Shit, there it was again. This was getting monotonous. He wasn't sure which was worse, the dreams or the threat from outside. This time, however, he was better prepared. Into his clothes in a flash, he was quickly out into the kitchen and able to locate the torch easily on the worktop without putting the light on. Shuffling into his overcoat, he grabbed the hazel staff for good measure and gently unlocked the back door.

It wasn't as dark outside as the night when he'd discovered the over-turned dustbin. A wan moon shone weakly between fast moving clouds, as a cold brisk breeze snatched at his coat, flapping it around his legs. He wasted no time on an inspection of the outbuildings. No, the cracks had come from over the far side, nearer the main drive, or out beyond in the woodland. Still gripped a little by fear, but shored up by an irritable grumpiness due to lack of sleep, Bartholomew advanced around the side of the house. The moon continued its dance with the clouds, moving in and out, creating a swathe of flitting shadows across the lawns and rhododendron bushes.

Crack! He ducked instinctively, as the latest explosion echoed out across the grounds. Bartholomew reached the corner of the building and peeked out down the main drive. There was nothing in sight. He now realised, however, that it wasn't really a crack after all. That had been in the dream. Curiously – in the circumstances – able to muster the thinnest sliver of humour, he debated with himself: when is a crack not a crack but a bang? Or vice versa? No. It was a bang. A wider, larger noise. Like artillery going off, or a huge firework taking you by surprise with its shocking retort.

He continued to hesitate by the corner of the building. The sensible thing to do would be to retreat to the flat, pick up his mobile and call the police. That would mean losing the opportunity of a sighting of the perpetrator, though. At least he had the heavy torch and staff with him. Deciding, against his better judgement, to risk it a little further; he cautiously stepped out from the building and slowly made his way over the gravel down towards the main drive.

Five minutes later he halted, half way down the avenue under the trees, where it was almost pitch black under the thick foliage overhead. He flinched, as another large bang went off to his right. Bartholomew crouched down by the base of one of the gnarled old trees and looked up, out across the paddocks, to the thin line of woodland that bordered the estate wall. It's up in there, whatever or whoever it was, he now knew. What if it was someone with a shotgun blasting rabbits, he worried. If he approached, he might get mistaken for a wild animal and get a couple of barrels full. No. He knew enough about shooting to judge this was something else. Rabbit shooting at night meant lamping. Powerful torches, dazzling the prey, so that the killing can be done on an industrial scale. One thing was for sure, these bangs were going off in the dark.

Oh well, he concluded, somehow managing to block out the pervasive, wind inducing fear – I've come this far, I might as well go on a little bit further. Still crouching down, he scurried quickly across the nearest paddock and dropped into the line of trees adjacent to the wall. Slowly but surely, trying his utmost to make as little noise underfoot as possible, he gradually crept up along the estate wall.

Ten minutes later, he was still moving slowly in a northerly direction. Apart from the chilly wind whistling through the trees, there was no other noise at all. Then, in a trice, there was another enormous bang up ahead. This time he got a view. The explosion seemed to emanate from the branch of a tree at head height. What it provided, though, was a brief illumination of the whole immediate landscape. And there, beyond, just about on the edge of the lit area, he caught a glimpse of a shadowy hooded figure, carrying what looked like a string of thinly shaped onions over his shoulder.

"Oi you! Stop that!" Bartholomew yelled out, shining the torch in the direction of the figure, now that the illumination had subsided. He waved the hazel stick in the air, hoping, rather pathetically, that it might make the intruder put any thoughts of a confrontation out of their mind. He needn't have worried. The hooded figure stood stock still for a moment, before rapidly legging it away up the line of the estate wall.

Bartholomew followed as best he could, but, in what he gauged to be less than twenty seconds, the figure had distanced themselves enough to be beyond the beam of the torch. He kept going and after a minute or two he heard the unmistakeable roar of a motorbike engine. This was followed a moment later by a quick ratcheting up through the gears, as the rider, or riders, accelerated off into the distance.

He walked on a little further and paused by a tall oak, panting heavily, more from the fright than the physical exertion. Once he'd recovered, Bartholomew spent the next twenty minutes traversing up and down the line of trees, trying to discover any evidence of the source of the explosions. It was fruitless, he decided. He couldn't find a thing. Exhaustion crept up on him like a silent assassin. He knew it was the adrenaline now deserting him. Time to get back to the flat and call the authorities. He'd had about enough of this. There was one thing that now needed no further explanation or confirmation: the overwhelming fear he'd seen in Mrs Goode. It was the reason she couldn't get off the estate fast enough. Tonight and the events of yesterday had not been the first time the environs of Minsham Court had been exposed to noisy and unwelcome visitors. And knowing what he knew now, his primary thought was that Kennedy had some serious explaining to do.

At ten o'clock the next morning, he was standing in exactly the same spot as he had been the night before from where he'd glimpsed the hooded intruder. This time, though, he had a thin, wiry and seemingly unhelpful Detective Sergeant as his companion. The pair of them stood silently, looking around, before deciding to walk slowly up the line of trees and, like Bartholomew had done the night before, inspect the ground carefully for any evidence of the explosions.

Following his useless search in the dark, he'd beaten a weary retreat back to the flat and dialled 999. Within approximately thirty minutes, a police car, all lights flashing and siren blaring, had roared up the main drive, much to Bartholomew's wry amusement. Aping Channel 5's *Police Interceptors* was wasted somewhat out here in the sticks in the dead of night, he cynically observed. Two burly, stocky PCs, who looked like they spent most of their time in the gym, jumped out and, after a couple of minutes of questioning, headed out on foot to investigate. The result was much the same. Twenty minutes later, they returned with nothing to report. There wasn't much they could do in the dark, apparently. It was best to wait until the morning. With reassurances about a further visit and exhortations to lock all doors, windows, re-set the alarm and not to confront any intruders again, they shot off back up the drive, lights and siren blaring away once more.

It was 4 am before Bartholomew had been able to drop off into an edgy, nervous sleep, so his introduction to Detective Sergeant Baxter on the mobile at eight-thirty the next morning had been a short and tetchy one. The conversation later that morning, out by the estate wall, seemed to carry on in the same vein.

"What exactly did you say you call yourself, sir? I mean in your line of business?" asked the Detective Sergeant, with just the slightest hint of sarcasm.

He was a short and very wiry; the build of a flat race jockey. His thin, weary face and dead pan eyes spoke of a lifetime of hearing all sorts of cock and bull stories. What he lacked in physical presence, though, he seemed to be able to make up for in acid articulation.

"I'm a house-sitter," replied Bartholomew, trying hard, but not altogether successfully, to keep the tone of his voice as even as possible.

"So, that's a caretaker, is it, sir?

"Yes, if you say so. Look, if you don't mind, I've been up half the night dealing with these intruders. I'd like to know what you are going to do about it. Is this sort of thing a common occurrence around here? Had any reports of similar incidences lately?"

"As a matter of fact, no," replied the Detective Sergeant, scrutinising Bartholomew carefully, as if searching for some missing clue. "Tell me again," he continued. "How exactly did you end up here?"

"Look, Detective Sergeant, I've already told you. I'm a professional house-sitter. I work for The Kennedy Agency which is based in London. It provides a house watching service to wealthy clients in the UK who own large properties. I've been assigned to Minsham

Court, for an as-yet undetermined period, starting a couple of days ago. I heard some unusual noises the other night outside the flat I'm occupying at the back of the building. I thought nothing further of it, as it was probably a feral cat knocking a dustbin over. But yesterday, there was someone creeping around the outside of the main house, trying to scare me and wind me up by scratching window panes and then disappearing into thin air."

He didn't mention the photo frame in the drawing room had been moved. Or the idea that someone, somehow, might have been *inside* the house. He thought the distrustful Detective Sergeant would probably discount it as over-imagination or that he was just sensationalising.

Bartholomew continued: "Last night's antics however have just underlined the position. Someone is up to no good. As to what they are hoping to achieve by their actions, I haven't a clue, other than it's bloody well driving me mad – and to be frank, it's not great on the nerves."

Baxter didn't immediately reply and an uneasy silence hung between the pair of them. He could sense the policeman was waiting for him to say something further. Bartholomew, eventually giving in to the game of cat and mouse, enquired:

"Why do you ask, Detective Sergeant? You seem a little suspicious."

"Maybe," came back the desultory reply. "You see, it's just that what you do is a little itinerant, if you don't mind me saying. In my experience, itinerancy comes with one thing: trouble. The two usually go hand in hand. Move in, stay a while, and move on, before the pigeons come home to roost – so to speak." He laughed humorously, looking up at the sky as if in search of a flight of the feathery creatures.

"Detective Sergeant, I think you are way off the mark here. Call Kennedy, my boss. She'll fill you in. This is a bona fide assignment on behalf of Mr Eves, the owner."

"Had many assignments before, sir? Or is this your first little venture for The Kennedy Agency?"

"Yes, as a matter of fact. A number. And I'd be grateful if you check the facts out first with my employer before you start viewing me as a potential suspect."

Bartholomew gritted his teeth. In the privacy of his own mind he assuaged himself by imagining the acerbic retort he would have liked to have given the doubting Detective Sergeant, had the position been different.

"Oh, I will. You can be sure of that," Baxter retorted firmly. "You see, there are only going to be a limited number of explanations for what may be happening here. Or number of causes. It's either going to be connected with the owner Mr Eves – which I doubt, as for a start, from what I understand, he's hardly ever in occupation. Or with you. But according to your whiter than white protestations, that's a dead end too. Or, it could involve a third party – which also looks unlikely, don't you think? I mean, why would someone go to the lengths that they have to break into the estate, and, essentially, make a lot of noise for no obvious purpose?"

"I don't know," replied Bartholomew, unable this time to conceal the irritation in his voice. "You're the detective here, not me. It's your job to find out."

"Hmmph," concluded Baxter, seemingly deciding that this particular line of questioning had reached its natural conclusion, for the moment.

"Ok," he resumed, after further thought. "So, your story is that on hearing the bangs go off, you left the flat, skirted the main house and crept, SAS style, down the main drive. There, due to your clever stealthy manoeuvring, you managed to spot one of the would-be intruders with an odd-shaped string of something or other slung over his shoulder, who then legged it up over the wall and made *The Great Escape,* by motorbike, before you could say Jack Robinson."

"Yes," replied Bartholomew, strongly stifling the urge to tell the Detective Sergeant bluntly that he was an extremely repetitive twat.

"Right then. Let's take another look up along the wall, shall we? See if there is anything to back up your assertions."

They set off again, closely scrutinising both the ground and the tree line, as they shuffled along in short, careful steps. After another half hour, however, the search ended as empty handed as before.

"This is wrong," Bartholomew exhorted. "I didn't imagine it. Look at me. Do you really think I'm the sort to be fantasising about chasing gangland hoodies around in the dark? Do I look like the wannabe paint-ball warrior type?"

Baxter was clearly about to make another clever quip in response to Bartholomew's concerns. Instead, his gaze seemed transfixed by something in the branch of a nearby tree. He walked over, without once taking his eye off the object, and plucked it off the bough. It was a small beige tube with a tassel at its base. He stood for a moment under the large tree inspecting the object minutely, turning it over in his hands. Finally, he put the tube up to his nose and inhaled deeply.

"Thought so," he sagely concluded.

"Thought so, what?" asked Bartholomew, crowding in, anxious to partake of the Detective Sergeant's apparent investigative wisdom.

"You may not have been imagining things. D'you know, someone's even been back here since you surprised them at – what was it – about one o'clock in the morning?" He looked at Bartholomew questioningly, who nodded in return.

"You see, you obviously scared them off. However, it also appears it was important to them to ensure no evidence was left behind. So they returned to clear up. Probably whilst you were having forty winks back in the flat, if what you've led me to believe is true. But they were in a rush, and didn't quite finish the job properly. Hence, this was left behind. Handy for us."

"What is it?" asked Bartholomew, staring down intently at the battered tubing that looked very much like a spent firecracker.

"It's the remnants of a bird scarer. They come on a long string. You hang them intermittently on the branches of a line of trees and they're designed to go off at anything from ten to thirty minute intervals. Keeps the pesky birds off the field crops. Or in this case, I think it was designed to keep whoever is currently residing in Minsham Court awake all night!"

With that said, there was nothing much further to do out by the wall. Baxter made a promise that the police would carry out the standard enquiries into whether any members of the public had witnessed a motorbike in the vicinity, or any unusual behaviour. He hastened to add it was unlikely, though, that anyone would have seen a thing. After all, it was in the early hours of the morning. He also confirmed the local patrolling police car would include the Minsham boundary on its rounds.

"Well sir… I must be off. Thieves to catch and all that. One last thing. Please do not try and engage with these people should they turn up again. They are likely to be extremely unpredictable and dangerous. Call us straight away. One thing I can't quite understand, though," he hesitated at this point. "You're quite right. You don't really strike me as the vigilante type. I would have put you more in the mould of *'discretion is the better part of valour'.*"

"You trying to tell me something, Detective Sergeant?" shot back Bartholomew. "If I'd called you when the first bang went off, then gauging by how long it took your two colleagues to turn up – all ever so brave with their lights flashing and siren blaring – then our friends would have been over the wall and long gone without any of us catching even the tiniest glimpse of them!"

"Just an observation sir…"

Then, after a moment's further thought, Bartholomew added,

"D'you know, though. I'm not quite sure why myself. I don't really know what came over me. Must be the country air. Perhaps it's turning me a little feral too."

With the Detective Sergeant finally gone, he returned to the flat and decided to see what he could assemble from the larder for a scratch lunch. He was going to need a good feed before he tackled Kennedy on the phone.

First things first, though. He rustled up a bottle of the *Saint-Julien* from the store and poured himself a large glass of the ruby nectar. Something to steady his nerves? he asked himself. Or just reward for services over and above the call of duty? Who bloody well cares, he decided. What really mattered was it tasted superb. He proceeded to award himself a generous top-up, just for good measure. In any event, he'd dissembled a little with the Detective Sergeant. He'd certainly been frightened out in the Park last night, but, he had been there before – enough that is, to at least understand it was all part of the experience.

That savvy had come by way of a ridiculous spur of the moment decision he'd made just after leaving college. On a crazy, misguided whim, which had virtually made his father disown him, he'd walked into an army careers centre and enlisted as a private in a county infantry regiment. He wasn't ever quite sure which his father had hated more – that he'd joined the Army – or he had joined as a squaddie. Either way, by the time he'd arrived for basic training what his father thought was the last thing on his mind. The first was what a monumental mistake he had made. But his father' point did eventually sink in. He'd lasted barely eighteen months before being invalided out with a perpetually weakened ankle but the experience was seared deep into his consciousness. Getting the almighty shit kicked out of you every night in barracks, out of convenient earshot of the NCOs, just for being considered 'sort of posh', was something that either destroyed you, or, as in his case, made you very quickly connect with your animal instinct for survival – and somehow overcome the debilitating effect that comes from the shock of violence. He just learnt to scrap back. The beatings became fights – ones he mostly lost. Some of the losses began to convert to an even outcome, with the protagonists, cut, bloodied and frustrated, hesitating to continue. Once he'd won twice, the targeting stopped altogether. Or, as is the way of the world, it didn't *really* stop: it just became some other poor unfortunate's turn.

Turning his attention to matters much more savoury, Bartholomew ducked into the larder and pulled out some basmati rice, red onions, sultanas, a head of garlic, eggs, soy sauce and Tabasco, along with the leftovers of a small piece of roast pork he'd consumed the previous evening. Whilst the onions and garlic were frying, he washed the rice thoroughly and then steam boiled it.

Chopping the pork into small cubes, he added it to the onions and garlic with the sultanas. With the rice cooked, he transferred it to the pan and then slowly worked in a decent slug of the soy and a few drops of the Tabasco.

"Ah!" he exclaimed. "Nearly forgot." Fishing out a small packet of cooked prawns from the fridge, he popped them into the mix, stirring contentedly, as the warm blended aroma of dark brown glistening rice, pork, soy, garlic and shellfish, wafted deliciously up towards him.

Finally, whilst the fried rice continued to cook gently, he whisked some eggs with milk and made an omelette. Then, the pièce de résistance: placing the omelette whole, like a magnificent crown, over the top of the fried rice to finish off the dish.

Twenty minutes and two large helpings later – along with a little Manis Ketjap he'd managed to source, to spice things up further – he almost felt his old self again. Shortly thereafter, it was in the same spirit of equanimity that he drove through the estate gates and headed down the road to Brilcrister, for a much needed change of scenery and to stock up on some more provisions.

The peace was never going to last for long. Three hundred metres past the gates, his mobile went off. His heart sank as Kennedy's name came up on the display. Letting it ring on gave him some small petty pleasure, but after a further minute of deliberation, he decided to face it head on. Pulling over to the roadside, he switched off the engine and called her back.

She sounded preoccupied and slightly harassed. Must be a busy afternoon in Raulo's, he surmised.

"Bartholomew. Good of you to call me back," opened Kennedy, with her usual charm.

He took a deep breath and squeezed the steering wheel tightly with his free hand.

"I was expecting an update from you today. But instead I've had an insinuating prick of a policeman on the phone. Baxter, I think he said his name was. Told me you've been up to all sorts of mischief. Chasing people around the Minsham estate in the middle of the night, calling out half the county Police Force! Bartholomew – what the hell have you been up to? Didn't I tell you to keep a low profile down there and just do your job? Last thing I want is Mr Eves being contacted. I will not tolerate you tarnishing my reputation with the clientele through your stupid, cavalier behaviour!"

"Come on Kennedy" he replied, standing his corner. "That's hardly fair. I've had three instances now down here of all sorts of strange goings-on in the night! Noises, bangs, hoodies breaching the barriers! Who exactly is this Mr Eves – some sort of Russian gangster with a price on his head? Do you know why is this happening? You seemed happy enough to send me right into the thick of it. You…"

"Belt up Bartholomew!" she barked down the phone. It seemed the sometime soft spot for him was not at the forefront of her mind today. He also knew there was no way Kennedy was sitting in Raulo's. No, it was somewhere far quieter. More likely in the privacy of her own home in Bayswater, where she could use maximum venom, if necessary, without being overheard.

"Mr Eves is a perfectly respectable UK citizen and has no reason to cause anyone any nuisance, *or* engage in any contentious activity!" She continued, heatedly. "Whatever is happening down there must just be a local oddity. A couple of likely lads fancying their luck in the big house. The policeman said they would keep an eye on it and that they would probably go away. As long as *you* don't go getting up to any more superman antics that is! Stay indoors. Keep the house locked and alarmed, and call Baxter if you hear anything further suspicious. I do not want this getting into the media, even if it's only the Turnip Townsend Times or whatever the local rag is called! Or gossiped about for that matter. As they say – gossip is currency!"

"Kennedy," Bartholomew persisted, knowing he was endangering what little amount of indulgence she usually afforded him, but up against it enough to push back. "You knew about this before I came down here. It's why Mrs Goode refused to stay."

In his mind he could just picture Mrs Goode lying in bed at night, on her own, in the middle of bloody nowhere. Seriously crapping herself, wondering when – not if – whoever it was that was out there was going to try and break in.

"Honestly, Kennedy, it must have been really worrying for her to have been on an assignment like this…"

"You'd better watch what you're saying, Bartholomew," hissed Kennedy, not at all pleasantly. After a moment's pause, she added in a similar vein:

"What's really the matter with you? Is it that you are a bit out of your comfort zone down there? Is that it? Getting a little tetchy, because sleeping off the hangover keeps on getting interrupted? Well, don't worry yourself any further. As I've said, just stay in the flat. No need to try and do a Jack Reacher. Call the cops if you hear anything and contact me when…"

"All right then Kennedy," he cut over her, finding himself with nowhere else to turn. "I thought you cared a little bit – well, at least for my own safety. But I think you're going to have to find someone else for this assignment. Just like you did for Mrs Goode.

It's only right you replace me. I'll give it 48 hours more - which could be a very long time considering the sort of things that go on here. After that, I'd like to return to London please. Assign me another job. I'll take anything you've got."

Hardly to his surprise, Kennedy just laughed down the phone. Like a worldly wise parent, who'd heard their child's protestations once too often.

"Don't try and tell me what going to happen, Bartholomew," she resumed, sounding more like her old self once again. Superior, back in control, but perhaps liking him a little again. Only a little, that is…

"No, Bartholomew, I don't think you're going to do that. What exactly is there for you to come back to anyway? I have no other suitable assignments at present. So: no work, no money. Why, I bet you've already blown what you've earned on this assignment so far on *Chateau Margaux* galore. No, you are going to stay down there and finish off the job. I will consider replacing you in due course, but it's going to be nigh on impossible to organise a handover during the Christmas period. Let me tell you one thing though," she added, her voice lowering a deadly notch. "You walk out of there, without an arranged handover, or if Mr Eves gets wind of something untoward, I'll make sure you *never* work again. For me *or* anyone else. Trust me on this one, Bartholomew."

He held the phone away from his ear, and for a moment, thumb hovering over the end button, nearly cut her dead. Although he didn't entirely believe she'd destroy him if he left Minsham Court without agreement, as she had so adroitly outlined, somehow he found himself hesitating.

He heard her laugh, almost as if she was with him in the pickup, and had witnessed his indecision.

"Good," she purred, contentedly, but still with enough warning in her voice. "I'm pleased you're seeing some sense at last. Give me a ring in 24 hours with an update. I'm sure it'll be as quiet as church mice down there from now on and you can lounge away the hours to your heart's content. Goodbye, Bartholomew. Remember what I said…"

He sat in the pickup and bitterly cursed the world, its tardiness, its inequality and especially its Kennedys. She was right as usual. Knew just where to hit his soft spot and twist the knife in, deep amongst the tattered shreds of his personal and economic circumstances. He vowed to himself, this was the last assignment he would ever do for her.

With that thought firmly in mind, he cranked the ignition, rammed the gearstick into first and wheel spun the pickup back out onto the road.

It was, however, without checking the rear-view mirror. He completely failed to spot the van coming up fast from behind. With a screech of brakes, the driver just managed to swerve out of the line of the pickup and half mounted the bank beyond in a spray of mud. After jack-knifing from side to side along the verge, the van eventually re-entered the highway and screeched noisily to a halt, some forty metres ahead.

Bartholomew braked sharply and jumped out of the pickup, knowing full well there was going to be a confrontation. He had realised, in a split second, where the van was from and who the driver was. She came flying down the road towards him, hair framed wildly about her furious face, eyes ablaze.

"What the fuck do you think you're doing?" she yelled at him. "Don't you look in the mirror?! You could have killed me!"

Pumped from the Kennedy exchange, and, with half his mind still bent on malicious redress, he decided in a moment to kill two birds with one stone.

He strode over and gently grasped her by the wrists, with a look that was about as sincere as he could muster in the circumstances.

"Roxy, you're ok! Thank God for that. Looks like no more harm done than a bit of burnt rubber. I'm really, really sorry, I was a little distracted; let me make amends. D'you know, I was just on my way down to Haddlewell to see you? You were right all along… we should dine in style. Seems a shame to have all that grand accommodation available and not put it to good use. Shall we say tomorrow night, at Minsham Court, at about eight o'clock? Make sure you're dressed for it," he grinned cheekily. "And please, do come to the front door."

Her ability to switch emotions, as if at the flick of a switch, caught him by surprise once again. From snarling tiger to sexy pussycat, all in an instant. She took a deep breath, composed herself, smiled like a super model and proceeded to assure him the near accident was a mere trifle and that she couldn't wait for tomorrow evening.

As she drove off, gaily waving out of the van window, he wondered what the hell he'd let himself in for. Who cares, he concluded, once again refusing to remonstrate with himself. If Kennedy wanted to keep him down here, then she'd just have to accept that the flat he'd been provided with was way too small for formal entertaining.

Chapter 8   The Master

In Brilcrister, he managed to park in the same space in the market square. Nearby he found a decent fishmonger, a stone's throw from the independent butcher he'd used on his last visit. It was shellfish he was after, more prawns, but really decent ones this time, not the supermarket variety he'd scoffed down at lunchtime. Moving quickly on to Edgars, he purchased a neck of lamb and some choice pork ribs too, just for good measure.

On the drive down to town, his mind for once had been on something other than food. More, that he had no formal clothes with him whatsoever on this assignment. He'd only shoved jeans, shirts, jumpers and a few small personal items into his Gladstone bag for the stay at Minsham Court. Indeed, clothes shopping filled him with dread. Although on reflection – he grudgingly had to ask himself – as he stowed the food items away in the pickup, wasn't it really more of a question about the precarious state of his finances?

He was hoping to locate a suitable charity shop in Brilcrister. He needn't have worried. Like most towns of a similar size, a number of such stores figured prominently in the High Street – rammed full of books, DVDs, bric-a-brac and musty clothing galore. In one, at the back, stuffed onto the end of a hanging rail, jammed in tight beside a jumble of chronically unfashionable menswear items, he found a vintage dinner jacket, still in good condition. Double breasted and hand-made, he judged, on closely inspecting the tailoring. Definitely not one of your usual off-the-shelf variety. After matching a similar pair of trousers in a sister shop two doors up, his mood lifted even further as he hit the jackpot once more. This time with a pair of smart black brogues, surely never used, and on offer at a fraction of what would have been their original retail price.

Judging that a second-hand shirt for the occasion was perhaps a bridge too far, he purchased a new, white cotton, button-cuffed number from a gentleman's outfitters nearby (although in the past he had bought plenty second hand, without a qualm). After all, he mentally concluded, he could still give himself a big pat on the back that the three recycled items together cost only half as much again as the shirt on its own. Conveniently ignoring the stark reality that his decision making had been entirely based on an empty wallet, as opposed to that of Save the Planet.

Back at the entrance to Minsham Court, he pressed the clicker and sat waiting in the pickup for the gates to swing open. The weather continued on in its sombre mood. The foreboding clouds which had swept along overhead during his return from Brilcrister, finally decided to discharge their freezing contents over the landscape. The noise was all encompassing as he drove down the drive under the canopy of trees.

Parking up, he legged it with his purchases as fast as possible across the yard, to avoid a total soaking. Back in the flat and shaking off what drenching he'd been unable to avoid, he decided he'd had quite enough for the day; it was time to light the wood burner and put his feet up. He shortly discovered the draw from the little cast iron stove in the sitting room was excellent. With a few scraps of paper, dry kindling and split seasoned logs from the covered barn, he soon had the wood burner roaring away. Half an hour later, it just remained to be seen how far he needed to tamp down the oxygen intake to maintain a nice, cosy fug.

Plugging his iPod into a wall socket, Bartholomew sank into the tired old leather armchair, closed his eyes and soaked up a bit of Ocean Colour Scene. Nearly twenty years old but still classy as hell, he judged. The enveloping heat gloriously bowling out of the wood burner, a cup of the Italian coffee and a seriously decent nip of *The Famous Grouse* all fostered an agreeable ambience. Eventually, after a good hour, he pulled himself out of his *Grouse* induced torpor and decided that a read would round off the evening nicely. He'd finished the Rose Tremain novel earlier – with a touch of relief, he had to admit – and so dug into the second paperback he'd purchased at Casper's.

✳✳✳

It was sometime after eleven that he shook himself awake. Still in the leather armchair, with the fire gone out and mug over on its side, the remnants of the coffee spilt carelessly across the floor. It took him a minute or two to realise that he wasn't in the railway waiting room with the World War One Secret Service Agent, Ashenden, and the Hairless Mexican; waiting for the train in Naples Station whilst Ashenden deciphers the secret cable, the one which tells him that the man the Hairless Mexican had assassinated earlier that evening at the hotel hadn't actually left Piraeus yet; where Ashenden, to his horror and anger, realises the Hairless Mexican has killed the wrong man…

He dragged himself out of his dream-like state and flipped the dog-eared Somerset Maugham collection off his chest onto the floor. At least returning to a waking state had no equally worrying scenario waiting for him in real time. Or so it seemed. Bartholomew lay still, sprawled in the armchair, listening carefully. The rain had ceased and the wind – which earlier had been vigorously rattling the window panes – had tapered off too. All seemed quiet. He wondered for how long.

He picked himself up and made the decision to do the rounds of the main house before he went to bed. In the utility room, he de-activated the alarm and stepped out into the main hall. Sliding his hand up the inside wall to locate the bank of switches, he eventually succeeded and flipped them all on with his fingertips. The vast hall, chandeliers brilliantly illuminating the glossy, chequered floor, stood as empty and silent as ever. Like a ghost of its former self.

Bartholomew stood and stared at the space, speculating as to the entertainment that must have taken place here in years gone by. Hunt meets and balls, birthday parties, musical evenings perhaps.

All the local gentry no doubt, dazzling in their hunting red or evening tails, dancing the night away whilst the servants stood about, boredom just about hidden away behind attentive masks, or, freezing outside in the icy December darkness as they waited patiently by their masters' carriages. No longer though. The interior of the house was all very pristine, possibly in a better state than in its heyday, but now empty and soulless. Seemingly the preserve of one person. Its elusive and mysterious owner. Or perhaps it was just a trophy. An acquisition, to show off the trappings of a lifestyle that fifty years before you were only ever likely to experience if you were born into it.

Bartholomew moved through the hall and into the drawing room. It was the same as on every other visit he'd made. Not a cushion or chair out of place. The photo frame was once again in its original position. He'd pushed it back after the last episode – perhaps in a sub-conscious attempt to deny it had ever been moved in the first place.

Moving on to the kitchen, he ran his eye over the gleaming appliances. The previous afternoon, the lady from the contract cleaning company had spent over six hours going over the house and he could see she wasn't the sort to skimp on the work, or move anything an inch out of position. There wasn't a patch of dust in sight. He wondered whether she had OCD. He'd met a number in the past, at the various jobs he'd done, and it was a consistent theme. Like bees to honey. The ones who did a spotless job often said they just couldn't help themselves. They wouldn't be able to stand it if a thing was left out of line, a pillow un-plumped, a sink not forensically scoured, a chrome plug left anything but gleaming.

He had to admit to himself that working away at the back of his mind, throughout the inspection, was a little bit of planning for the next evening. *Diner à deux*. Looking around, he thought he might as well give it a sense of theatre: use all the available props; light a magnificent fire in the hall; set a grand table in the dining room. What would Kennedy think? He laughed to himself. Well, in any event, she was never going to know but it gave him some small pleasure to think of her reaction if she were to find out. The word ballistic came to mind. Strolling on, still chuckling mischievously, he realised he'd have to get the over-zealous cleaner in afterwards, for a comprehensive, much earlier than normal, spring clean. Mr Eves would have to pick up the tab. Giving it no more than a moment's thought, he vaguely hoped it wouldn't be too big a supplement.

Back out in the hall he headed for the stairs. It seemed the wind had picked up again as he could hear a kind of fluttering, like the sound of a pack of cards being flicked through with ones thumb. He halted and listened harder. The fluttering continued, intermittently, although always at the same speed. Keeping entirely still, Bartholomew tried to imagine what natural occurrence could produce such a noise? The leaves of a tree being repeatedly whipped against a wall? – or drawn across a windowpane?

Moving over to the door of the drawing room, he realised how exposed he felt in the glaring light of the hall chandeliers. He pressed the light switches just inside the door, bringing the room to life. The fluttering had ceased in the last minute or so, but out of the corner of his eye, he caught a flash of a low indistinct shape retreating from the far window. Striding rapidly over to the corner, he rapped angrily on the glass with his knuckle, driven on by his surging nerves. Unable to contain his frustration, he screamed at the darkness beyond: "Why don't you just leave me alone! Or come to the front door and show yourself – if you've got any balls. You won't though, will you? Stalker!"

He stood back from the window, fists clenched, trying to control his ragged breathing. After a minute of forcing himself to calm down and think rationally, he listened once more. There was nothing to be heard bar the familiar night time background noises, the wind in the rhododendron bushes, a light splattering of rain: just as he would have guessed. Whoever it was out there would be a hundred metres or so away by now, slyly camouflaged in the inky blackness, safe in the knowledge that any chase Bartholomew made would be futile.

I'm going to bloody well ignore it, that's what I'm going to do, he silently determined, refusal to give in to the intimidation and mind games just about gaining the edge over his jumpy state. Calling the police tonight wouldn't help, either. A search to try to apprehend the stalker – or whatever it was – would prove fruitless. And yet, at the back of his mind lurked a needling worry, like an ever invasive parasite slowly eating away at him – questioning whether it was all just in his imagination – that maybe, he was simply losing his grip on reality.

He walked back into the hall and mounted the stairs two at a time. He hadn't checked through the bedrooms since the day before yesterday, so he moved to the far end of the corridor on the side of the house facing the drive and inspected each room, half expecting some further fright. Once he was satisfied, with no small relief, that all was as it should be within the sequence of identical guest suites, he arrived back at the top of the stairs, outside the master bedroom. Pushing the door open, he stepped inside.

He hadn't really taken it in before. As he stood next to the vast double bed, lushly draped with a deep blue silk cover, this time he registered the wardrobe arrangements. Or – to be more precise – the mirrored wardrobe arrangements. It was, essentially, a complete room of floor to ceiling mirrors. Apart from the door to the hallway, the two large sash windows overlooking the drive and the ceiling itself, the entire bedroom was one continuous, revolving bank of reflection. Even the door to the private bathroom in the far corner of the room had its outer face similarly clad. Crumbs, he thought, almost humorously, grateful for any diversion from the events of earlier – no place in here for the shy and retiring, He wondered who had commissioned the bedroom to this particular specification. Someone, clearly, who was not afraid of the fact that every crack and wrinkle would be on display, from every conceivable angle. Apart from above, that is.

Strangely embarrassed, and chastising himself for his prudishness – for God's sake, he was on his own after all, well, hopefully, that is – he quickly turned the lights off. He stood for a further couple of minutes in the dark until his eyes accustomed themselves to the gloom, before moving over to the left hand window. He caught sight of a pair of headlights slowly traversing the road that bordered the estate wall. They seemed to hover slightly as they passed the main gates. Or was that just his over-active imagination again? Yes, it was. The lights continued on, until they faded away in the direction of Evensthorpe. Stop winding yourself up, he told himself as he stepped back out onto the landing. Finish your checks and get yourself off to bed. He'd had more than enough unwarranted excitement tonight, so to hell with anyone else thinking of disturbing him.

Wishful thinking was the trick, he concluded the next morning. Within twenty minutes of the tour of boudoir mirrors, he'd got back into the flat, locked the door to his bedroom for extra security and tucked himself up snugly under his duvet. Managing a good six hours of uninterrupted sleep had been a treat. If his nocturnal joker friends had visited, well, he hadn't heard them. Ignorance is bliss, as they say.

Feeling more like his old self in the morning, and with the superior advantage of daylight, he took a quick tour around the house and outbuildings. All looked as it should. Back in the kitchen, brewing a cup of the Italian coffee whilst poaching a couple of eggs, his mobile suddenly rudely vibrated on the kitchen table.

"Bartholomew," he answered shortly.

"It's Detective Sergeant Baxter," came back the dry reply. "Just checking in with you, sir. To ensure you've come to no harm overnight."

"Well, thank you very much Detective Sergeant. For your conscientious enquiry" Bartholomew replied flatly: bitterly thinking: a bit late now… I could have been burgled and assaulted, and they'd never have been any the wiser. Until that is, they got down their routine checklist and decided to pick up the phone.

"It's not my conscience, sir, just standard procedure. We agreed we'd speak this morning and I know you would have called me at the slightest alarm following our little chat yesterday – the one about you not playing James Bond any more. Anyway, just to let you know, our community spirited police car did a couple of turns around the near neighbourhood during the night, which included the road adjacent to Minsham Court. I'm told they neither heard nor saw anything untoward. I'm assuming their report matches your own experience?"

Bartholomew refrained from off-loading to Baxter about what had occurred in the drawing room. He knew he wouldn't come out of it well, regardless of how he explained it. Besides, afterwards he'd been sparko for most of the night in a drug-like exhausted state and in any event, probably wouldn't have heard a further thing. Instead, he enquired:

"So, any leads? By now you must have an inkling of who these people are or what their agenda is?"

"Still working on it. It's not uncommon for it to take a little time to generate some results from our local enquiries. But don't you worry. We'll get to the bottom of it. Tell me, sir, what are your immediate plans?"

"What do you mean – immediate plans?"

"Well sir, not thinking of taking off anywhere are we? Moving on to your next assignment or whatever you call it?"

"Of course, I'm not – I've told you already, I'm contracted to house-sit Minsham Court until my employer lets me know otherwise. Why do you ask?"

"Just wanted to keep up-to-date with your plans, that's all, sir. Our initial investigations have revealed nothing as yet with regards to a motive for these disturbances. I told you yesterday, we are looking down all potential avenues – and I have to remind you, sir, one of those includes yourself. So please do not leave the vicinity without letting me know. I can assure you we will find you if you decide to move on – unobtrusively that is."

"And as I told you, Detective Sergeant Baxter, you're barking completely up the wrong tree. You need to spend your time searching for the real villains, not speculating on some bizarre motive that you think I may have. I mean, are you trying to tell me something I don't know?"

"Keep calm sir. It's just routine. Stay in touch. That's all I'm asking."

"So, can I take it your boys will be out patrolling over the next few nights? For when, no doubt, our friends turn up yet again?"

"Oh yes, don't worry – we certainly will be. Anyway, have to go, sir. Please let us know immediately if you hear or see anything further untoward."

Bartholomew didn't bother to reply, just grimaced, index finger stabbing hard at his mobile to end the call. The guy was a donkey. It was just a wind up, he knew, but it worried him that the local police would be pushed to get a result. No doubt it was a small world in these parts and word got around quickly. It would be easy to pin some jacked-up story on Bartholomew, the outsider, that he was a plant for some gang or other. None of it made any sense. Why go to the trouble he'd gone to to report the disturbances?

And why make any disturbance at all if all you wanted to do was to get into the estate and burgle the house?

The frustration of it all was driving him mad. He decided to get some fresh air and exercise to clear his mind. Donned in his usual apparel, he grasped the hazel staff and quickly exited the flat, heading off down the drive at a rapid pace, only slowing once he began to approach the main entrance gates. Still dwelling on Baxter's little mind games, he began to walk up along the estate wall at a more measured pace, checking to see if he could spot any further evidence of intrusion.

After an unproductive thirty minutes, he had to conclude there was no indication of further activity. Either on the leafy floor, or hanging from any of the numerous trees he now sauntered morosely under.

Finally, bored, and no less frustrated, he crossed the grassy paddocks and headed off up into the wood. Within a few minutes, he had pushed through the initial belt of trees and reached the edge of the pit. He decided, for no particular reason, to gently trot down the side of the bowl and stand once again in its centre. He waited there quietly, gripping the staff with both hands, as he listened hard for any sign that his shadow might have joined him once more. There was nothing to be heard though, other than the gentle swish of branches high above in the raw, wintry breeze.

He clambered up the far side of the pit and made off again at a leisurely pace to connect with the usual path which cut north through the gloomy wood. And yes, sure enough, there it was: he discerned some slight movement in the trees over to his right.

Well, well, he thought. Here we go again. Just keep walking, he told himself. Keep on the track and have the staff ready. He grasped it even tighter, holding it now in a horizontal position, and moved along the path, taking sideways steps this time so he was ready to meet the challenge directly from the trees.

"Eves, I thought it had been made clear to you. This is Rissborough land!"

Bartholomew almost jumped right out of his skin and swung frantically around to meet the new threat. Not from the right but from directly in front – coming along the track towards him. It was two men, silhouetted from behind by the weak sun which had, at that instant, surprisingly broken out from behind the heavy clouds. It lit up the whole length of the path bisecting the wood.

It was not the men themselves though, nor the verbal challenge that captured his attention so completely. More, the blue-black barrels of a 12 bore shotgun, which were pointing directly at his kneecaps.

He wasn't sure which of the pair had challenged him. Both men must have been well over six foot in height and he could just about make out that one was much more heavily built than the other. The voice, however, was one of authority. Of the Establishment. A voice that sounded like it was very much used to getting its own way.

"I said – I thought you had already been made aware that you are not on Minsham Court property here. This is part of the Rissborough estate. What exactly is it that you don't understand?"

The shotgun hadn't wavered an inch in the minute that had passed since the beginning of the stand-off. With the sun passing once more behind the clouds, Bartholomew was now able to make out that the owner of the patriarchal voice was not the one holding the 12 bore. His companion was silent, just concentrating on the task – that is, of ensuring Bartholomew's legs remained fully in line with the direction of the rock-steady barrels.

Holding his hands out wide, Bartholomew faced the pair full-on. After tilting his head back, so they could see his visage under the fedora, he replied as calmly as he could:

"I think you're mistaking me for someone else. I'm not Mr Eves."

For a moment neither man reacted at all to this statement. Then, finally, they caught each other's glance and a look of mild perplexity passed between them. The welcome outcome, though, was for the silent one to lower the barrels of the 12 bore, just enough so that it was more or less pointing at the ground, albeit still a couple of narrow inches from Bartholomew's toes.

Bartholomew now had a chance to take a good look at his aggressors. 'Patriarchal' was clearly not only the owner of the wonderful voice, he was most definitely the more richly attired. His top of the range French wellingtons protected the lower half of legs clad in expensive tweed breeks. He wore a dark blue padded jacket – of the type Barbour now produces at silly prices – and, on his left wrist, Bartholomew caught a flash of an antique wristwatch set on a subtle, classy, light brown leather strap.

It was the face that really caught the attention though. Brown hair, beginning to go grey at the temples topped a profile that was,

Bartholomew had to admit, handsome and suave. He was a bit of a John Kerry look-alike. The look of an international statesman, leader of the pack, the big influencer. But it was the eyes that really told you what you needed to know about this man. Slightly hooded, the colour of pale grey and intensely piercing. Looking right into you and through you, with a fierceness that left you in no doubt he wasn't the type to suffer fools gladly, or let anything stand in his way.

His companion was no less intriguing. He was dressed in clumpy, polished brown brogues and matching tweed breeks, jacket and flat cap. All very nicely worn in. The tweeds were of the slightly rough cut style – the ones you see the gamekeeper wearing. Not the master. And that was the slightly odd thing about it. Bartholomew knew enough about game shoots to be able to recognise the stereotypical fit of the man who spends a good amount of his time outside. Country born, often ruddy-cheeked and one who moves about with a sure-footed ease across the varied terrain of the English countryside.

This individual looked different somehow. The image of a bodyguard or finely tuned athlete sprung to mind. It was the rigid, erect posture, the tapering of broad chest into narrow waist, the sinewy cords sticking out in his neck. Bartholomew wondered – with humour being the only prop he could muster in the circumstances to help stifle his fear – if when he spoke would it be with a Russian Mafioso accent. Not a true country brogue, chirpy and instructive, piped out of a thickset body in the usual gamekeeper mould.

Like his master though, he had unflinching eyes. Unflinching eyes and a sure and steady grasp on the shotgun, which was still aimed menacingly close to Bartholomew's sensitive and mightily put-upon toes.

"Is there any chance you could point that thing somewhere else?" Bartholomew asked.

In the circumstances, he ensured he made his request in the politest possible manner. Not quite a beg, but, it had to be said, not far off one.

"Jeavons – break open the gun and stand back," Patriarchal finally instructed the hulk, after a further bout of scrutinising Bartholomew.

Well, at least they'd given Mr Mafioso a decent sounding surname, thought Bartholomew. Even though he knew the chances he'd been born with the surname of Jeavons were absolutely zilch. He wasn't about to mention it though. He gauged that would be about as welcome as a fart in a space suit.

The look that remained etched on Jeavons' face, as he broke the gun and hung it over the crook of his right arm, only served to provide a clear, unambiguous signal – that is, the slightest miss-move on Bartholomew's part would categorically result in an immediate re-closure of the weapon.

"I'll ask you then," Patriarchal pointedly challenged once more, hands in pockets, still holding onto Bartholomew with those laser like eyes. "Who are you and what are you doing in these woods?"

"I'm working at Minsham Court. Which, as I imagine you know, is on the other side of the woods that way," Bartholomew answered, jerking a thumb over his shoulder.

"I'm the house-sitter. Simple as that. I need to ensure the property and estate are kept secure. So I conduct a daily inspection through the gardens and grounds."

"You're not on Minsham Court property here though, are you?" came back the frosty reply. "This is part of the Rissborough Estate."

"Well, I have to say, it's not very well marked. I mean, apologies if I've inadvertently strayed onto private property, but I've an old OS Map back in my flat and, from the look of it, it would appear that the Minsham boundary extends all the way to the edge of this wood. Overlooking Rissborough Hall itself."

The effect of Bartholomew's words seemed to release some sort of explosive valve inside his interrogator's head. Patriarchal's face reddened in contorted fury. His facial muscles twitched ferociously in the half light as he clenched his lips tightly together in an effort to stop himself spouting out some instruction to his companion, that Bartholomew sensed, would almost certainly be life-threatening. The reaction struck a distant chord with Bartholomew, but for the life of him he couldn't remember from where.

Eventually, after a minute of further internal struggle, the man seemed to calm down and regain some of his previous, aloof veneer. Jeavons still looked on manically, as if to say: shall I close the gun now, sir, and give this trespassing motherfucker both the barrels he deserves?

Partriarchal gestured downwards with his arm for Jeavons to back off. Bartholomew had seen enough now to decide that goading this man further was not an option he would choose lightly again. He wondered who was the scarier of the two: the hulk or his loose-cannon master?

"My family have lived on this estate for nearly three hundred years. The boundary hasn't changed in all that time. Fences, estate walls or other means of demarcation are not necessary here. The position is clear and always has been. It is just outsiders who are new to the area who like to play games and treat the position with less than the respect it deserves. If I, or Jeavons here, catch anyone trespassing, then you can see for yourself," he said, nodding over in Jeavons' direction, "they will have to face the full consequences."

"Ok, I get the picture," Bartholomew replied evenly.

He just couldn't stop himself though. Couldn't resist one last niggle.

"What about the shadow?"

"Eh?" replied Patriarchal.

"As I've explained, I've walked this wood pretty regularly over the last few days. I keep on hearing strange movements in the trees as I cut along this path. It's as if someone is watching me but always wants to remain out of sight. I even caught a glimpse of whoever it is the other day. It was in pretty bad weather, so I couldn't be sure, but it looked like someone wearing a black Lycra running suit. One of those all-in-one types, with a hood. Unless, of course, it was one of you two guys. Out stalking trespassers."

Patriarchal, or Gerald Rissborough as Bartholomew now guessed he was, glanced over to Jeavons, who shrugged his shoulders and shook his head.

"No, we've not had that particular pleasure, but rest assured, we will keep a close look out for your friend in the future."

He then glanced at his scrumptious wristwatch and humphed.

"Bloody hell, is that the time? I've got meetings to attend. Time for you to about turn and head back from whence you came, Mr House-Sitter. Just this side of the pit is where the Rissborough boundary ends. Make sure you stick to the other side of it from now on."

"Alright, point taken, Mr Rissborough," quipped back Bartholomew, as he began to saunter off from whence he came.

"Wait there a minute. How do you know my name?"

Bartholomew halted once more.

"Ah well, it was a bit of a long shot really, but I put two and two together and came up with the conclusion that funding the sort of clothes and watch you're wearing, as well as the fittest gamekeeper I've seen in a long while, could only be the preserve of one man in these parts. To be precise, the owner of the biggest house in the neighbourhood. It is, after all, only just through the trees over there."

Bartholomew thought he might have provoked another seismic reaction, but instead, Rissborough seemed to take it all as a compliment and smiled. Almost charmingly.

"Well, you are right of course. I am Gerald Rissborough."

Bartholomew swore he could almost see the man's chest swell by at least six inches.

"And you? I can't continue to call you Mr House-Sitter. Or I suppose I could. But I won't. What is your name?"

"Bartholomew."

Rissborough's head seemed to make a little funny movement, as a quizzical look passed across his features. He took a couple of steps towards Bartholomew and leant forward, as if peering in. After a further thirty seconds of scrutiny, he stood back again and his body seemed to relax. Whilst the questioning look remained in place, he seemed somehow to have moved on, and appeared now almost accommodating. Bartholomew was confused. He didn't usually have this effect on men of Rissborough's standing. In fact, quite the opposite.

"It's just Bartholomew, is it?" Rissborough enquired further. "Anything else?"

"No, that'll do."

"Well, pleased to make your acquaintance. D'you know, I actually rather like your sense of humour. Kind of irreverent, wouldn't you say? Amusing – a bit alternative. Wouldn't you agree Jeavons?" he turned to ask the brooding gamekeeper, whose lack of response provided Bartholomew with an unequivocal answer as to what his view entailed.

Ignoring, for the moment, the gamekeeper's stance on the matter, Bartholomew thought: Crumbs, I can almost feel my own chest inflating half an inch or two.

Rissborough placed a thoughtful finger under his chin. "Look, I'd like to extend a bit of hospitality. Now that we are near neighbours – for a short while at least, that is. Let's say I'd like to make amends for the bad start out here today. All a bit of a misunderstanding, I think. You are probably right. New to the area and how were you to know about ancient boundaries. Your employer should have warned you."

On that note, Rissborough seemed momentarily to wobble on the charm offensive and some of his previous menace resurfaced. It was obviously a bit of a sore point. Recovering his equanimity once more, he resumed in pleasant landlord mode.

"We always hold a lunch time drinks party each year at Rissborough. On New Year's Day. Why don't you join us? I'll send an invite over. It's just family and old friends. Mainly county people. Looks like you are the sort who can hold your own. Put a jacket on and don't worry. We won't shoot you if come on foot through the woods. Ha! Indeed, please do. You can have a couple of glasses and not worry about drinking and driving. Make your own way back safely. It will be all on private land, so to speak."

Bartholomew was slightly bemused by the sudden turnaround, but in the circumstances felt it best to be obsequious. He indicated his acceptance with a polite nod of the head and bade the pair goodbye.

Jeavons gave him one last lingering look as he turned away with his master. Just to remind Bartholomew: Mr Rissborough might have reversed his original stance but don't for one instant think I won't cut you down in a trice if you put a foot out of line. Christ, thought Bartholomew with a shiver, as he passed the edge of the pit once more. Shades of Solville.

He eventually met the tree line and crossed the paddocks in a slow meander back towards the house. What he'd really like to do was to push all thoughts of the last few days out of his mind altogether. It was nigh on impossible though. An acid, dissembling boss, an enigma of an owner, an SAS style stalker, sinister hoodie intruders in the parkland and possibly even the house plus two psychos in the woods ready to put him in a wheelchair were not to be easily disregarded. Not to mention an accusatory copper bursting to blame Bartholomew for an inside job. Lucky I'm not the sensitive type, he laughed to himself mirthlessly. One could get a complex around here.

As to what it all added up to, he really didn't have a clue. Clearly, locally, it didn't look like Mr Eves was a particularly popular man. Bartholomew knew though, he couldn't put up with the goings-on for that much longer. There was definitely another conversation with Kennedy to be had. Without a doubt, she had the wrong house-sitter profile in place here. Either that, or she was having some sort of twisted, wicked fun with him. That had crossed his mind too. Nevertheless, if it came to seriously risking his health, he would be out of here at a moment's notice. Whether Kennedy liked it or not.

Not quite yet though. If the assignment demanded far more of him than the usual remit, then it would have to have its perks too. He would think of it as Bartholomew time.

In conjunction with his mood brightening, his pace picked up once more as he crossed the final manicured lawn. It was early afternoon, and the thought of cooking for the evening ahead gave him a lift – as it always did. For one night only, this particular Master of Minsham Court was about to entertain in the style to which he would like to become accustomed.

Chapter 9 The Confused Texan

For the sake of ease, he decided to suppress his envy of the magnificent Aga in the main kitchen and instead utilise his own battered work horse in the flat. He had direct access to the larder and, although he would need to heat and cool his proposed fare in the house itself, he judged there would be less mess in the aftermath.

Donning the grubby apron, he set to on the worktop for the first course. Ramming The Kings of Leon up to full volume on the iPod, he grabbed a jar of Hellmann's mayonnaise from the fridge and whacked a good dollop of it into a mixing bowl. To this, he stirred in a couple of decent slugs of the Ketjap Manis, lemon juice, Worcester sauce and a few drops of Tabasco.

Retrieving two fine cut-glass champagne flutes from the main house dining room, he set them on the kitchen table. He proceeded to ease the Brilcrister prawns into the mixture, ensuring they got a good dousing, and then carefully divided it all between the two glasses. With a slice of lemon jammed onto the rim. It was pure 70's chic, if he didn't say so himself.

Placing the flutes to chill in the fridge, next he began to construct the Moroccan Lamb. In a large bowl, he mixed ground cumin, cinnamon, ginger, chilli powder, black pepper and a few saffron threads. To this, he added some lamb fillet and getting his hands into the bowl gave it all a jolly good mix before frying the meat in batches. Adding three cans of chopped tomatoes, lamb stock and a cinnamon stick he then put the whole lot into a casserole dish and shoved it in the lower oven of the Aga. That's good for about three hours he decided. Now time to sort out the rest of his planned menu: shortbread, lemon posset and a raspberry coulis, all quickly assembled and popped into the back of the fridge too.

Waiting for the Moroccan Lamb to cook through, he decided a cup of tea was in order. He put his feet up on a chair at the table and slurped his Earl Grey happily. The Kings of Leon continued to make one hell of a racket.

Onto the last leg. He retrieved the dough from the fridge. Rolling it out, he cut it out into some shapes. Stars and moons seemed to come to mind. He wasn't sure why. Carefully placing his artwork onto a flat tray, he realised he was going to need a cold shelf for the Aga. What are the chances, he wondered, of there being one in the kitchen? Much to his surprise, however, there it was, leaning on the back wall of the larder. A little cobwebbed and warped, but perfectly serviceable. He slid the cold shelf into the top of the hot oven and then shoved the flat tray onto the grid shelf beneath.

The shortbreads looked pretty good too on close inspection. Enough cooking for the moment, he decided. Moving into the main hall of the house, he lit a fire in the huge hearth. He gauged a pre-dinner drink in the high back armchairs in front of a roaring log fire would set the scene nicely.

Bartholomew laid the table in the dining room for two. Grandly, at either end of the vast table, with two huge ornate candlesticks in between. If Roxy wanted to be entertained in style then he might as well create the right ambience. He flicked on the switch for the chandeliers in the hall, and all the side lights in the drawing room too, to get just the perfect effect. Let's hope it doesn't screw up all the automatic timers, he grimaced.

Experiencing only the minutest twinge of conscience, he phoned Kennedy to report that all was quiet on the estate, here on his own. As indeed it was, at the moment. He was lucky. She sounded distracted and not willing to spend any time with him on further detail – which in the circumstances suited him perfectly. Mind you, he thought darkly to himself, he was going to have to have a very different sort of conversation with her once he'd got this evening out of the way.

After moving the food through to the main kitchen, he retired to the flat for a good soak in the bath. Shaved, and having pulled a comb through his shampooed hair for the first time in a week, he donned his new shirt and the charity dinner suit. At the stroke of eight, just as he had pulled on the new shoes – which he now realised, regretfully, pinched his toes a little – he heard the intercom go in the kitchen.

"It's me," came her sultry voice out of the wall when he pressed the buzzer.

"Hi there," he replied, trying to sound as cool as possible. "Bring your car round to the main door, I'll meet you there."

Bartholomew strode from the kitchen – nobly ignoring the minor pain from his squashed toes – through the utility room and out into the main hall of the house like a true member of the landed gentry. He'd quite decided he could really get into the theatre of it all. Arriving at the huge front door, he pulled it open just in time to catch Roxy ascending the main steps. She had a blue beret on and was wrapped up tight in a knee length Burberry. Very coquettish, he thought appreciatively – and then, a little mischievously – not unlike Michelle from *'Allo 'Allo*."

"You going to invite me in or shall we both just stand out here freezing on the doorstep?" she asked, arching her eyebrows. Bartholomew gave her a fixed, beaming smile in return. More on his part, it has to be said, to suppress the giggle bubbling inside that at least she hadn't opened with: "*Listen very carefully, I shall say this only once.*"

Stroppy or not, she looked a million dollars. He stepped back and ushered her into the hall. Moving inside, Roxy looked around in open appreciation at the sparkling chandeliers and roaring log fire, whose reflecting flames caressingly flickered across the black and white chequer floor.

"Wow," she sighed. "Now that's what I call a real hallway." She slowly pulled off the beret, shook her dark bob out and gave him a full-on, smouldering, catlike smile of a greeting. Wow indeed, he thought, taking in those eyes and that sensuous mouth again.

They moved over to the high backed chairs, as Roxy passed him a heavy paper carrier bag.

"This is for you, Bartholomew. My contribution for the evening. I trust you have a cocktail shaker in the house?"

He peeped inside. A bottle of gin accompanied one of vermouth and a couple of limes.

She added; "You'd better. I'm the queen of the dry martinis so lead me to the kitchen and I'll fix us a couple."

Perhaps this is more *007* than *'Allo 'Allo!*, speculated Bartholomew, struggling hard again to quash the inane giggle that was threatening to ripple violently up through his torso. He couldn't but help ponder on what other impressions she might have up her sleeve.

They reached the kitchen. He pulled out a cocktail shaker and glasses from one of the swanky eye-line cupboards, whilst Roxy had a good nose around. She seemed mightily impressed. What wealth and riches does for some, he mused. Perhaps he'd got a little too blazé about his surroundings, after a few too many Kennedy assignments. Wheeling out some ice and crushing it for her in a tea towel, he looked on while Roxy quickly and expertly fixed the martinis.

"You're right – quite the dry martini queen. Let's have these in front of the fire. Can I take your coat?"

Roxy set the shaker down by the readied martinis. Un-buckling the belt, she shook off the Burberry, before flipping it over the back of one of the central island stools.

Jokes aside, he was riveted. Simply dressed in a sleeveless black cocktail dress which came to just above the knee, Roxy was one of those women who needed no prop to demonstrate she was a true thoroughbred.

Judging that to share the equine analogy would hardly be tactful in the circumstances, he kept his compliment to a simple 'you look great' and just enjoyed the rear view of sheer stockings and high heels as he followed her back out into the hall.

She eyed him amusingly over her martini, as they reclined in the high back chairs.

"You don't look too bad yourself, all scrubbed up. You know, I haven't had the chance to tell you, but I like your curly hair. When you wash it."

She was laughing at him again with those eyes. He'd only just taken a couple of sips of his cocktail when Roxy suddenly downed hers, and told him to hurry up. Before he knew it, she'd slid out to the kitchen and returned in a shake with a couple more of the liquid bombs.

"Bottoms up, Bartholomew!" she chortled, and then proceeded to knock the martini back in one.

Right, he thought, a little taken aback. Better get on with the food. He took Roxy's arm and escorted her into the dining room, seating her at the far end of the long table.

Soon they were spooning the prawn cocktails down. He'd opened a bottle of Chilean Sauvignon Blanc and sat sipping the white wine, whilst watching her eat.

Roxy indicated her appreciation of the starter by nodding her head and exuding a long, deep, satisfied mmmmm... She proceeded to silently tease him, with her best impression of... what was it now, he tried to recall... yes... it was coming back to him: the scene in the Sixties movie starring Albert Finney, in Fielding's *Tom Jones*. The scene with Tom and Mrs Waters at the Inn. Bartholomew decided it was quite indecent the way Roxy held his eye and slowly sucked the cocktail sauce off the long slippery bodies, even though the martinis and white wine had already taken a good hold of him. Thoroughly indecent. But mesmeric.

Over the Moroccan Lamb, which he'd garnished with a sprig of coriander and served with couscous and a green salad, he tried to engender a bit more conversation. Although he wasn't quite sure if that was entirely the point of the evening.

Pre-occupied by the heavenly rich flavours of the dish, Roxy vaguely confirmed she'd been brought up locally and it was her ambition to run her own livery yard. Other than that, it was difficult to extract a lot more from his dining companion.

"So Bartholomew, what about you?" Roxy enquired brazenly, after wolfing down the rest of the lamb and whacking back half a glass of the claret. The one, that is, he couldn't really afford.

"Have you had your heart broken a few times along the way?"

He didn't answer for a moment, suddenly feeling a little morose.

"No. Actually – yes. That is to say, only twice. Once, a long time ago, which was unrequited, and then another time, just a few years back in London." He shivered, as if trying to throw off an unwanted memory, like shaking the rain drops off an umbrella.

"Ooh, look at you, all so serious. Sorry I asked the question. Can I have a top up please?"

He re-filled her glass, cleared the plates and retreated to the kitchen to assemble the pudding.

Bartholomew realised he was pretty intoxicated already. It was, though, hardly difficult to create the impression he wanted on the pudding plates: the lemon posset shot glasses on one side; the coulis smeared across the other into a point; and a couple of the star and moon shortbreads, strategically placed, to finish off the look.

Triumphantly carrying his offering back into the dining room, he arrived to find Roxy's seat empty. Setting the puddings down, he swiftly moved back out into the hall. Where the hell has she gone now, he groaned? The girl was a wandering minstrel. Concerned she would be poking around in the owner's drawers or other valuable objects, he dashed in and out of the kitchen and drawing room, but his guest was nowhere to be seen.

Finally, just as Bartholomew was heading back towards the stairs and the entrance to the flat, where he guessed she now must be, he spotted something out of place. To the left of the staircase, a door stood slightly ajar. It was decorated in exactly the same light cream colour as the rest of the hall panelling, which was probably why he'd never seen it before. That and the expert joinery of its snug fit, he realised on inspecting it further.

Pulling the door open, he saw it led to a descending flight of stairs. The room at the bottom was dimly lit. He now also knew to where Roxy had so mysteriously disappeared. The noise from below gave away the room's purpose in an instant. He could hear her staggering around, muttering to herself, and the unmistakable chink of bottles.

Bartholomew stepped down slowly and carefully, in light of his inebriated state. Arriving at the base of the stairs, he was confronted by a long, brick-arched ceilinged wine cellar and the sight of a very nicely rounded rump bending over a wine rack. A couple of dusty bottles of wine stuck out from under an arm.

"For Christ's sake, Roxy!" he blurted out. "What the hell are you doing down here? This is the owner's private bloody collection! C'mon on, we've got to get back upstairs."

"Oh, belt up Bartholomew!" she laughed harshly, grabbing a third bottle from the rack and tottering back towards him. "You've run out in the kitchen and I'm certainly not driving to the Spar in Haddlewell for a top up. Stop worrying all the time! Have you seen how much he's got in here? Two or three bottles less won't make a jot of difference. Anyway, don't you want to have a good time?"

She was right about the wine, the collection was vast. Racks and racks of the stuff. He just wanted her out of there as fast as possible and so quickly ushered her back upstairs, before she decided the three vintages she'd pilfered already were not going to be enough.

They both staggered out of the disguised doorway and into the hall. For some reason – probably as a result of the schoolboy thrill of a successful heist – they both almost skipped over to the fire, giggling away hysterically. This is not going in the right direction, thought Bartholomew, unable, though, to suppress the euphoric thrill of it all. In fact, all he could think of was – what the hell.

Roxy – who had somehow managed to obtain a corkscrew and glasses without disappearing from view – quickly proceeded to fill the goblets and demanded a down-in-one toast to the pair of them. Putting his nose to the classic vintage, Bartholomew knew it was an absolute sin not to savour the wine – but shut his mind to sensibility and did exactly as he was told.

And so it continued. After the third round, he managed to persuade Roxy to at least taste the wine, although by now he knew it was academic. She obliged for the next five to ten minutes, but half way through the second bottle got bored, and once more reverted to the manic toasting.

What they toasted he couldn't later quite recall. It might have been the discovery of the hidden wine cellar, the dwarf in *Game of Thrones,* or just Uncle Tom Cobley for all he knew. It was all a bit of a blur. His puddings lay lonely and unappreciated on the dining room table, as Roxy continued to ply them both with the wine of the gods. Finally, she staggered to her feet and informed him she needed the loo. Thankfully, and with no little relief, he directed her towards the bathroom in the flat.

Ten minutes later, as he stared into the fire in a *Grand Cru* stupor, he suddenly wondered what was taking her so long. Pulling himself to his feet and swaying slightly, he retreated back down the hall. As he neared the grand staircase, he realised that the lights were now on up on the first floor landing. Oh God, he sighed – what now? He'd planned to end the evening back in the flat. If Roxy was upstairs poking around, he needed to get her back down pronto before she created any more havoc.

Grabbing the varnished oak handrail to steady himself, he mounted the stairs, listening hard to see if he could quickly locate her whereabouts. To his consternation, or relief – in his muddled alcoholic state he wasn't quite sure which emotion applied best – all was quiet as he reached the landing. Darkness enveloped one side of the house at the first floor level. On the other, it was only the master bedroom landing area which was brightly illuminated. He checked down the shadowy corridor beyond the main suite, through the bedrooms, one by one, but there was neither sight nor sound of his elusive guest.

Finally, he grabbed the doorknob of the master bedroom and pushed his way in. The room was fully lit, which worried him further, but as empty as its neighbours along the landing. He closed the door behind him and stepped over to the end of the vast bed, draped with the deep blue silk cover.

"What took you so long, Barty?" a purring voice asked from behind.

In his inebriated but startled state, he almost laughed out loud at the cliché. I knew she'd have more of a repertoire up her sleeve, he told himself.

Those thoughts, however, were forgotten in an instant as he took in all before him. He had turned and, with his back to the bed, now realised that Roxy had been in the bathroom all along. She closed the mirrored door firmly behind her and moved over towards him, with a couple of long model strides.

It wasn't the catwalk or the cliché that kept him silent. Roxy just stood there, hand on hip, the other slowly running her fingers through her hair. Aside from the stockings, high heeled shoes and God's natural cover, she hadn't a stitch on.

Bartholomew had a flashback to the Spar, to the very first time they'd met. He'd been tongue-tied that time too. He remained standing – albeit rocking ever so slightly – speech eluding him once more. Her figure was an incredible example of sleek toned bodywork, and, if he was to be frank, a natural shining radiance. She was a goddess.

Roxy shifted her weight ever so slightly onto her left leg, and a small muscle twitched at the very top of her thigh, just under the hipbone.

"I'll say it again," she silkily pouted. "You took your time. It was starting to get cold and lonely up here. Did you want me to come down naked into the hall, in front of the fireplace? Was that it?"

"I, umm… actually I thought we might end up in the den, down in the flat…"

"No, no, no," she replied firmly, moving closer. "I've told you before Barty Boy. If you want me then it's got to be Minsham Court proper, or nothing at all. I don't do the servant's quarters."

Before Bartholomew had the chance to quip – no, you're right there, we mustn't let the side down – she urgently reached for him. Pulling his head down towards hers with one hand, she stuck a hot, wet tongue deep into his startled mouth.

He decided not to protest any further, as clearly the sensation was not altogether unpleasant. The slippery face sucking went on for some time. Bartholomew, despite the copious booze on board, began to feel the stirrings of a mighty erection and automatically reached out to play with the various toys on offer.

"No, no, again," gasped Roxy, as she pushed him away, swatting down his clumsy octopus fumbling. "I want it my way. Ok?"

He wasn't allotted any more time than it took to give her a quick nod, before she swiftly unbuttoned his shirt. She pushed it off his shoulders and ran her smooth, cool palms fleetingly over his chest and nipples. Blimey, thought Bartholomew, still swaying drunkenly and now trying to cope with what had become a very tight pair of trousers. Best I do just as I'm told.

Roxy, eyeing him coolly, dropped onto one knee and unbuckled his belt. Tugging slowly and surely at the buttons of his flies, she finally eased his trousers down, removed his shoes and left him standing in nothing at all but his white Fruit of the Looms.

"Well, well" she cooed. "Just like pass the parcel. Down to the last wrapper." With that, she wrenched the jockeys down and out he popped, like a sausage balloon in the final moments of inflation.

Roxy didn't waste any time on viewing the presentation. Grasping Bartholomew with a firm grip, she pulled him back savagely in one motion, bringing an instant tear to his eye. Thankfully, the pain quickly morphed into pleasure, as Roxy lowered her head and his world once again became wonderful and rosy. How long this went on for he wasn't quite sure, but it seemed in no time at all she had got to her feet and stood face to face with him again. He reached for her – out of manners, he tried to persuade himself, rather than lust – to give her some reciprocal joy.

In response, she just laughed throatily and shoved him hard backwards, down onto the bed. Moving like a feline predator round to the side, she made one final cool appraisal of his prone form before straddling his thighs, her back to his face.

"What the hell are you doing?"

"For God's sake Barty! Where have you been all your life? Never done a reverse cowboy?"

He didn't want to admit he hadn't. Instead, he tried to reach up again with a caress but was met with a further swat and derisory snort.

"Don't worry Bartholomew," she cried out over her shoulder, almost contemptuously. "You don't have to provide any gentlemanly foreplay here. I'm not one of your soppy London lasses. Just lie back there like a good boy and enjoy the view."

She was right. The view was absolutely tremendous – so he decided in the circumstances not to argue any further and follow her instructions to the letter.

Roxy raised herself above him. With a deft hand she drew his extremely attentive appendage, like the arm of a derrick crane, up to the appropriate angle.

"You ready?" she squeaked and, before he had a chance to answer, lowered herself down onto him with a series of deep, satisfied grunts.

Slowly Roxy began to rock up and down. Bartholomew lay there, acquiescing gratefully, going along for the ride. The ride, however, soon stepped up a gear as she began a deep, regular, throaty groan, moving her head from side to side. He could now see her back, bottom and thighs were covered in a glistening sheen, as she gradually moved the motion into a new, greater, more urgent rhythm.

The rocking motion had now become more of a pounding. Bartholomew looked sideways and caught sight of Roxy watching herself in one of the mirrored walls. He looked around the rest of the room, and maybe it was the booze, but he thought he could see six of her now. He wasn't sure he could quite cope with being fucked by six women at once, so he stared up at the ceiling and decided to think of England instead.

On and on it went. The up and down was by now a bit of a battering. It was as if, for her, he wasn't really there. Christ, he thought, the woman doesn't want a lover; she needs one of those bucking broncos you get at a charity ball. One that preferably has a large pommel sticking up out of the middle of the saddle.

"Roxxxxxx…..yyyyyyy…...cannnnn………youuuuuuu……...slowww ww…...downnnnn……
aaaaa…….littttt……...bittttttttttt……...pleaseeeeeeeeee…….!

It was of no use and he got no answer. Just about managing to raise his head again, he looked sideways at the mirror. He could see Roxy, with her head up, eyes tightly shut, caught in an ecstatic trance, her expression gripped in frenzied concentration.

Well, he confusedly, drunkenly reasoned. It would be quite improper to deny the woman her satisfaction, but he wasn't quite sure if he could last the distance. He gripped the bed cover either side of him for all he was worth. Like an approaching sea mist, he could sense a grey shroud beginning to envelope his mind. A sudden, irrational, ridiculous fear pervaded his fuzzy consciousness that he was being madly shafted to death. Bloody hell, he thought; here am I, at the pinnacle of most men's fantasies, and all I can think of is will I make it out alive.

Roxy was bouncing him so hard and fast now that his breath was coming out in a sequence of rapid, explosive gasps. His abdomen felt as if it was imploding. She continued to grunt and snort above him, like a thoroughbred filly three furlongs out and ahead of the field by a length. As the alcoholic wave and sheer physicality finally began to overwhelm him, forcefully dragging his mind down into a deepening blackness, all he could imagine he could hear was the ecstatic wail of a siren, somewhere off in the distance.

Chapter 10   The Fall

Daylight had long pushed its murderous winter glare in through the two sash windows. Bartholomew opened his eyes and immediately shut them again, as agonising waves of pain pounded away against his temple. Waiting a moment for it to ebb a little, he very gently lifted his head. He saw he was in exactly the same position as before. Spread eagled on the master suite bed. Naked still, but thankfully alone.

Carefully raising his fragile torso, he swore he could see the beginnings of purple bruising across his stomach and hips. They ached like merry hell. That, and his tackle, which looked like a careless arrangement of battered, shrivelled walnuts.

Slowly, so as not to further antagonise the nasty hobgoblins stomping around in his head, he gently levered himself up onto his feet. Delicately, he picked up his clothes, which lay scattered around the foot of the bed.

Jesus Christ, he moaned, through clenched teeth, as he limped out into the hallway and descended the stairs. Never, ever again. Immediate priorities, he decided. Water and pills. In the flat he located both, partaking of masses of the former and as many as he thought was safe of the latter, before running a hot bath.

He'd had time to quickly check his mobile whilst downing the pills. One o'clock in the afternoon. He must have been sparko for a good twelve hours plus. Not surprising given the circumstances, he mentally, painfully winced. He wondered what had happened to Roxy? No, he thought; quickly, let's change the subject.

As he lay in the hot, steamy water – the pills finally just about defeating the hobgoblins – he heard the intercom go in the kitchen. Oh God, he cursed. Please, just leave me alone. There is no way am I going to answer that. The intercom continued to blare out a couple of times more and then fell silent. That's better, he sighed with numb relief. Peace at last.

A couple of hours, six pieces of unsalted buttered toast and two pots of coffee later, he finally felt human enough to go and inspect the damage in the main house. Actually, it could have been a lot worse, he reasoned. At least on the ground floor it was localised to the kitchen, hall and dining room. Back up in the master suite he threw the blue cover inside out over the end of the bed. I must be in denial, he grimaced.

It was time for a white lie. Needs must when the devil drives. Limping back to the kitchen in the flat, he pulled out the ring binder and located the mobile number for the OCD cleaner. She was not impressed he was calling her today. Why, he asked? Because it's Christmas Eve, why do you think? came back the disgruntled reply. Bloody hell, he thought – Christmas Eve!

Bartholomew apologised profusely and wished her merry tidings in advance. He proceeded to tell her the owner had dropped by unexpectedly last night, with a guest. Just for the evening. Could she pop over for a couple of hours to clear up? It was just that if he did it, it wouldn't be anything like up to her standards. There were bound to be all sorts of bits and pieces left out of place.

He could hear her brain whirring away. The tidiness portion warring with the rest and, finally, as he knew it would, overwhelming it. She just couldn't resist it. Ok, she agreed, unable to cope with the thought of her cleaning domain being anything less than immaculately arranged. She would be over in the next hour. He thanked her, told her to get it billed as usual, and that the master of Minsham Court would be ever so grateful. As indeed, this particular master truly was. He judged it would go unnoticed. The fact too that the cleaner would think it was Mr Eves hopefully meant she wouldn't gossip. Let's hope so, he ruminated.

Suddenly his mobile rang on the kitchen table. It was a message from Detective Sergeant Baxter. Something along the lines of: as he hadn't heard from Bartholomew, he was assuming all was ok. Plus that his patrol car had not reported any unexpected activity in the area. Bartholomew laughed out loud at this, wondering whether they were really making any checks at all. Thinking about it, the lights he'd had on in the house for Roxy were not really any different from the array set on timers each night. Clearly, they hadn't spotted Roxy leaving. If they'd have stopped her… well, she would have certainly blown their breathalysers right off the scale.

He checked in with Kennedy but thankfully she was on voicemail, so he left a message reporting all was quiet. Soon after the cleaner arrived with a worried look on her face. Bloody hell, what now he groaned. No, it was nothing, she said. She was just concerned about the untidy house. He agreed with her emphatically. He had the very same concerns himself. She scuttled off looking determined to get her cleaning fix. Oh, and by the way, she mentioned before heading off out into the hall, there was a white cardboard box sitting on the gravel outside the front gates.

Bartholomew left her to it and, pulling the overcoat on over his aching body, trudged round to the front of the house and up the drive. The weather was as depressingly grey and dreary as usual. At least no rain, he observed, trying vainly to look on the bright side. Beneath the leaden sky he loped, wincing occasionally at the pain from the abdominal bruising. At least his headache had retreated, leaving just the edge of a black dog gloom.

The gates swung open before him. There it was: a medium-sized white cardboard box with a delivery note sticking out of the top. He realised it must have been a delivery driver buzzing the intercom earlier, when he was in the bath. He ripped the note off and snorted amusedly, as he digested the contents. 'Bradley's Best Produce' it said. 'A gold medallion 16-pound turkey from one of our finest free range farms in Gloucestershire. Ready to cook with instructions provided. Giblets included in a sealed bag.'

The owner must have ordered it before his plans had changed, Bartholomew guessed. Just great, he thought, Christmas alone at Minsham Court with a 16-pound turkey. He'd be having turkey curry with the leftovers for the next three months. Well, he couldn't leave it out here, the rats would have it. Perhaps he'd drop it down to the Sally Army in Brilcrister later on today. He was sure they could use it. Picking it up, trying carefully not to let the box bash against his bruising, he lugged it slowly back to the flat and dumped it in the kitchen larder.

OCD was all frantic, noisy activity in the house, so he decided to get some more fresh air. It was nearing four and would soon be dark, but he thought a quick thirty minutes up to the woods and back might help with the recuperation.

He slowly made his way across the paddocks and wended his way into the edge of the darkening wood. As usual, he hesitated at the pit, and then decided a quick tour of the lip would be enough before he returned to the house. No infringement of Gerald Rissborough's boundary either. He could well do without any hassle from that direction today.

Half way round the far side, right on the lip, he spotted them on the ground: a wizened troop of mushrooms which had somehow survived and then been mummified in the winter freeze. Just beyond, he located a couple of clusters in the same state, close to the base of a gnarled tree trunk. Hands on knees and crouching slightly, to ease the ache in his stomach, he examined the mushrooms intently.

Until it was, that he heard the familiar crackle behind him. Bartholomew instinctively decided on a different tactic this time. Instead of moving away, he charged directly towards the source of the noise. Sure enough, it worked. He was almost upon the jogging black figure before it knew he was there. It looked around, startled to see him so close, before rapidly sprinting off. After a few strides, however, in a panic, it failed to navigate a tricky tree root and went bowling head over heels down onto the mossy floor.

Bartholomew was up and over the figure in an instant. Triumphant in finally cornering the shadow. Screaming internally at the searing pain which shot across his middle. He stood gasping, leaning over the figure lain prone face down on the floor. Apart from dark blue running shoes, it was, as he'd thought, covered in a one-piece black Lycra suit. Including a balaclava style head covering.

The shadow was heaving with exertion, and groaning ever so slightly. He could see its left foot was twisted.

"Get up whoever you are!" he demanded. He was fed up with the subterfuge. He'd had more than enough intimidation recently to want to bother with any pleasantries.

"It's my ankle," came back the pained reply. "It's twisted. You are going to have to help me."

"My God," he thought, taken aback. It's a woman. Crouching down, he carefully assisted the black lycra clad body into a sitting position. The shadow's frame was very slender he now realised. She still didn't look up, keeping her head in a lowered position between her legs.

"Look," he said, now somewhat calmer, and, it had to said, more than a little curious. "Let me try and get you standing so you can test the weight on your foot." The woman nodded and then – as if reluctantly – ever so slowly, pulled off the balaclava, raised her head, and looked him directly in the face.

It was the mass of tawny hair and ultimately those intense green eyes that shocked him so much. He reeled back, hardly believing. Suddenly he was back on a Cypriot hillside, thirty years before.

"Olivia? No… you can't be… Olivia? The words fell out of his mouth in a loose jumble, even as his mind was playing catch-up and telling him not to be so stupid to think this could be the girl he had roamed with during that apocalyptic summer, a million years ago. He couldn't keep his eyes off her. She continued to look at him in a way he couldn't quite determine, almost apologetically, bemused, guiltily. He presumed it was just the awkward circumstances.

"Bartholomew? God! Well… yes… is it actually you? And me. What a surprise! Here in the middle of nowhere. On the floor. Although in slightly different circumstances from the last time we saw each other."

She tried to laugh at the sardonic humour, but then winced as she moved her leg, grabbing it quickly. "I don't think it's broken, just badly sprained," she gasped. "Can you help me, because it's going to get really dark in here soon."

"Of course," he replied, all thoughts as to why she was running in the woods in the first place pushed right out of his mind.

He got her on her feet. With her arm across his shoulders and his around her waist, they made their way out of the wood at a snail-like pace. Eventually, they reached the edge and rested, looking down at Minsham Court in the gathering dusk.

"Umm," he asked haltingly, still in mild shock that he was back with Olivia again, from what was, after all, a lifetime ago. "Where did you run from? Sorry, what I mean is – where do you live?"

"I've got a cottage in Evensthorpe," she replied, concentrating hard on not putting too much weight on her foot. To him, she felt incredibly slender in his grip. Well, he reasoned, he knew she ran a lot.

"Look, Bartholomew, can you call me a taxi? I need to get home and take my weight off this." She stared ahead – not wanting, it seemed, to look him in the face. "Is this where you live?" She nodded towards the house.

"No, I mean, yes. I'm the caretaker, or house-sitter if you like. Just here for a few weeks. And of course I'm not going to call you a taxi. I'll run you home. Hey, I can't believe it's you. After all these years. What a great surprise."

"Me too," she replied. He couldn't see her face as she was still looking down at her foot. He didn't care. All he could think of was how pleased he was to be with her again.

They reached the flat and leaving her leaning against the wall of the barn, he retrieved the pickup keys from the kitchen. OCD had presumably gone as there were no other vehicles in the yard. He'd inspect her work later. He had other more important matters to attend to now.

Shoving the double doors open, he helped Olivia into the front seat and then manoeuvred the pickup out and up the drive. It wasn't more than a couple of miles to Evensthorpe. Just as he'd remembered Sheila the postie describe. Olivia sat quietly, almost thoughtfully, her face still a pasty white.

They passed a sign on the left for Gallion's Stud. Unwelcome imagery flashed through his mind from the night before. For some reason his abdomen suddenly ached. Guilty pain? he asked himself. Bloody torture more like, he grimaced, blocking out the memory as quickly as he could. He knew he would do absolutely everything in his power from now on to avoid bumping into Roxy again.

They entered Evensthorpe, which turned out to be the typical picturesque village. Twee thatched cottages were strung out either side of a main thoroughfare. A village pub dominated the centre, the harsh down lighters above its sign illuminating the picture of a cunning fox grinning lasciviously over a hen coop.

"It's just over here on the left." Olivia motioned with her finger. He could see a small box-like cottage, nestled cosily in a terrace of three. He parked at the kerb and helped Olivia out. At the front door she instructed him to look for the key under a cracked flower pot, rammed half buried in the adjacent border.

Retrieving the key, he assisted her across the threshold. The ground floor of the cottage was a simple arrangement of hall with staircase and a kitchen and sitting room on either side. He caught a glimpse of contemporary furnishings, a small, decorated Christmas tree and a smart wood burner with a holly garland decorated mantel above in the sitting room, before turning left and helping Olivia onto a chair in the kitchen. In the hall, he shoved his overcoat on a row of pegs by the front door alongside a jumble of scarves and hats. Back in the kitchen, he was able to take a closer look at his surroundings – the room décor and arrangement there were pretty charming too. Slightly funky and trendily down-to-earth. He thought to himself: if you were happy with someone you loved, it was the sort of cosy bolt hole you could walk into and never, ever, want to leave again. Get back to reality, he cussed, giving himself the proverbial slap. Dream on. Shaking his head a little, he continued his inspection of the kitchen and was pleased to see Olivia had a little Rayburn, tucked in neatly between two oak worktops at the far end. Without asking, he proceeded to fill the kettle at the sink and stuck it on the hotplate.

"Have you got any ice?"

She nodded towards the fridge in the corner, whilst pulling off her running shoe. Bartholomew, grabbing a tea towel and fashioning a string of cubes into a sort of bandage, wrapped it around her ankle and then helped her park her leg on a chair. She looked up at him with a neutral expression; although he hoped what he also saw in her eyes was something akin to gratitude.

"You've been really helpful. I'd have been stuck in the freezing dark up in the woods if it hadn't have been for you. Thank you, Bartholomew."

He had his back to her as he filled the teapot. "Surely you mean: if it wasn't for me you wouldn't have had a fall in the first place. You'd have made it back here in one piece all on your own."

There was no immediate answer, so he continued, still with his back to her.

"I mean, I have to say, Olivia, I've seen you now a few times in the wood. Or glimpses of you. I got the distinct impression I was being shadowed. It put me on edge, if you really want to know – that's why I ran at you. I suppose you'd call it something along the lines of: attack is the best form of defence."

He turned and walked over to the table, bearing the teapot and two mugs.

"I'm really sorry if I spooked you, Bartholomew." She looked up at him with wide eyes. "I'm wary of bumping into people. I can't stand road running – it's the cross country stuff I like. It would be nigh on impossible to ask every single local landowner round here for permission to run on their property. Frankly, the odds are most would flatly refuse. The type of terrain I like is where you have to cross boggy fields, or where the challenge is to avoid rabbit holes or tree zig-zag. I'm just not one of those gym bunnies on a treadmill with a set of headphones on. So again, I'm really sorry if you got the wrong impression. When I see someone on my runs, I tend to take evasive action and keep a safe distance. Most of it is on private property, after all."

He watched her face. Half trying to read what lay beneath the surface – the other half transfixed by her evident beauty. Even in the SAS style running kit. Transfixed, like all those years ago.

It seemed she had her reasons. In a way, she was right, he thought, bringing to mind an image of Gerald Rissborough and his shotgun-carrying henchman Jeavons as a point in case. Her cautiousness was justified. He made a note to warn her about the pair. Particularly as he had now regretfully alerted them to her regular presence in the wood.

"Don't you need to get back – I mean, to your job?" she asked, not unkindly. "I don't want to hold you up. Hopefully I should be ok now. She stood and moved on the foot a little, still gripping the back of the chair.

"No, it's fine, honestly. I'd like to make sure you are all right."

To be really honest would be to tell her that meeting her again was the best thing that had happened to him in a long time. It was an infinitely, preferable million miles away from the events of the previous evening.

"Let me get your wood burner going and cook you some supper," he suggested, hopefully. "You haven't seen me for so long, I can at least show you I'm fairly useful around the place."

Olivia looked at him searchingly, as if trying to decide what to read into his offer.

"I'm sure you're very good at lots of things, Bartholomew. For one, you've already made it obvious this afternoon that you still care. For people that is. I remember that as always being something important to you."

It was quite the most disarming compliment he'd received in a very long while. Bartholomew couldn't remember a time in recent years when someone had really thought something positive of him. He wondered, disparagingly, standing there in the tiny cottage with a beautiful woman he'd only really known as a child: what had become of his life? Why was he just treading water?

"Heh…" she said, now concerned. "Did I say something out of line? Looks like I might have struck the wrong note. If it helps, you know we've all got our regrets in life. Whatever it is you are thinking – don't be too hard on yourself."

She touched him lightly on the shoulder and he shook himself out of his mini gloom.

"Ok, then," she continued. "You can make me supper. You'll have to make do with whatever is in the larder. I'm going to have a bath. You alright fending for yourself?"

"Of course," he nodded, with a wry half-smile, as she hobbled out into the hallway and headed up the stairs. "That's something I'm pretty good at too."

He quickly got the wood burner going with some kindling and a couple of small logs from a stack on the hearth. In the larder, he had a swift poke around, but in seconds knew exactly what to cook in the circumstances: Aglio Olio Peperoncino.

He boiled a pan of water and threw in a fat handful of spaghetti. In a frying pan, he poured a glug of olive oil, to which he added crushed garlic and dried chilli flakes. He heated it gently, 'til the garlic had turned lightly golden.

Next, he grated some fresh parmesan. When the pasta was *al dente*, he drained it, and threw in the contents from the frying pan. Bartholomew was just mixing it all up when Olivia appeared in the kitchen looking fresh as a daisy, wrapped up in a huge towelling robe. She perched on a chair and sniffed the air.

"Umm... That smells really good. What is it?

He told her it was the simplest of dishes but designed to give a bit of a kick. Just what she needed after this afternoon. He served it up on plates, garnished with fresh basil leaves, which he'd found in a pot on the kitchen windowsill and had ripped into small pieces. He'd also managed to locate a bottle of Chilean Malbec in a small rack at the back of the larder, from which he filled two glasses.

They sat at the table and looked at each other over the steaming pasta.

"To old times," he toasted.

"To old times," she repeated, and he felt the unspoken memory of Michael and the fissure from all those years ago pass between them. The private nightmares surfaced too, in his own mind – the ones featuring a revengeful Jerome. He wasn't going to raise either, and if Olivia decided it was best left alone, then that was fine by him.

"How's the foot?"

"I'm not sure an ice bag and then a hot bath is the correct procedure, but actually it's not too bad. I can at least hobble around. I stuck it over the rim anyway!"

"See what it's like in the morning, I guess," he replied. "Which, by the way, as I keep on forgetting, is Christmas Day! Are you going to family? Sorry, I haven't asked about your parents. Are they…"

"Look, not at all," she replied, twirling the pasta on her fork. "Sadly both my folks passed away in the last couple of years. Father had a stroke and my Mother had a long battle with cancer. Not a good time, but we're passed it now. No, you probably don't remember, I have one sister. She lives in Kent with her husband and kids, so I'm off there in the morning for three or four days."

"How about you? Do you go to your parents or your own family?"

He realised she was asking him if he had someone in his life. "No," he laughed dryly. "My parents are well and still around, thankfully, but they don't live in the UK. At the moment I think they're in…"

He was interrupted by Olivia's mobile phone going off on the table. She looked down at the number and frowned.

"Excuse me," she said, struggling to get out of her chair. "I'll have to take this."

"Would you like me to go next door?" he suggested, partly rising out of his seat.

"No, no," she waved him down and limped out into the hallway.

He could just about make out a deep, gruff male voice, before she moved out of earshot into the living room. He heard her raise her voice once but it quickly ceased. Almost as if she had been drowned out.

A few minutes later she returned. "Sorry about that." She apologised with what he could only interpret as a tired and resigned expression. She raised her eyebrows but avoided eye contact with him. He sensed she was not going to share whatever it was, and wanted to move on.

"So," he continued. "Is this your permanent base?"

"No, it's my out of town get away. I live in London and get up here at weekends. Sometimes during the week too. Depends what's on really. I'm an Arts journalist. Freelance. My work is based mainly in London, but I do have to travel occasionally. Usually it's the opening of a new museum, or a collection somewhere. I'm just back from New York last week. Home for Christmas. Oh sorry… I think you were saying about your parents?

He filled her in on his parents' overseas wanderlust, which had not abated since his father's retirement from the services.

"Actually, I'm not really into the Christmas thing," he admitted sheepishly, pulling a face but laughing a little. What's that old fashioned expression? The one that fits me... bah humbug? I'd enjoy the cooking though, if I had enough of a party to do it for."

"Yes, I can see that," she mumbled, hungrily finishing off her plate, as he re-filled their glasses. "You obviously enjoy throwing bits and bobs together."

"Yes," he nodded, now reluctantly serious. "It's one of the few things that gives me some peace and harmony."

"What?" she pushed again. "No Mrs Bartholomew around to keep you company?"

"No," he replied, pausing a moment, before deciding to continue. "Once, a long time ago there was nearly a Mrs Bartholomew, although, knowing her, I'm not sure she would have taken my name. It didn't quite work out. It was almost an escape at the altar, if the truth be told. It's easier on my own."

"Oh, I'm sorry to hear that. Were you still in the same business back then? It's just that..."

"What you mean is: why am I in a dead end, probably very poorly paid job that any numbskull could do?"

"No. Sorry. I didn't mean that exactly, I just thought..."

"It's ok. I'll be frank. It suits me most of the time – the different assignments I'm given, that is. It's low key, mostly hassle free (apart from this particular gig, he inwardly cursed) and I'm able to be my own man."

He continued looking down and added, somewhat unwillingly, "I did have a previous life. In London, where I still live and own a small flat. I was in the property business. Let's say my participation in it was something akin to from rags to riches and then, fairly abruptly, quite the reverse: from riches to rags. It's a long and not particularly savoury story involving a collection of ruthless exploiters and me as the naïve fall guy, and I'm sure you don't want me to bore you with it."

"No, not at all," she continued, but he managed to cut her off, before she pried any further.

"What about you? Someone who can still look like a million dollars – even though they're decked out like a military sniper. You must have a queue of admirers lined up?"

She didn't react at all to the flattery. Positively or negatively. Just looked at him steadily, without saying a thing. The overriding impression he got from the gaze, though, was one of sadness. Of regret.

"Same as you, I guess, really," she eventually answered. "Life's complicated isn't it? Never turns out quite the way you expect it to. For some, you can never throw off the shackles of the past."

Bartholomew didn't know what Olivia was referring to, but he felt inclined to agree with her anyway. In his experience, life could certainly be a bitch.

"Look at the pair of us," she suddenly exclaimed. "Too maudlin! Come on, finish your wine and then you must be getting back."

"Ok," he agreed. Summoning up the courage, he ventured; "As I'm down here for a while, can I have your number? I mean, it would be good to see a bit of each other."

She looked at him uncertainly. As if she wanted to keep him at a distance. But not quite able to shut him out altogether.

"Don't worry," he laughed. "I'm not asking you out on a date… just to keep in touch."

She nodded slowly, the tiniest smile appearing at the corner of her mouth. "Ok, Bartholomew," she agreed. "Just to keep in touch."

They sat in amiable silence on the big sofa in the living room, as they finished their wine and watched the flames leap high in the glass fronted wood burner. For him, it must have been the effect of the night before, and for her, the shock of the fall. He woke suddenly, to realise they had both nodded off. Like a couple of oldies, he thought, companionably knackered.

He must have dropped off once more, as the next thing that woke him was the soft feel of her head on his shoulder. She had fallen on him and, in her sleep, nestled in. He sat there, feeling more content than he could remember in a long time. Enjoying the closeness, and her warm, natural scent.

It seemed only a moment later he awoke again, to find himself alone and the glow of the wood burner down to a low ebb. Reaching for his phone, he saw it was 2 am. Christ, he thought. Minsham Court. Got to get back. Hesitating at the bottom of the stairs, he thought about it and then climbed them two at a time. Peeking his head around the first door he came to, he saw that Olivia was tucked up in a large double bed, fast asleep like a contented cat. Good, he thought, and experienced that unfamiliar wave of happiness surge through him once more.

In the kitchen, he scribbled a quick note to say Happy Christmas and then, after a pause, put a comment to the effect that she should be wary of running again in the local woods – in his experience landowners could be very unpredictable. He fervently hoped it was enough of a warning to put her off.

He grabbed his coat from the peg. As he shoved his arm into a sleeve and pulled it over his shoulders, he stopped for a moment. There was something familiar in the air. He couldn't quite put his finger on it. Bloody hell, he cursed. It's two in the morning and your mind is playing crazy tricks on you. Pull yourself together and get on back to Minsham Court. He closed the cottage door quietly behind him, got into the pickup and drove away slowly into the freezing, black night.

Half a mile out of Evensthorpe, the engine conked out. He looked at the fuel gauge. "Bollocks!" he swore loudly. He couldn't believe it. But then again, he hadn't exactly taken much notice of how much diesel he had on board since he'd started using the vehicle. He sat there by the side of the road and contemplated the options. He wasn't going to return to Olivia's cottage. That would be too crass. "Oh, I've run out of fuel…Can I stay for the rest of the night?"

No. He'd have to walk the remaining mile and a half back to Minsham. Problem was, though, he didn't really want to leave the pickup out here on the main road. Not ideal. Grasping at a final straw he realised he might have one other solution. Pulling out his wallet, he located the grubby business card Cyclops had given him on his first day. He rang the number. Sure enough, he got an answer.

"Yes!"

"Cyclops? Hello. You may remember me. You took me from Brilcrister Station up to Minsham Court – about a week ago. I wonder if…"

Cyclops cut him off. "Yeah, I remember you. The housekeeper. Up from London."

"House-sitter, not housekeeper," Bartholomew retorted. "I'm a bloke, if you recall."

"It's often difficult to tell these days if you really want to know. You should see some of the sights I get to…"

Bartholomew cut over him. It was brass monkeys in the pickup.

"Look, I'm in my pickup and I've run out of diesel. I'm about half way up on the Haddlewell-Evensthorpe road. Any chance you can get me a couple of litres? Enough to get me to a garage in the morning?"

"What a twat! Running out of fuel on Christmas Eve!"

"Cyclops, I don't need an fffffing lecture. I need a can of fuel! I'll make it worth your while. Can you sort me out?"

"Alright, Mr House… Sitter, or whatever you call yourself. Keep calm and I'll try and carry on. You're lucky. I've just dropped off my last load of drunken knobheads down in Brilcrister and was heading home. I've got a can in the back. See you in a mo."

Wonders will never cease, thought Bartholomew; and sure enough, round the corner, fifteen minutes later, puffed the smoky Lada with old one eye at the helm. From a rusty can Cyclops had pulled from the boot, they had soon poured enough diesel in to get him home and back out to a garage in the morning. After re-stowing the can, Bartholomew eyed Cyclops across the bonnet of the pickup.

"You've saved the day Cyclops. Or should I say the night. What do I owe you? And don't forget to add on a good tip."

"I don't charge for emergencies," Cyclops replied. For once his voice was empty of sarcasm. "And it's Christmas after all." He moved away to get back into the ancient Lada.

Bartholomew was taken aback. Christ alive. Twice in one day. Two people being kind to him. It was almost too much to take in. An idea came to mind. One, probably also driven by a cooking urge. But a charitable idea at least, he reasoned with himself.

"Well, that's really generous of you, Cyclops. Much appreciated. I suppose you're looking forward to Christmas day with the family?"

He'd guessed the answer already,

"Nah, that's all bollocks," came back the reply, the sarcasm returning with a full vengeance. "Don't do family. Haven't got any, anyway. It's a Fray Bentos pie for me. Oven tatties and frozen peas. Love it!"

Bartholomew made his proposal: "Well, what about this – save your dodgy horse meat pie for another day. I'll cook you Christmas lunch. The full works, at Minsham Court. In the flat that is. To return the favour. I've a huge turkey I've got to get rid of and aim to serve you up a royal feast. And I won't take no for an answer!"

Bartholomew moved to get back in the pickup. He knew Cyclops was probably a loner and would quite happily sit at home watching the telly, all on his lonesome. But the temptation of a sumptuous Christmas lunch catered for by someone else, and at no cost to himself, would be too much to resist.

"Alright. Suppose house-sitters should know how to cook. He pondered for a little longer, trying to play down his keenness. What time then?"

"Well, it's late now. So let's say – be at Minsham Court at 3pm for a pre-lunch drink and I'll aim to serve it up around four. Sound good?"

He received a small, almost grateful grunt of acknowledgment in return. With that, he gunned the pickup and sped off into the night.

Chapter 11 The Bone

He arose at 12.30, bleary eyed. Late to bed had thankfully meant no nightmares, although he was still experiencing some discomfort across his lower belly. A reasonable trade-off, he told himself. Fixing a pot of the Italian coffee, he took stock whilst sipping away at the aromatic blend and then immediately began to plan the rest of the Christmas lunch.

On returning to Minsham Court half way through the night before, his mind still full of Olivia, he'd decided to kick off part of his preparations at once. 3am in the morning had seen him – after, that is, knocking back a generous tooth glass sharpener of *The Famous Grouse* – manhandle the bulky turkey, breast up, into a large Aga tray on the kitchen table. He'd grasped the bird by the back end and gradually worked his fingers up between the skin and the breast meat. Eventually, after carefully edging his hand forward, he'd separated as much of the skin away from the rest of the bird as he was able. Grabbing a decent handful of butter, mixed with a little rosemary, he pushed up into the pocket, gently edging it in, so that the whole of the breast meat was covered with the sticky mass, before gently pulling the skin tightly back over.

Next, as he had no sausage meat, he cannibalised six large pork sausages. Adding the sausage to a bowl of breadcrumbs, chopped hazelnuts, apricots, lemon zest and seasoning, he roughly mixed it all up by hand. Grabbing handfuls of the stuffing, he shoved it up into the turkey's cavity, before pinning the ends back down with a couple of toothpicks. To finish it all off, he draped a half a dozen layers of streaky bacon over the top of the bird.

Bartholomew sat at the table, partaking of more of *The Famous Grouse*, whilst he gave the turkey a good thirty minutes in the hot oven of the Aga. After retrieving the bird – its juices already beginning to flow in earnest – he created a foil tent over the top, transferred it down to the lower, cooler oven, closed the Aga door and shambled gratefully off to bed.

The rest was easy to assemble in the early afternoon of Christmas Day. Bread sauce, infused with cloves and finely grated nutmeg. Cranberry jelly (admittedly from a jar). Parsnips, carrots and potatoes, peeled and ready for roasting. Plus, of course, the Brussels sprouts – although, if he were to be honest, he was a little wary of their potential effect – visualising that Cyclops would undoubtedly have an appetite at the larger end of the scale.

At three o'clock on the dot, the intercom blared its merry greeting. Bartholomew didn't bother to ask who it was and just pressed the entry button. A couple of minutes later, the puffing Lada pulled up outside the flat. Cyclops heaved his bulky torso up and out of the rust bucket, before casually sauntering into the kitchen, carrying a heavy plastic bag.

"Merry Christmas, Cyclops!" Bartholomew greeted his guest. He was mildly surprised to receive a reasonable half grin of acknowledgment in return.

"Bought you a Christmas present. Well, one for us to share and then one for me," grunted Cyclops, by way of further greeting.

From the plastic bag he pulled out a Co-op ready-to-microwave Christmas pudding and six cans of strong, dry cider.

"Well, that's very kind, Cyclops – but I don't drink cider."

"That's my present to me," came back the gruff reply.

"Ha! Only joking. Thanks for the pudding. Good idea, as my plans hadn't stretched that far. Anyway, if I had planned it properly I should have made it twelve months ago! C'mon, let's have a drink."

They sat quietly in the kitchen: Cyclops ploughing through the cider, Bartholomew on a bottle of decent sparkling wine, whilst they waited for the potatoes to crisply brown. Once he'd laid the table, Bartholomew rested the bird, and, after adding some flour, stock, Lea & Perrins and a decent slug of the claret, he made a deep, rich gravy in the bottom of the roasting pan.

Finally, they managed to sit down opposite one another and survey the feast before them. Bartholomew offered Cyclops a glass of the astronomically priced *Saint-Julien*, but he refused, stoically insisting on sticking to his West Country tipple.

As he served up a huge plateful for his guest, he was reminded of a story an old friend used to laugh about. She would recount how she'd shared a house with a couple of student lads at college. When it came to a roast lunch, the two lads would place the large joint of pork – or whatever variety of meat they were having that Sunday – atop a carving board, directly between the pair of them, as they sat up to table. Instead of carving slices off the joint – as one would expect – such was their appetite, they would simply cut the joint in two and plonk a steaming half on each of their plates.

Cyclops could probably match them pound for pound, observed Bartholomew, sipping his wine, as he watched the taxi man work his way through his third large helping. He had to admit, though, to taking a certain amount of pleasure from seeing his cooking appreciated on such a colossal scale.

An hour later, they sat bloated and comatose-like on the sofa, blandly absorbing the best of what the BBC had to throw at them on a Christmas evening. It wasn't long before Cyclops was away with the fairies and snoring heavily. Bartholomew, after gently freeing the last can of cider from his dining companion's dangling hand, left him to it on the sofa before heading off himself, similarly exhausted, to his own lumpy bed.

As he might have guessed, rich food and heavy wine gave rise to the usual night-time demons. He woke abruptly and reached over to the bedside table, to check his mobile. Just gone 4am. He lay there under the duvet as it slowly began to dawn on him – that again, this wasn't a nightmare – the bumping noises he thought he'd heard in his sleep were for real.

He sat up. Bloody hell, he worried away. There it was again. Bump, bump, bump. In his jockeys, he scrambled out into the kitchen, the fear of it all making him break out into a mild sweat, despite the night time cold. As he made his way over to the sitting room, the noise was repeated twice more. Bump, bump. Almost a thud, as if someone or something was being gradually dragged along, bit by bit, over a number of obstacles.

In the flat, the previous night, he had closed the sitting room door on his way to bed. He now wrenched it open again in the hope that Cyclops would assist him in dealing with whatever was out there in the main house. For there was one thing he was absolutely certain of now: the noises were coming from that direction.

Whatever idea of help he thought the belligerent Cyclops might provide, was swiftly quashed. He opened the sitting room door, and, after a peek inside, quickly shut it again. Cyclops was dead to the world, flat on his back on the sofa, still snoring seismically. But it wasn't the comatose state that made Bartholomew retreat so hastily. It was the intense, pungent fog of Cyclops's Brussels sprout emissions that hung in the air like a thick, heavy cloak. At this point, dealing with some unknown, potentially dangerous intruders on his own, seemed a far preferable option than to wade through the stench from hell and try and wake the taxi driver.

He took a long, deep lungful of fresh air in the kitchen to clear his befuddled head. Slowly gathering himself together, he gingerly crept out into the utility room, still clad only in his jockeys, gripping his mobile phone.

He flicked on the lights and immediately spotted that the alarm was in de-activated mode. He was confused. Thinking back to last night, he was sure he'd checked it was on after leaving the snoring Cyclops and heading off to bed. He pushed the door open into the hall and put on the chandelier lights. He stood still, listening intently. It was so quiet it almost made him think someone was holding their breath. It was when he moved to the foot of the stairs that he spotted them: two of the classical urns, from the first floor landing. Neatly positioned together, as if a couple of removal men were coming in the morning to pick them up and stack them securely in a van.

Oh fuck, he swore, the sweat breaking out all over him once more. They're in the house. *Jesus Christ*, what the hell is this, he asked himself again, still desperately peering around, grasping onto the slim forlorn hope that someone *had been* in the house; whilst knowing – in his heart of hearts – that someone *was in* the house. Still in denial – and knowing, again, that he should call Baxter immediately and retreat to the flat, to hide under Cyclops's sofa – he stupidly found himself mounting the stairs. As he reached the left hand landing, he thought he sensed something back down in the hall below, and turned round to look. At that precise moment, a hooded figure barrelled out of the master bedroom, hitting him side on, smashing him violently to the floor, before flying headlong down the stairs.

In his stunned, knocked-down state, Bartholomew groggily realised the crashing sound he could now hear below must be the intruder knocking over the urns on the stairs, in his urgent haste to exit. Clumsily relocating his mobile from the floor, he scrambled to his feet and managed a pathetic "Oi!" before limply staggering back down the staircase in pursuit.

Chest heaving, at the bottom he guessed the hooded figure must have bolted back in through the utility room. Sheepishly hesitating before the door, in case the intruder was waiting for him just inside with something nasty and blunt to finish him off, he finally found the sense to call the police. Locating Baxter's number, he waited desperately as it rang and rang, until finally he heard the familiar insinuating voice answer.

"Yes, sir. What can I do for you? Bit early in the morning for our usual chat, isn't it?"

"Baxter," he sighed in sheer relief, on hearing the Detective Sergeant's caustic reply. "Thank God. Get over here now. We've been burgled. I think there's still one in the house, I'm not sure if I should …"

Wallop. To his utter consternation, he was viciously flattened for the second time. This time though, from behind. Bartholomew was bowled over onto his front, mobile phone flying from his hand once more, the device spinning wildly across the floor of the hall.

By now, partly sobbing with the enormity of it all, prone on the floor, arms out in front of him, Bartholomew had a clear view of hoodie number two racing into the utility room and making a beeline for the window. Garnering a sense of self-respect from somewhere deep within, not for the first time that night Bartholomew dragged himself to his feet, and followed. Rudely bashed down twice in the space of a couple of minutes was, after all, a lot for anyone to take.

In the utility room, two stark facts were apparent: Firstly, hoodie number two was desperately trying to make his escape out of the large sash window, encouraged, it seemed, by his accomplice, who was by now on the other side. Freedom for this one, however, was clearly not as straightforward. Hoodie number two had got his upper body through the gap, but the waistband of his baggy grey tracksuit bottoms was caught on the window frame latch, pulling them down. All Bartholomew could see was a bare, hairy bottom, wriggling frantically, trying desperately to escape, but held back by the tracksuit bottoms which by now were caught up around the intruder's lower thighs.

Secondly, the state of the turkey. He'd moved the half-consumed bird, loosely covered in foil, out into the utility room the night before. The kitchen larder shelf had not been wide enough to take the wooden board it sat on.

He stared at the first in amazement and the second in sheer disbelief. The thieving heinous bastards, he cried. They've desecrated the turkey. Ripped the foil off and helped themselves to the bird, like a couple of wild prairie dogs who'd frantically torn the carcass to pieces. Turning its neat, partly carved state into a carnivorous bomb site.

It was a step too far. Fear of engagement now furthermost from his mind, Bartholomew ran over to the bird in a couple of determined strides. Grasping a huge leg of the turkey, at the meaty end, he ripped it off the carcass. Turning to confront his assailant with a grim, determined gleam in his eye, he cantered across the room. In a burst of furious culinary indignation, swinging his arm in a low arch from behind, he rammed the leg, bone end first, as hard as he could, up and in between the wriggling bottom cheeks of his aggressor.

"Take that right up there where the sun don't shine!" he screamed out, laughing manically, as, with an almighty shriek of pain, hoodie number two was propelled, rigid with shock, like a rocket, up and out of the window into the enveloping blackness beyond.

"And don't ever come back! Dare touch my food again and you'll get the other leg to boot!" he bellowed crazily after them.

Bartholomew moved back from the window and collapsed onto the floor. The adrenaline had suddenly deserted him. It was as much as he could do to glance up and register a shambling Cyclops enter the room looking mildly bewildered.

"What the effing hell you doing in here, you twat!? You should try sleeping somewhere more comfortable. No wonder you get nightmares, dossing out here on the floor. Sofa's not bad you know. Where've you put my can of frigging cider?"

Bartholomew groaned, lay back, and stared bleakly up at the ceiling.

Chapter 12 The Revelation

Brilcrister Police Station Interview Room Number 1 was like a sad imitation of an American cop drama. Bartholomew looked around, tired and irritable, at the faded paintwork, scuffed wooden table and stark fluorescent lighting. Only two chairs too, he noted with grim humour – just like in *CSI*. He wondered vaguely whether Detective Sergeant Baxter was at this very moment scrutinising him through the one two-way mirror on the wall.

For why he was in the police station in the first place was a mystery to Bartholomew. It was the day after Boxing Day. The day after the attempted burglary. A number of events had occurred since he had successfully (in his opinion) expelled the intruders from the house.

Within minutes of the two hoodies escaping into the grounds, various police cars had roared up the drive. Bartholomew had got Cyclops to open the gates a few minutes earlier and soon the house was swarming with officers. They had quickly searched Minsham Court from top to bottom. It was all clear. The place was empty. It also transpired the pedestals were the only items that had been moved. Baxter gauged Bartholomew must have disturbed the burglars early on in the raid.

Back in the kitchen, recovering over a cup of strong tea, he had waited to be railed at by the Detective Sergeant for intervening again, but the policeman had remained strangely quiet. Perhaps he didn't want to look ungrateful in front of his colleagues.

Bartholomew somehow doubted it. Knowing Baxter's *modus operandi*, he was certain the policeman would have something uncomfortable to say to him about it all, sooner, rather than later.

News of progress came through almost immediately. Baxter took a call on his mobile in the kitchen and answered it with a series of good, good, goods and well dones. It was the two beefy coppers in the police car. They'd apprehended two men by the estate wall and were now in the process of transporting one to the police station and the other to hospital. It seemed they had only managed to catch the men because one could hardly walk, having to rely on the other for support. It was something to do with a third leg apparently, or so Baxter informed the assembled kitchen audience comprising Bartholomew, Cyclops, numerous police officers and the now attendant forensic team. He couldn't quite get the gist of it over the phone. The officer talking to him seemed to be finding it difficult to explain the facts clearly, without having to take long moments to collect himself. Baxter had concluded it would have to wait until his return to the station, before he could get to the bottom of it all.

And that was how it had been left. By midday, the forensic teams had done their bit and Minsham Court was all Bartholomew's once more. He'd expected an update call from Baxter later that day. Indeed, just as he'd phoned Kennedy to let her know what had happened he'd got the call to report to Brilcrister Police Station at ten o'clock the next morning for interview. Why me? he'd asked Baxter pointedly. Who's the victim here after all? Baxter, however, was all circumspection and formality, repeating that Bartholomew was required at the station in the morning, at the appointed time, and not to be late.

Kennedy had been her usual treat, too. It was as if it was all Bartholomew's fault. How had someone been able to de-activate the alarm? How was she going to explain it to Mr Eves? Bartholomew decided he could only deal with one protagonist at a time and so had cut the call short, saying he'd update her once he knew more from the police. First things first. He'd deal with Kennedy later on, when he could give her his full focus. One thing was for sure though. As regards the assignment, this was a watershed. Morosely calculating how next to deal with his conniving boss, his thoughts were suddenly cut short by Detective Sergeant Baxter briskly entering the interview room.

The thin, weary looking policeman sat down in the chair opposite and regarded him balefully. It was as if he was waiting for Bartholomew to volunteer some information, or perhaps provide an explanation. Fine by me, decided Bartholomew – and launched in:

"Detective Sergeant, I'm happy to assist in any way I can, but is it really necessary for me to attend down here? You've caught the culprits red-handed. And really, the only question I have for you is why did they go to all that trouble of banging dustbins in the night, rattling window panes and setting off crop scarers? I mean – before they decided to burgle the house?

"Furthermore, I'd also like you to confirm that you'll be objecting to any bail application. Just so I can report back to my boss, who can then reassure the client that the burglars will be kept locked up – that is, at least until full court proceedings. To ensure the client's property is at no further risk."

"First things first, sir," Baxter replied, with a stony expression. It was an unsettling look, thought Bartholomew. One that implied he was about to say something rather unpleasant.

"We're not sure either at this stage. About the pair's tactics, that is. We're still conducting interviews, but we think they probably did it in the knowledge that the property is not regularly occupied by the owner. It may be they had hoped to scare off the hired help, so they could ransack the house undisturbed."

"Too right," Bartholomew agreed. "About scaring the hired help!"

"But that doesn't quite match with what I want to talk to you about this morning, sir," Baxter continued, still holding Bartholomew in a steely gaze.

"Sorry, I'm not quite with you, Detective Sergeant."

"I have to inform you, sir, that two very serious allegations have been made against you."

Bartholomew tried his utmost not to gulp. Oh God, he groaned under his breath, feeling a sense of dread bubbling up inside. What now?

"To put you in the picture, the two men arrested at Minsham Court are well known to us. They're local lads, with a long history of house breaking. In fact, we were on to them as potential suspects just before the incident occurred."

Oh yeah, thought Bartholomew. That all sounded rather contrived and easy to say after the event. That is to say, once Bartholomew had intervened at his own personal risk, disabled one of burglars and facilitated a swift arrest!.

"The two men being held are a Mark Cudmore and a Ryan Hollins. Thing is though, sir, they've been singing rather freely in the interviews we've conducted with them so far. It would appear, from both their accounts, there was a third person involved. A ringleader, so to speak. That individual has now also been arrested, interviewed and is currently being held downstairs in the cells."

"Ok, but what's that got to do with me?" replied Bartholomew, somewhat bemused. "That's your business to sort out."

"The ringleader of the gang is a Miss Roxanne Halsall."

Baxter scrutinised Bartholomew's face carefully as he made the pronouncement.

"Roxy!" he blurted out. "Bloody hell – you're joking?!"

"It's not just that, sir. You see, Miss Halsall has been singing too. Although, she seems to be keen on an altogether different tune."

Bartholomew looked at the policeman with a horrible sinking feeling, guessing now what was coming next.

"Miss Halsall is alleging that you, sir, have acted as the inside man. She admits she's met you once or twice. And sure, she knows the lads too, from down the local. But her position is she had nothing to do with the burglary, or any other nefarious activity. The lads just took her into their confidence one night about their little scam, over a few beers. How their leader is you: the inside man. You, who provided details of the house layout, security alarm code and an idea of which items were valuable. She is saying the plan was for you to be out for the evening. But she's guessing you bottled it. Stayed in instead. Contriving to look innocent by tackling the intruders and alerting the police."

The bitch! Bartholomew somehow managed to hold his tongue, whilst thinking desperately for a suitable riposte to the policeman's charge – knowing if he got it wrong he would be sunk. He cursed the day he had ever set eyes on Roxy. He could see it all now. His own bloody ego hoodwinking him. She'd taken him for a fool, reeled him in and used and abused him for her own personal as well as business ends. Now she wanted to shift the blame off herself by pointing the finger directly at him. For Christ's sake, the vixen had almost shagged him to death a couple of nights ago! What more did she want!

Inwardly gathering himself together, he mustered the coolest look he could manage in the circumstances and replied:

"Surely you've not been taken in by that load of old claptrap, Detective Sergeant? I can tell you exactly what has happened here. No doubt, you know Miss Halsall works part time at the Spar in Haddlewell. Strangely enough, she was very insistent she made all the deliveries herself – of items that I needed up at Minsham Court. You can double check with Sheila the post mistress. She was there when Miss Halsall turned up. I was cooking in the flat kitchen and was distracted. When I turned around, she'd gone out into the utility room. I got hold of her just as she was about to try and enter the main house."

"What about the security alarm?" asked Baxter, still looking sceptical.

"She would have seen the alarm panel on the wall in the utility room. She must have searched for the code in the house file at the kitchen table, while I had my back turned at the Aga. Ok, sloppy on my part, but you wouldn't really expect the local delivery girl to be planning a heist under the guise of fetching your supply of Italian coffee, would you?!"

Thinking frantically, Bartholomew knew there could be possible flaws in his defence that might yet fell him. In a moment of inspiration, he decided to take a specific line of attack.

"Anyway – I bet she was there in the house with the two lads," he added. "She just wasn't stupid enough to get caught on the night. Why, your forensic team must have found her fingerprints all over the place."

He knew OCD would have done a spanking good cleaning job in the master suite and downstairs rooms after his evening with Roxy, but surely even she wasn't a match for forensics.

"You are right, sir, as a matter of fact. Miss Halsall's fingerprints were found in the hall, kitchen and all over the master bedroom suite."

"There you are then. My case proved. Her story about me is a load of old cock and bull. Why, I bet she can't even prove where she was on the night in question!"

The look on Baxter's face told him he'd hit the jackpot. The old clichés are the best, Bartholomew gleefully triumphed. Nothing ventured, nothing gained.

"Miss Halsall, as it happens, has provided an alibi. The trouble is she has no one to verify it. So, one *could* venture to say she might have been in the house that night, with the others.

"Too bloody right, Detective Sergeant. You know that's what happened."

"We'll see, sir," replied Baxter, still maintaining an accusatory air. "Do you have your mobile with you?"

"Of course. Why?"

"Please give it to me, sir. We'll be checking it for all incoming and outgoing calls made over the last two weeks. Just to see who you've been talking too – locally that is, sir."

As Bartholomew handed the mobile over, he metaphorically raised his eyes to heaven and thanked the Lord. The gods had smiled on him for once. For he now recalled, although Roxy had left her number on a yellow post-it, stuck to a vase on the kitchen table, he had never saved it onto his mobile. Why, ironically, he even had Kennedy to thank. If she hadn't called him that day to give him a bollocking, he'd never have driven Roxy off the road. Or proceeded to ask her – in person – to dinner at Minsham Court. Firmly bolstered up now, he casually leant back in the chair and folded his arms.

"You were saying there was something else, Detective Sergeant?"

"Yes. As you are aware, sir, one of the men had to be taken to hospital.

My heart bleeds, Bartholomew silently commiserated, trying very hard not to look smug.

"As aforementioned, we've managed to interview Mr Hollins – in his hospital bed. That is, after the four hours of surgery he endured yesterday morning. We understand a full team of surgeons were required to… ahem…" Baxter coughed at this point, almost choking on his words. "To… ahem… remove an article from Mr Hollins's back passage. Apparently, there was a high degree of concern about the possibility of splintering. Suffice to say, these concerns proved unfounded and the said… ahem… leg, was successfully retrieved."

Bartholomew could have sworn he caught sight of a miniscule tremor ripple once, then twice, through the policeman's torso. His jaw was clenched tight and tiny little muscles began to twitch convulsively in either cheek. It was the sight of a man trying his utmost to keep his professional demeanour intact. Bartholomew wondered, if, for a little personal sport, he could tip the Detective Sergeant over the edge with a clever retort. Before he could summon up a suitable witticism however, Baxter seemed to collect himself, and once again adopt a stern, judge-like expression.

"Mr Hollins is demanding we put you on a charge of GBH, in respect of the assault upon his person. He is also vowing to take you to a civil court and seek substantial compensation for his injuries. Although the latter, of course, is not a matter for the police."

"Assault!" protested Bartholomew bitterly. "What about the assault on me! Those two bastards flattened me twice in the house. They're lucky I have no visible injuries. Just the mental ones to give me nightmares for the rest of my life! If anyone is going to be pressing charges, it'll be me. The only GBH Hollins has suffered is to his precious pride!

Calming down somewhat, Bartholomew thought about it for a little longer, before chortling out loud:

"Detective Sergeant, you know damn well this talk of civil action is a total non-starter. Think about it. Hollins – down the pub, with his mates. Boasting, after a few pints, about all the lovely lolly he's going to get from a large compensation claim. Telling them how he's managed to burgle a grand country house and get himself nicely injured in the process. Awesome Hollins!, his mates will crow in admiration. Wicked! Show us your battle scars. How did you get them? Fighting off ex-military security guards? Grappling with ferocious guard dogs? No, sorry lads. It wasn't quite like that. I was… umm… umm… I was trying to escape out of a window and a weedy caretaker came up behind and managed to shove a huge turkey bone up my ass."

This time Bartholomew definitely clocked the tiniest uplift at the corner of Baxter's mouth.

"So you see, Detective Sergeant, this is not going to go anywhere. Other than to the very bottom of Hollins's memory bank. That is, once he's got his head together and his delicate arse stops hurting. So unless you are going to charge me, if it's ok with you, I would like to take myself back to Minsham Court. In fact, for your information, I'm planning a trip up to London tomorrow. To see my employer. About terminating my work contract."

Baxter studied him carefully for a few seconds, as if making his mind up about something

"Ok, sir. That will be all for now. I'd like you, though, to stay closely in touch. Let me know when you get back from London. I assume you will be back for one more time, before you depart? I'll keep you apprised of events. Be prepared though. My gut feeling is we haven't seen the end of this saga yet."

"And my mobile. When can I have it back?"

"Drop by in the morning on your way to the railway station. We'll have scrutinised your records by then – and ascertained as to whether we need to extend our hospitality to you here. Goodbye, sir. Look forward to seeing you in the morning."

Chapter 13 The Bonus

Bartholomew pushed in through the doors at Raulo's, straining his neck around the large and not very accommodating front of house to check whether Kennedy was at her usual table.

He'd travelled up on the train to Waterloo that morning, leaving the pickup tucked away in a corner of Brilcrister Station car park. On the way, as instructed, he'd stopped by the police station. Baxter wasn't on duty but a surly and disappointed looking desk sergeant had grudgingly handed over his mobile phone. Bartholomew didn't bother to thank him. He judged the 'told you so' look on his face was a clear enough message for the sergeant to relay back to Baxter.

Going through the barriers at Waterloo Station he'd passed the Caribbean ticket inspector – the very same one as on his first visit to Brilcrister. Things must be looking up, decided Bartholomew. The inspector regarded him without the slightest indication of anything being out of the ordinary, even nodding and calling him sir, as if he really meant it.

First things first. Back in town, he'd headed over to Earl's Court to check on the flat and pick up his post. The reality was depressingly familiar on both fronts. The apartment was freezing cold and, he had to admit, looking really run down. What else did you expect? he asked himself. That someone magically overhauled the place whilst you were away? Dream on.

The post wasn't a lot more exciting either. A load of unpaid bills. A letter from his pompous wine merchant, threatening legal action if he didn't settle the invoice for his last three cases of claret. Lastly, a blatant flyer for a statuesque Eastern European hooker, with a purported 48 inch bust, which also informed you she was your very near neighbour and could be with you within ten minutes of your call. He'd shoved most of the paperwork in the bin, including the flyer. Funny that. He thought the area was supposed to be coming up in the world, undergoing the inevitable re-gentrification. Clearly, not quite yet.

Kennedy was in her usual spot. Nattily dressed in an expensive light blue silk shirt. Short hair gelled back, tortoiseshells on. Mobile glued to the ear. Ever so the businesswoman.

Bartholomew crossed the brasserie floor. José spotted him from the far side of the room and made a motion with his hand, as if taking an espresso. Bartholomew shook his head firmly. Now was the time for straight talking, not sipping conversational coffee. He sat down uninvited, just as Kennedy ceased her financial doodling, with a Montblanc pen on a paper napkin, and raised her head. He saw the fury explode in her eyes.

"What the fuck are you doing here?" she hissed, keeping her head down, furtively looking around to make sure there were no mega-wealthy clients that might overhear.

"Why the hell do you think?" he shot back. "Came down to see you in person. Now that the debacle at Minsham Court has been sorted out."

"Debacle? Yes! Of your sodding making, Bartholomew. Do you know how much trouble you've caused me? The comfort and counselling I've had to give the client. They've been on the phone half a dozen times since I informed them of the break in. Instant and informative updates is how they phrased it. That's what they expect. In other words: don't dare fuck this up! Get it sorted out pronto – or your reputation is on the line!

"Bartholomew, do you know how well connected this client is? To everyone who is anything. And I mean to everyone who is worth north of half a billion. It's that big, I'm telling you. In addition, I've also had that dickhead of a policeman on the phone again, asking all sorts of personal questions about you. You're bloody lucky I didn't give him some juicy tit-bits about your ill-starred past. You'd still be in the cells down there in Backwater or Brilwater, or whatever the bloody place is called!"

"It's Brilcrister, Kennedy. Don't you read the file? *Look,*" he continued, just about maintaining some semblance of a respectful employee tone in his voice - *you're going to have to listen to me here*. It's not making any sense to say it's all my fault. All I've had since I've been down there is one continuous stream of shitty hassle – ascending in severity from people behaving badly to a couple of guys trying to put me in hospital. Anybody in the same situation would have reached the end of their tether by now..."

"I told you to keep out of the main house, Bartholomew," Kennedy swiftly interjected. "Just to keep an eye on it. And to stay quiet in the flat."

He wondered whether she had somehow got wind of his dalliance with Roxy. Or discovered that a few bottles of vintage wine were missing from the cellar. Did she have a little watcher on the payroll, amongst the Estate contracted staff? Or had Baxter passed her one or two mistruths; deliberately lobbing in a couple of hand grenades, just to see whether they threw up anything? He decided – no. It was all front. Kennedy's usual tactics, to put him on the back foot.

"The burglars are the only ones who have entered the house uninvited, Kennedy," he told her firmly. "Ask the police."

He thought; take that whatever way you want, Mrs High and Mighty. Indeed, she did look a little perplexed.

"Kennedy, you sent me down there in the full knowledge there were serious issues afoot." Finding no other way to say it, Bartholomew plunged on: "I'm no longer convinced my well-being is of any importance to you. So I'm handing in my notice with immediate effect. I'll go back down there tomorrow, to pick up the rest of my things – but, after that, I'm going to be returning to London on the very next train. And I'd like my money in cash now please. You at least owe me that, after all I've been through."

Kennedy, unusually silent, regarded him stony faced. Eventually, she tilted her head to one side, and, looking at him almost coquettishly, asked: "What do you want, Bartholomew?"

"What do you mean, what do I want?"

"What do you want to stay on at the house for one more week? That's all the time I need to find someone suitable to replace you.

One week only. Ok, I admit you've had a little bit of a rough time. Over and above the call of duty, so to speak. So, name your price."

This was a turn up for the books. Kennedy acquiescing for once. What's behind that, he wondered?

"I'm not interested. I've told you – I can't continue with the assignment. This has been the last dance for you and me." And finally losing all patience, he barked: "For fuck's sake Kennedy! My health is worth more than a paltry week's pay!"

"Come on, Bartholomew," she persisted, disturbingly soothing and polite. "The gang that's been causing all the trouble are behind bars. It's plain sailing from now on. Just a normal job. Feet up in the flat for a week."

"Nope, I've said it. I'm out of there." He began to get to his feet.

"Day rate and a half for a week, with an extra day thrown in *gratis*. What do you say? Think of all the fancy claret that could buy!"

"Fraid not, Kennedy. I'm not that desperate. And you know full well the day rate you've got me on is a pittance. Hardly enough to live on, let alone buy a decent vintage."

"Ok. Final offer. Double the day rate for a week *and* two extra days *gratis*. Take it or leave it."

He thought hard for a moment, before responding.

"Ok, Kennedy. For one week only. But here's the deal: double the day rate, two extra days *gratis*, *and* a really decent lunch when the job's finished. For *two*. Why, you might even enjoy it. I think *The*

Savoy will do. To include aperitifs in the American Bar. Actually, thinking about it, let's eat in *The Savoy Grill*. A little bit of Gordy. One final condition. I get to choose the wine and menu – for both of us. Now – you take it or leave it."

Hopefully that would make her blanche. He knew she would find it galling to have Bartholomew in control of Kennedy spending money on Kennedy. She looked at him for a long moment, seemingly juggling something in her head. Ever the poker player our Kennedy, he scornfully observed.

"Ok, Bartholomew. You've got yourself a deal. But I want you back down at Minsham Court by this afternoon, at the very latest. I can't have the client thinking his valuable asset is being left unattended. Get going now. Check in with me as soon as you get there."

Marginally surprised, he stood up and walked off without so much as a goodbye. In any event, it wouldn't have made a jot of difference. He wasn't going back down to Minsham Court for Kennedy, a precocious client, wads of cash, or the best that Gordon Ramsay could throw at him.

Kennedy was never going to know, but the reality was he would have gone back down to Minsham Court without any inducement at all. For as long as it took. He had one, far more pressing matter to attend to. Against which all the side items he'd negotiated with Kennedy were a mere trifle. For he was going back to see Olivia again.

Chapter 14   The Content

Bartholomew waited patiently on the doorstep of the terraced cottage in Evensthorpe, with a bag of food shopping in each hand. It was six o'clock in the evening, the day after his return from London.

As instructed by Kennedy, he'd returned directly to the country on an afternoon train and was ensconced in Minsham Court a brief couple of hours later. All had seemed quiet back down on the Estate. OCD had been in and cleared up, now that the police had completed their procedures. The only change had been the empty spaces on the first floor, where the two urns had stood. They, or rather their broken remains, were now safely locked away in Brilcrister Police Station, ready to be used in evidence at the forthcoming legal proceedings.

If he was to be honest with himself, it all felt a little bit flat – the peace and quiet. Almost an anti-climax. With his erstwhile stalker caught and now pleasingly identified, plus the goings-on in the night resolved too, he felt different somehow. He rationalised that ever since he'd arrived at Minsham Court, he'd had to live with the tension. No longer though. Perhaps he could finally get a couple of good nights' sleep on the trot. You never know, he ruminated wistfully.

Sheila the Postie had turned up the next morning and been full of the local gossip – primarily about the burglary. Apparently, it was all the talk of Haddlewell and she'd even been asked about it in

Brilcrister. No-one was surprised about the involvement of the two lads. Their pasts were common knowledge.

It was more Roxy. Gallion's Stud had fired her immediately and the Spar had also closed its doors to their now-former employee. The only real information Bartholomew had gleaned from Sheila – which he didn't particularly like the sound of – was that all three were now out on bail. From what Sheila had been told by her postie colleagues in Brilcrister, who delivered to the administration offices of the Courts, there was general surprise that the trio had received the assistance of a senior brief to argue bail with the judge. He'd have to ask Baxter about that one next time he spoke to him. It worried him a little that the gang were out on the loose again. He supposed they'd be mad now to come anywhere near the Estate, with court proceedings looming. Unless, he thought, still worrying away, he was unlucky enough to bump into one of them at some other neutral location.

Aside from Sheila's news, there was thankfully not much else for him to report back to Kennedy, other than that all was in order at Minsham Court. He toured the grounds, inspected the house twice a day, checked the alarms and slept heavily. Via Sheila, the promised invitation to the New Year's Day lunch time drinks party turned up from Gerald Rissborough. Or rather, from Mr and Mrs Gerald Rissborough. My, he speculated, with some sympathy, what she must have to put up with. He'd placed the thick, heavily embossed card up above the Aga, on the empty, dusty mantelpiece. He didn't think he'd go. Not really his sort of thing after all, hobnobbing with all the county worthies.

He'd texted Olivia on the evening of his return. Suggesting he pop around and see how the foot was recovering. He hadn't got a reply until the next morning, which had played on his mind a bit. Stop behaving like an anxious schoolboy, he'd told himself. Worrying, he wouldn't get a second date. Why, let's face it – he hadn't even had a first. Olivia had finally texted that morning to say she'd just returned from her sister's and needed to sort a few things out first. But, if he felt it necessary, he could come around for a quick half hour in the early evening.

Bartholomew put one of the bags down on the doormat and rang the bell again. Christ, it was bloody freezing out in the street, even in his thick overcoat. A light came on in the hallway and, before he knew it, there she was in the doorway.

He had wondered, most selfishly, whether his mind had been playing tricks on him in the interval since he'd last seen her on Christmas Eve. About how simply beautiful she was. He was pleased to note, however, his memory faculty for extremely good-looking women was still in first-class working order. Olivia was dressed in a V-neck, light beige coloured sweater, above a pair of powder blue jeans. Her legs, it seemed, went on and on forever – down to a pair of flat court shoes. The tawny hair, pulled up into a ponytail, only seemed to accentuate the green eyes, which now regarded him with a mixture of warmth and, if he had to admit it, an element of caution.

"I couldn't help it – brought supper," he began, holding up the two bags. "You wait till I show you what I've got in store for you this time. Absolutely impossible to refuse!"

She gave him that fathomless look once more, as if it all might be too troublesome, but then motioned him in with a tiny smile.

"God you're incorrigible!" she laughed lightly, closing the door behind them. "How's a girl supposed to keep her figure with you around? Better be healthy. And simple – remember, you were just popping around for a quick chat!"

It was the sense of ease between them that he really noticed. It seemed the most natural thing in the world – the way they slotted in together: unpacking the shopping, opening a bottle of wine, her telling him all about the time with her sister, nieces and nephews. How it had been fun, but that she'd soon looked forward to getting back into her own routine. She didn't say if she'd thought of him whilst she'd been away. He couldn't tell her, he had thought of her for just about every spare minute of the day. Which for him – the house-sitter – was a lot of minutes.

He'd decided not to mention the attempted burglary and the arrest of Roxy's gang. No doubt, she'd hear about it locally. But all that could wait. In any event, he didn't exactly want to spend a lot more time thinking about it himself.

"So how's the foot?"

"It's coming along. I'm walking fine, but I think I'll give running a miss for a week or two. Just to be sure it fully recovers."

Good, he thought. There's a silver lining to every cloud. It would keep Olivia well away from any mad gentry in the woods.

"So, do you want to give me a hand?" he asked, after they had sorted the groceries out on the kitchen table. "I mean, it's pretty straightforward and you can hardly not have guessed what's on the menu!"

"Yes – I'm not so clueless, Bartholomew! I don't fancy cutting up the ribs though, but show me what else I can do."

And so he did. He'd pulled two large sheets of pork ribs out of their wrapping, and cut up them up with a fearsomely sharp butcher's knife Olivia had fetched from a block on the worktop. He then arranged them loosely on a baking tray, meaty side up.

Bartholomew asked Olivia to slice up two large red onions and a lemon, whilst he diced up some extra portions of pork, which he then pushed under the layer of ribs. He demonstrated how to generously cover the ribs with the onions and lemon, before popping the tray into the Rayburn.

"We'll just leave it in for thirty minutes, to brown a little. C'mon, let's sort out the sauce."

Between them, into a saucepan, they measured out a little light brown sugar, vinegar, Worcester sauce, tomato ketchup, a few drops of Tabasco, water, and finally some crushed garlic.

"How did you know I had enough Worcester and Tabasco Sauce?" she enquired, with a quizzical expression. "I'm always running out."

"On Christmas Eve. Don't you remember? You told me to help myself in the kitchen. Sadly, I have to admit; with regard to larders,

I have a near photographic memory. If you tested me, I bet I could name ninety five per cent of the contents you have in there. Oddly, the memory doesn't function nearly as well when it comes to paying parking tickets or the household bills."

Once they'd heated the mixture to boiling point, it was time to retrieve the tray from the Rayburn. On the worktop, Bartholomew carefully poured the sauce all over the arranged ribs, leaving a good sea of it in the bottom of the tray.

"God, I can tell they're going to be good already" Olivia exclaimed, appreciatively sniffing the vapour wafting up from the tray." What 'type' of spare ribs are these?"

"Spare ribs are spare ribs, I guess, but these are the French Canadian variety. Courtesy of my mother's kitchen, via some old friends they knew many years ago from over the water. I tell you, I used to go into a seriously heavy swoon whenever I heard they were on the menu. Guaranteed good mood all round!"

Olivia raised her hands to her face and wrinkled her nose. "Ugh, the raw onion's not so hot though."

He'd been moving over to wash his own hands, so they arrived at exactly the same time. Both, with their legs pressing into the front of the deep butler sink.

He pushed the single lever tap, and picked up a bottle of squeezy soap from the kitchen window shelf. With her close proximity, all he could think about was the warmth of her thigh against his own, as she accepted, with a little gasp, a dollop of the soap in her cupped hands.

"Water too hot?" he asked, trying it himself too.

"No, it's not that. I think I may have a couple of small paper cuts on my fingers. The onion's got in and it stings a little."

"Here, let me help." He knew exactly why he wanted to, because it was nigh on impossible for him not to touch her. With a little of the soap, he gently picked up her hands and with the lightest of possible caresses, avoiding the sensitive areas, he carefully worked it into her palms and in between her fingers.

"There," he said, soothingly. "That should do it."

When he was finished, he pulled her hands into the steady flow of warm water, still encased in his own, and held them there for a while. Eventually, he reached up with one hand and turned off the tap. There was a deafening silence in the kitchen. Bartholomew and Olivia stood side by side, looking down at his remaining hand, still softly clutching her long delicate fingers.

Finally, almost as if in slow motion, she raised her face, so that her intense green eyes held his in a long – and what seemed to him – wondrous, but fleetingly sad regard.

He broke the gaze and felt himself drawn forward, trance like, to lightly brush his lips across her cheek. Held there, inhaling her warm, intoxicating, natural scent, as he had that night in front of the wood burner on Christmas Eve.

She whispered: "Bartholomew – I can't do this. It's complicated. It's just not…"

"I know. I tried to stop myself. But I can't. Tell me you can stop."

"I can," she almost sobbed, but then, as if involuntarily, her head turned fractionally towards his face, so that their foreheads were touching like two samurai wrestlers, sizing each other up before the final round.

"We must stop this now," Olivia whispered again, as she reached up and slid a hand around the back of his neck, pulling him into her. He held her gaze the whole time, drowning in the deep green of her wide fathomless eyes, until, finally, he leant forward and ever so slowly, kissed her properly for the first time.

"You can stop," he whispered back, between ever more urgent kisses. "But it would be the biggest mistake of your life."

"You! I don't know what." She laughed, kissing him back now, the heat of the exchange rapidly overwhelming the pair of them, as she matched him for urgency. "How long do your ribs take, Mr Chef?" she asked, teasing now, continuing to shower his face with tender pecks.

"Oh – about an hour and a half to two hours," he managed to reply under the loving assault, the food part of his brain still functioning totally untroubled. "They should be basted occasionally but it doesn't matter if the ribs are a little blackened on top – it's tastier that way."

"Well, what are we waiting for then?" she replied and, with a conspiratorial smile, led him out of the kitchen in the direction of the stairs.

It only seemed a moment later when he awoke. In Olivia's bed, with her soft, slender body nestled snugly into his under the duvet.

He was having one of those funny feelings again, he smiled to himself, in the semi-darkness. The one where he feels amazingly happy and content. Where it was difficult to imagine that anything better existed on the planet. Olivia moved in her sleep before cuddling closer into his body, with a deep satisfied murmur. Something else though was going on in his head – but he couldn't think what the hell it was. Until finally, with a shocked "Shit!" he sat bolt upright in the bed.

"What is it?" cried out Olivia, leaping up too, looking around alarmed.

"Christ! The ribs! – they'll be burnt to death. Quick, I've got to rescue them!"

He leapt out of the bed, trying to dash for the door. Catching his foot on his discarded trousers he was sent flying, crashing to the ground. "Shit!" he cursed again, crawling to the door as Olivia flopped back onto the duvet, giggling helplessly.

Down in the kitchen, he realised the curtains weren't drawn. Quickly grabbing a tea towel, he hung it around his waist as best he could. Needless to say, as he pulled the blackened ribs from the Rayburn, the flimsy cotton covering fell to the ground. Oh well, he sighed, giving up. The great and the good of Evensthorpe might just have to get an unexpected eyeful on their way home from Evensong.

More importantly – and on closer inspection – he was gratified to see the ribs were perfectly done. Within ten minutes, he'd cooked basmati rice. He carried the offering of oozing sauce, ribs and steaming rice, back up to the bedroom on two large plates. Olivia was sitting cross legged, quite naked, in the middle of the bed.

He put one of the plates down in front of her with a fork and a square of kitchen towel.

"My God!" she exclaimed, inhaling the rich, deep aroma lifting off the plate. "I see what you mean."

She picked up a rib and chewed off a piece of pork. After a couple of further mouthfuls and rapidly licking the sauce off her fingers with great relish, she caught his eye and asked in all seriousness:

"Are there any seconds?"

He laughed, calling her a greedy puss and pointing out that she hadn't even finished her first helping. He sat there, unusually for him, only picking at his food. His hunger eclipsed by the sheer pleasure of watching Olivia lose herself in the primeval act of uninhibited, naked scoffing. Finally, with a finger, she wiped around the plate, a mound of ribs piled up on the side. Picked entirely clean. She leant over the edge of the bed and put the plate on the floor.

"More?" he enquired. "I thought you already had your seconds on order?"

"Oh, I'm having seconds alright" she answered in a low voice, and, with purposeful eyes, moved on all fours towards him. "Of both."

Chapter 15 The Nose

The wood burner in the sitting room of the flat wasn't half as dinky as the one in Olivia's cottage – but it certainly matched it for heat output.

Bartholomew stretched his legs out contentedly in the old leather armchair and reflected on the last couple of days, as he absently watched the logs blaze away through the glass-fronted burner.

It was late morning, New Year's Eve. He'd spent the last two nights at Olivia's cottage, returning during the day to Minsham Court to do his usual rounds. He'd checked in with Kennedy to report all was quiet, leaving out the bit about his nocturnal whereabouts. He didn't give a fig what Kennedy thought, regardless of their deal. The house seemed fine when he returned each morning and the likelihood of further aggravation was surely minimal.

If Kennedy had sacked him on the spot for abandoning his post, or refused to pay him the promised bonus, he would have laughed in her face and told her that was fine. In any event, in less than half a week he'd be out of here and back up in London.

Meanwhile, his happiness had continued unabated. The two nights he had spent with Olivia were easily, he judged, the best two nights of his entire life. They had laughed, cooked, made love, slept, snacked, laughed and made love again. When he was with her, in the tiny cottage, it was as if the rest of the world didn't exist. All the rubbish things that had ever happened to him, the disappointments, the let-downs, the cruel outcomes – and the consequent gloom that they brought on – were now banished from his thoughts. He even wondered whether his sub-conscious had been wiped clean. He hadn't experienced a nightmare now for four days. This was virtually a record for him.

Olivia had an existing commitment for New Year's Eve, in Notting Hill, and was heading off on the train that morning. She'd said it was something to do with an old client friend. They'd made their farewells on her doorstep: Olivia wrapped tightly in her towelling robe, he kissing her goodbye, making arrangements to see each other the evening after New Year's Day, whilst his mind was still half pre-occupied on what lay beneath her robe. She had pushed him gently away, with one of those faraway looks she still occasionally gave him, which he didn't understand, but was far too happy to be bothered to try and decipher.

No, he thought, buoyantly, as he reclined in the leather armchair. Minsham Court was history. The future lay ahead in London. His head was full of thoughts of life after Kennedy. He'd look around again and get himself a decent job. A job that really meant something. Re-decorate the flat, cut his wine consumption down and, of course, cook as much as possible.

He speculated on whether he and Olivia would spend most of their time at his place, or over at her pad in Maida Vale. Perhaps some travelling was in order, too. He'd always had a yen for a trip down the spine of South America. On a never-ending railway journey, writing a travel diary, sipping Chilean *Sauvignon Blanc*. Just a glass – or maybe two.

In fact, that's what he needed right now, he decided. Some decent reading matter. And a couple of good travel guides, so he could plan ahead and sow the seed of the idea in Olivia's mind next time he saw her. He would spend a lazy New Year's Eve here on his own, in front of the wood burner, with a raft of good travel literature, envisaging the future.

He piled more logs into the wood burner and tamped down the oxygen flow, to make it last until he returned in the afternoon. Heading out into the utility room, he grabbed his overcoat and the fedora.

Shrugging on the overcoat, he suddenly froze at the sound of a couple of harsh raps on the kitchen door. The nerve jangling feeling he'd hoped he'd permanently left behind re-surfaced in the blink of an eye. Grabbing the hazel staff, he headed out warily into the kitchen. On the basis this was a serious intrusion – no buzz from the main gates intercom but a presence right outside the flat, albeit one that had actually announced itself – he wanted to make sure he was prepared for any eventuality.

He needn't have worried. Ripping open the kitchen door, staff held rigidly in front, he was confronted by a small, middle-aged woman in a tweed skirt and head scarf that somehow reminded Bartholomew of film clips of the Queen from the 1960's.

"I'm Leonora Rissborough," she announced, holding out her hand. She had a soft, pleasant voice and the immediate impression Bartholomew got was one of honest candour.

"Bartholomew," he replied, lowering the staff and leaning forward to shake her hand lightly, feeling slightly foolish now at the sight he must have presented.

"I'd heard from my staff that there had been a bit of trouble at Minsham recently" she continued, with a small understanding smile. "Don't be embarrassed on my behalf."

The moment having passed, he reasoned it was justified for him to assume his professional demeanour once more. "It's just that visitors to Minsham Court are expected to ring from the main gate. Neighbours too."

"I'm so sorry, force of habit of old. My great-aunt used to live here many years ago. I'd visit as a young girl. She was childless herself and treated me like her own daughter. I'd often come for tea and when I used to stay for longer during the summer holidays, I used to roam the grounds, sometime on my pony, sometimes on foot. I know the estate like the back of my hand."

"Look" he said, feeling once again somehow disarmed and deciding now the woman deserved some hospitality, despite her unorthodox entry. "Please, come into the kitchen and have a cup of coffee. I expect you could do with one after a tramp through those gloomy woods."

She smiled appreciatively and said "Alright, a quick cup then. It's very kind of you."

Taking her coat and scarf, he sat her at the kitchen table and began to assemble the coffee.

"So, I take it you didn't bump into your husband crossing the estate boundary, or that fun loving gamekeeper of his?"

"No, Gerald is out on business today. As to Jeavons, well, I'm constantly told he's an integral cog as far as the running of the estate is concerned. Or should I say, the running of the estate *correctly*. Funny, in my father's day, gamekeepers used to look so very different."

Bartholomew instinctively liked the woman and her approach. Despite her bright smile he noticed her eyes were tired and sad. Resigned, would be an accurate description. He'd seen that look somewhere before.

"Rissborough's nothing to do with your side of the family, is it?" he enquired casually, a little curious about the family dynamics having now met both Mr and Mrs Rissborough.

"No. All Gerald's. My aunt's occupation of Minsham Court was just a co-incidence. I grew up in Shropshire."

Placing the coffee pot and cups and saucers on the table, Bartholomew reached into the larder and grabbed an old square tin. Leonora did not seem bothered at all by the relaxed etiquette as he prised off the lid and offered her a slice of homemade flapjack directly from the container.

"I can tell you know the way to a woman's heart is through food" she laughed, leaning forward, clearly appreciating the aroma rising up of ever so lightly burnt oats and golden syrup.

He watched her pick out a crusty edged square. "I just get a sense sometimes when someone could do with a little treat," he smiled back warmly, genuinely meaning it, somehow feeling that despite her position and apparent good fortune in life, this was not a woman who had had a lot of attention spent on her recently.

"Who taught you how to make these so well?" she enquired, "Your mother, I expect."

"Of course. I lived in Cyprus for a while as a kid. I was a Service brat, my father flew jets. Some days in the summer it would get so hot outside you just couldn't get on your bike as usual and roam around the base with your friends. It seemed a crazy thing to do, as you'd have thought cooking in that heat was mad but we had large ceiling fans so it wasn't so uncomfortable. I perfected the art of flapjacks on one of those very hot afternoons.

After munching a little of her square, Leonora looked up with a concerned frown. "I don't like to pry, but are you ok here, even after all the goings on? I appreciate you're a professional house-sitter, or caretaker – Gerald told me as much – and doubtless used to being in places on your own, but isn't this a little much, just for one person?

He laughed and shrugged his shoulders. He appreciated her concern and for a moment contemplated giving her chapter and verse of his experiences to date. Instead, he decided he didn't want to dwell on it any longer and with another rueful grin replied: "Let's just say the perpetrators will never interfere with a food lover again. They're all locked up now, and I'm still here, cooking."

She looked a little confused but had the good grace to laugh. To return her kindness, he asked: "Would you like a tour of the house? To bring back a few old memories?"

She looked wistful for a moment, then got up and retrieved her coat and scarf from where he'd left them hanging over the back of a chair. "No, I don't think so. I sense – like you – that sometimes things are better left untouched. Anyway, it's so bitterly cold outside I better make sure I get back soon before someone starts worrying about me."

Bartholomew helped her on with her coat as she thanked him for the coffee. As Leonora made off briskly across the gravel, in the direction of the woods, she called back to him: "You will come to the drinks party, won't you? I really would like it if you did."

He waved her off. "I'll think about it. It's very kind of you both to ask," he shouted back, guessing, as he said it, she'd know that he was only partly dissembling.

***

The cold frost on the ground outside clearly wasn't going to release its grip all day. Bartholomew carefully guided the pickup down the drive and out onto the road, pointing the vehicle towards Brilcrister. For reasons he attributed to the conversation with Leonora, about his childhood, a yearning came to him to see if he could find any copies of the old Henry Treece trilogy he'd read as a boy. Perhaps something else too, but he thought it would be fun to pick up the old Norse tales once again. And *Casper's* was the bookshop that might just have a copy in stock.

The road down into Brilcrister was treacherous. There were a couple of empty cars left on the verge, clearly abandoned by their owners having failed to navigate the incline in the icy conditions. Taking it slowly, the ancient pickup grinded carefully down the slope, the four-wheel drive proving its worth.

Just as he hit the outskirts of Brilcrister his mobile rang. Looking down, still with half an eye fixed on the icy road, he recognised Detective Sergeant Baxter's number. What now, he thought, unwilling to speak to the policeman if it meant further hassle – which, undoubtedly, it most certainly would. Oh what the hell, he decided, and carefully steered the pickup over to the side of the road before answering the call.

"Hello Detective Sergeant, what can I do for you?"

"Hello, sir. Just thought we'd touch base as we haven't spoken for a while."

Trying to keep a modicum of humour in his voice, Bartholomew replied: "Why is it, Detective Sergeant, that I always get a little nervous when you open every conversation we have along the same lines? Is it because usually, within a couple of minutes, you seem to have me lined up on a serious charge? Or, at the very least, you're informing me I'm your number one suspect?

"I suppose you're phoning to let me know another country house in the locality has been broken into and I'm about to be arrested," continued Bartholomew, still trying his hardest to maintain a marginally jocular tone. "I mean, usually it's itinerants that are the trouble, Detective Sergeant. No proof of permanent residence, transient, no records, used to disappearing quickly when the heat is on. Ha! must be something like that – don't you think?"

There was silence at the other end of the phone as he sensed Baxter trying to determine whether Bartholomew was really jesting or not.

Finally, he responded. "Not at all. I know you're only poking fun sir, but what people don't realise in these situations is that we have to follow a thorough procedure, check out every avenue. Most crime, after all, has an obvious trend if you don't mind me…"

"Ah, there you are! You've just proved my point, Detective Sergeant," shot back Bartholomew, laughing now.

"Well, perhaps you should have more faith in the police force, sir – or in your own standing, if I may…"

"Hang on a minute, Detective Sergeant let's not get personal.

"Ok, sir, I can see this conversation isn't going anywhere. So I'll get to the point The reason for telephoning is to pass on some information to you about Roxanne Halsall and Ryan Hollins."

"Oh, yeah" Bartholomew continued, laughing again now. "What now? I suppose they've told you I'm the orchestrator of a dozen other major burglaries in the county and at this precise moment I'm on my way down to London to Buckingham Palace to case the joint!"

"Not exactly, sir. In fact quite the opposite. Miss Halsall has informed us she wishes to amend the statement she made on Boxing Day. To the effect that she *was* in the house at Minsham Court in the early hours of Boxing Day, with Mr Hollins and Mr Cudmore. She has now also confirmed that you had nothing to do with the crime. She has admitted to meeting you a couple of times, but has clearly stated you had no involvement whatsoever in the burglary. Or, with any of the other nocturnal activities that have been going on in and around the estate grounds.

This time the deafening silence came from Bartholomew's end of the line. He sat back slowly in the driving seat. It wasn't as if he really had a suitable riposte to the sergeant's news.

"Are you still on the line, sir?" asked Baxter, quite coolly.

"Yes."

"Good, then I'll continue. Additionally, both Mr Hollins and Mr Cudmore have indicated that, at the upcoming court hearings, they will now be entering a guilty plea.

"Mr Hollins has stated that, on reflection, he is withdrawing his request that you be put on a charge of GBH. He has also confirmed that it is definitely not his intention to pursue you for any form of civil damages. That is, sir, in respect of your actions on the night in question with the… ahem… turkey leg. Now, or in the future."

Baxter hesitated, clearly hoping for a reply from Bartholomew. It seemed the policeman was thoroughly enjoying himself.

"Overall, sir, it looks like you are fully in the clear. Now that we have been able to interview Miss Halsall with a bit more information – and put it to her in no uncertain terms that her alibi does not stack up – she has decided to come clean. After all, the fingerprint evidence is overwhelming. It would seem common sense has prevailed. Especially since we've explained to Miss Halsall that admitting to the crime in full should hopefully motivate the judge to pass a minimal sentence – as she is a first time offender."

"As for Mr Hollins, well, we both know he's been blowing a lot of hot air. I gather his physical discomfort is somewhat reduced now and I'm sure he'd rather put the whole episode behind him. Although – I'm not sure that's entirely the right analogy to use in the circumstances.

"Which is why, sir – if I may be so bold – I said earlier you should have more confidence in the system. You see, we usually get there in the end. Anyway, I have to go on another call now, so unless there is anything else you need from me, I'll be signing off. Just to let you know: we'll still need you for any witness requirements in respect of the court proceedings but we'll be in touch about that separately. Good bye, sir. And may I say the very best of luck with your next assignment – wherever that may be."

Bartholomew resisted the urge to make a final quip at the Detective Sergeant. Instead, he just ended the call. He sat for a while in the cab thinking it through. Well, that was a turn up for the books. Things just seemed to be getting better and better for once. In view of the bigger picture, Roxy must have decided to live with the fact that the police believed her to be in the house on the night of the burglary, based purely on fingerprint evidence. For as far as Bartholomew was aware, there had only been three people inside the main house at the time in question – and one of them was him. Still, it made no difference what version of the truth was to be believed. There was nothing to stop him now making a clean break of it back to London, as planned. There'd be no potential charges or lawsuits to see out after he'd departed from Minsham Court.

It rankled though, the way the policeman had constantly twisted the turn of events to suit his own purposes and paint the force in a good light. It was more police-state behaviour than rural constabulary. He turned the ignition and, as he began to guide the pickup out onto the icy road once more, decided to forget about it. Let them all disappear from view. Park all that unwelcome noise where it belonged – in the past.

He manoeuvred the pickup into a slot in the market square, just as the last of the morning stall holders were finishing packing away. He was hungry and remembered a little brasserie along one of the alleyways leading off the square.

Sure enough, it was not only open and bustling inside, it also had a little outside kitchen unit. A cheery, red-haired chef, in a stained apron and with ten-day old stubble was stirring a giant sized pan of paella with an enormous wooden spoon. An impressive column of steam rose from the pan into the freezing air, sending out that uniquely intoxicating aroma of chicken, seafood, chorizo sausage, spices and rice roasting in oil. Even in the cold, the town was busy with people, still sorting out their New Year's Eve purchases. A queue of hungry shoppers lined up before the stall, stamping their feet to beat off the freeze, nostrils collectively twitching. Trade was brisk, as the ginger chef spooned out large dollops of the paella into takeaway polystyrene boxes, as fast as he decently could.

Bartholomew joined the queue and not long after was ambling in the direction of *Casper's*, whilst struggling to shovel in mouthfuls of the paella with frozen hands and a plastic spoon.

He could hear the voice of his father in his head, admonishing him: never eat whilst walking along in a public place. Oh well, he reasoned, it's far too cold to sit down anywhere. What was that saying about when you are a parent, always a parent? Worrying about your offspring even when they are mature adults. Was there another one – one that said in a corner of your mind you are always a child?

He turned the corner into the long terrace where *Casper's* was situated and spooned down the last of the rice out of the polystyrene box. Near the junction, where the terrace met the modern shopping precinct, he searched for a bin. Like everywhere these days, it proved to be a difficult task. Eventually, he found an overflowing receptacle, partially hidden, just inside the precinct entrance. After shoving the box in as far as he could, without getting coated in all sorts of other assorted greases, he crossed the road and headed towards the peeling façade of *Casper's*.

He put his weight into the entrance door to get it to open, whilst absently watching a small group of pensioners, wrapped up in heavy coats, scarves and woolly hats, at a bus stop across the street. They were huddled together for warmth, corralled by their assorted pull-along shopping trolleys. Collectively, like a gaggle of geese, they were craning their necks forwards towards what seemed to be a traffic altercation going on at the far end of the terrace. From what he could see, it looked like a council recycling lorry driver was having a bit of a standoff with the owner of a large, black vehicle. Lovely, he observed. It seemed like the Christmas spirit of goodwill to all men was already wearing off. Why, it could be time for a New Year's resolution.

Casper's was extremely busy too. People using their Christmas book tokens with a vengeance before the public holiday. Or rather, discreetly returning those books they never really wanted in the first place, but were far too polite to say so over the canapés and sparkling wine.

Bartholomew searched along the travel section until he found two excellent guides on Chile and Argentina, both in pristine condition. Hardbacks, a few years old, but pretty good value nonetheless. Well, he thought, rather pleased with himself, he was recycling too.

For the next ten minutes he hunted high and low along the alphabetically arranged bookshelves for copies of the Henry Treece trilogy. Try as he might, he couldn't spot a single one of the series. Time for some help, he decided, and headed off along the central corridor for assistance.

Somewhat relieved, near the counter he spotted the hippy assistant who had rung the till for him the last time he was in the bookshop. Thank God, it appeared the old Dickensian look-a-like wasn't on duty today. After a quick word and a flick through the stock list on the computer, the hippy motioned for Bartholomew to follow him down the central isle and over to a line of bookshelves in the far right hand corner, near the front entrance to the shop. His luck, however, ran out there. As if by magic, from behind the last bookshelf, out sprang the doddery old assistant.

"Phillips! What are you doing away from the till? You know we never leave the till unattended. Get back to the counter at once!"

Phillips answered – in a somewhat meek and terrified voice – that he was only helping a customer. After providing a rather scrambled explanation of what Bartholomew was after, he scuttled off at high speed back up the central isle. Dickens scrutinised Bartholomew closely, up and down, before asking:

"Haven't we met before, sir? I have a funny feeling that our paths have crossed. He raised his head, looking down his long, thin, aquiline nose.

Oh my God, groaned Bartholomew, trying hard not to look up. Not the white sprouting nasal hair bushes again. He wasn't sure if he could look at the twin growths without gagging. He could feel the chorizo sausage swirling around in his stomach. Staring fixedly at the centre of the man's chest, he replied in as an authoritative tone as possible;

"Never! You must have me mistaken for someone else. This is my very first time in *Casper's*."

Dickens continued to stare at Bartholomew, somewhat unconvinced. Eventually, thankfully, he decided to move on.

"Who exactly was it you were after again, sir? Henry James? Henry Fielding? Henry Graham? Ehm – Graham Henry?"

"No. Not *Tom Jones* or the *All Black's* former coach – just Henry Treece. *The Viking Trilogy, which* he wrote in the 1950s."

"Ah! Why didn't you say so in the first place?! Of course we have some copies. Follow me."

Dickens lurched off along the last row of bookcases, followed by Bartholomew slowly shaking his head. On arrival at the far wall, he pulled out a couple of mobile stools and motioned Bartholomew to squat on one, whilst he proceeded to perch with surprisingly delicate ease on the other.

"Let me see," he pondered, tapping his bony fingers on the long nose as he scanned the bookshelf above. Bartholomew kept his own eyes deliberately fixed on the book spines along the row directly in front of him, not even registering the titles. Just maintaining a strict, no nasal hair view.

"Henry Treece… yes, first novel was written, if I'm right, around 1955. *Viking's Dawn*. Second was, let me think… yes, I know – *The Road to Miklagard*. Then followed, ha! unsurprisingly, by *Viking's Sunset*."

"Something like that," replied Bartholomew, dryly.

He could still feel the sausage churning around in his stomach. He hoped he hadn't eaten a dodgy prawn.

"Do you actually have any copies?"

"Hmm... yes," came back the vague reply, as Dickens continued to run his hands up and down the bookshelf, searching for the trilogy but not actually locating anything at all.

"I can remember the story now," he continued. "Harald going berserk in *The Road to Miklagard*. Quite my favourite episode."

"It's revealed Harald is a berserker in *Viking's Sunset*, not *The Road to Miklagard*. It's in the final book."

"No, you are wrong. It's in the second of the trilogy."

"I think you'll find it's the third."

"Second."

"Third. Look – do you actually have any Henry Treece?

"Of course; ah, there we are – finally!"

Dickens' long, bony fingers retrieved a slim bound volume from one of the shelves, right at the top of his reach. Bartholomew sighed with deep relief. There wasn't much more he could take. Nostalgia trips should be far more enjoyable than this. He was feeling really sick now.

"There!" Dickens triumphantly exclaimed, holding up a copy of *The Road to Miklagard*. "I can prove my point now."

He began to leaf through the book, humming to himself, as if he was entirely on his own and without a care in the world.

Bartholomew decided to give it a couple more minutes and then he was out of here, armed with a Henry Treece or not. To distract himself from his queasy stomach and thoughts of Dickensian sprouting, he absent-mindedly listened to the muted sounds of what appeared to be an argument going on on the far side of the bookshelf. It was impossible, really, to make anything out at all, as the participants were doing everything they could to keep a lid on it, almost whispering. He could sense though, from the low pitch of voices, that a serious disagreement was in train. *Casper's* seemed to have that effect on people, he concluded, depressingly.

Finally, he broke: "Look – I've had about enough of this. I may have it wrong. It could have happened in *The Road to Miklagard*. I don't care either way. Just tell me if you have any of the others in the series? If not, then please just give me that one there so I can go and pay!"

Dickens was about to answer when he stopped and raised his head. Bartholomew, inadvertently, got the nasal display full on and felt a rush of bile coming up from his stomach. He sensed he was about to retch, before bringing it back under control. Dickens, tilting his head back even further – whilst sniffing the air with his large, bountifully-filled nostrils – exclaimed:

"What is that?"

"Uh?" gasped Bartholomew, reeling now, one hand grasping his stomach.

"Rose petals. That's it. Pink, I think, although I'm not quite sure of their origin."

Bartholomew, his head in a fog, stared at the man thinking: He's gone completely off his rocker.

In the silence that ensued, Bartholomew froze as the climax of the ever-so discreet argument beyond the bookshelf reached its zenith. At that moment, the faintest hint of rose petal essence washed over him, making him absolutely certain that the street-food inside his stomach wanted out – now!

He stood up, not really sure of anything, anymore.

"I've… I've got to go. You keep the Treece. I think it's better the past remains in the past."

With that he ran for the door, desperately clutching his belly. Barging through, he lurched out onto the pavement and vomited copiously into the gutter, much to the chagrin of the on-looking pensioners.

Chapter 16 The Barman

For once the lack of sleep came from something other than a nightmare. He couldn't settle down, even for a couple of hours in the evening in front of the wood burner, nursing a glass of *The Famous Grouse*. The dwindling residue of the paella malaise had stayed on, leaving him with a dull, night-long stomach ache and too much time to brood.

Through to the late morning, Bartholomew gloomily stomped around the grounds in the immediate vicinity of the house, taking his time, pacing it out, until the cold fresh air had finally cleared his head. Just before midday, he returned to the flat and dug out the dinner suit and shirt from the charity shop. It'd have to do. He had no other formal clothes to wear and he knew for certain he couldn't just pitch up in jeans and a grimy fleece.

He'd made his mind up during the morning ramble that he would go to the Rissborough's lunchtime drinks party. In the circumstances, he'd now decided, it would be rude not to. Donning the dinner suit, he thought about it a little more, and after admitting to himself he'd look completely out of place in the evening attire, decided to ditch the jacket. Hopefully, the trousers would pass off as a trendy alternative to moleskins or chinos, or whatever it was the county set wore these days.

Pulling on the overcoat, fedora, and grabbing the hazel staff from a corner of the utility room, he headed out across the manicured lawns and paddocks. It was even colder than the day before, but now with a vicious biting wind which howled away, driving ruthlessly in from the east. The heavy frost crackled under his feet as he slogged up the incline, before he entered the familiar wood.

He followed the path around the lip of the crater and through to the track beyond, all the while shivering violently. He was absolutely freezing, realising too late that a fleece under the overcoat was exactly what was required, or at least until he got down to Rissborough Hall. To try to combat the freeze, he moved at an energetic pace and in no time at all reached the far side of the wood. Without breaking his stride, he swiftly loped on down through the Rissborough paddocks and was soon a tidy field away from the house.

It was enormous, close up. Minsham Court felt like a quaint little doll's house in comparison. Unsurprisingly, the vast sweeping drive was stuffed with all the types of vehicles you'd expect too. There probably wasn't a car or 4X4 there with a value under fifty thousand pounds. Including one shining beast – located in pride of place – by the front entrance. No doubt about who owns that one, Bartholomew sourly concluded.

He was just about to slam the gigantic lion's head knocker down hard on the left of the huge double-fronted doors, when they were parted by an elderly, stooping man, dressed in black tails. Bartholomew gave his name to the old boy, whom he assumed must be the Rissborough's butler, and was ushered inside. Just as the butler was relieving him of his overcoat – in a foyer which was larger than the footprint of a modern four bedroom house – Gerald Rissborough appeared, antique champagne flute in hand.

"Ah, Bartholomew. At last. So glad you were able to come. We weren't quite sure you were going to make it. The invite was RSVP…"

Rissborough, dressed in a tweed jacket, blue tie and mustard coloured chinos, gave him the professional host's full beaming smile, but the eyes remained as calculating and knowing as ever.

"Well, I had a couple of hours free in my diary today so I thought I could just about fit it in," Bartholomew eventually replied. "I wasn't really quite sure though, until this morning, whether I felt it really was the right thing for me to attend. I am now though."

"Oh good, I'm very pleased to hear it." Rissborough continued, the fixed smile still held rigidly in place.

"I've been so looking forward to us seeing each other again. I would have been most disappointed if you had decided to turn me down. Tell me, how was the walk over here? Pretty cold out there today. Big hoar frost. Wind's pretty evil too!"

"Yes, very. Enough to freeze the balls off a brass monkey, as they say. No loose cannons though to slow me down this time. I mean, shotgun wielding gamekeepers in the woods."

"Ha! Very droll. I'll have to pass that one on to Jeavons. I'm sure he'd be most amused! You never know, he might like a re-play at some point. In fact – I know he would."

At that point another guest arrived so the butler motioned Bartholomew into the next room. Rissborough gave him a final nod.

"Enjoy yourself Bartholomew. We're drinking a 96' vintage. You must make sure you fill your cup. And please, rest assured, we will catch up later."

The butler all but pushed him into what could only be referred to as the Great Hall. It had to be at least three times the size of the one at Minsham Court. The ceiling seemed to reach up to the heavens, or at least to the vast Italianate frescos decorating its capacious surface. The walls were draped with tapestries, denoting ancient hunting scenes. In two massive opposing fireplaces, cradling enormous medieval-style grates, with dogs at either end in the shape of magnificent stags, a couple of huge log fires roared away.

In the centre of the hall about forty people were gathered in typical cocktail party style, nattering away to each other loudly, in familiar little groups, champagne glasses gripped to their chests, or sipped from enthusiastically.

What was it all about, he asked himself, when a stranger – in his case a man – enters for the first time a room, in which a bunch of people who all know each other intimately are grouped together. It is as if we are not that far removed from a pack of dogs – and that it is only decorum that masks, or restrains, our true desired behaviour. There is a hum of conversation and, as the stranger enters, every head moves, just fractionally, to size up the newcomer. The women, who have already registered every other man in the room, many times over – the basic human instinct for evaluating partner suitability, sub-consciously or consciously – ask themselves if this new man is a potential match. Even if they already have a match, in this very room, the one they've had for the last twenty years or more. The men, on the other hand, eyes jousting, consider if this new contender is a threat to their status with their own women, or perhaps, to their position in the male pecking order in the room. If it were a pack of dogs they would have crowded round, sniffing the undercarriage of the intruder, hairs bristling on the back of their necks. Instead, human evolution holds them back. It's all done with the eyes, although, given half a chance, some of them would quite easily slip back into the old dog mould. He decided it would be rather disconcerting – a bunch of toffs, chasing him around the Great Hall on all fours, desperately trying to stick their over-bred noses up his backside.

An elderly gent, dressed in a loud Toad of Toad Hall checked suit, bawled out at him:

"Barman! I'll have a top up please. Where's the damn bottle?"

"I'm a guest. Not a waiter. Get your own drink… Toady."

"What? Oh gosh, I didn't quite get all that. I'm a little deaf. Bloody hell, sorry old man, thought you were one of the staff. Desperate for a top-up."

Toady managed to grab two flutes from a genuine passing waiter and handed one to Bartholomew, vintage fizz splashing over onto the flagstone floor. Sizing up Bartholomew's attire, he crooked a finger at him. Moving closer, he whispered:

"Want to know a secret?"

"Not particularly," Bartholomew replied, swigging back the champagne in one, whilst trying to gently move away.

"Well, I'm going to tell you one anyway. Two, in fact."

"Oh well, go on then. Put me out of my misery."

Leaning over towards Bartholomew's ear, in an alcoholic sway, he whispered:

"I bought this suit in a British Heart Foundation charity shop. Ten quid. What d'you think?"

Bartholomew was quite impressed. Bloody hell, Toady did look like the real deal. Just shows you *front* is everything. Grand setting, red walrus face, right accent, suit that once had cost a small fortune but you could now get for the cost of three pints of beer and there he was; looking just like Queen Victoria's son, a bloated Prince of Wales. Why, Toady was probably a plasterer for all he knew.

"And the other?"

Slurring his words, Toady belched under a raised hand, before whispering conspiratorially,

"Don't ever tell a soul, as no one else knows this but me – but try shopping at Lidl. You can actually get real German cheese and yoghurts. My God, man! You should see some of the deals on wine! Try not to look too much at the other shoppers though, or you might get mugged, but it's a real wheeze, I tell you. Remember, don't tell a soul." Toady tapped his veined nose. "You and I are the only ones in the know. Got to keep it that way!"

Bartholomew decided it was high time he moved away and grabbing another flute, ambled off over towards one of the magnificent fireplaces. Nearing the roaring fire, he hijacked a further passing waiter. This one was carrying a selection of canapés on a silver platter. Bartholomew quickly downed a couple of quail eggs and three thin pastry parcels of shredded duck, each coated in a rich, dark plum sauce.

As he was munching happily away he looked over to the far side of the fireplace. Jeavons was positioned there, muscles bulging under a tight black suit, hands clasped together in front, eyeing him stonily. Bartholomew broke the gaze immediately. There was absolutely no point in winding up the weight-lifting gamekeeper with any perceived cheek. That was for sure.

He moved further out into the room, but not before noticing a small group of men, of mixed age, observing him closely from just the other side of Jeavon's spot by the fireplace. They were dressed in the usual county set party apparel, akin to Gerald Rissborough's, and seemed to be talking and smirking amongst themselves, whilst continuing to follow his progress through the hall. Perhaps, he thought darkly to himself, he was the only visual sport on offer at this grand celebration; the outsider, looking like a fish out of water in his badly chosen attire.

Turning away from the group he bumped into a tall man in his forties, standing on his own. Bartholomew apologised and began to move away, however the man – shod in the most ridiculous purple Gucci loafers – decided to introduce himself.

"Septimus Felcher Frotherington."

"I'm sure," replied Bartholomew. "Sounds very painful."

"I'm sorry? I don't quite get your drift. Who are you?"

"Bartholomew."

"What do you do then? No, let me guess. I'm not fooled by your outfit. Met your type before. Likes the incognito look. Hedge fund manager?"

"Nope."

"Alright, wealth management?"

"No."

"Investment banker?"

"'Fraid not."

"Securities. Offshore funds. Foreign currencies?

"Look, let me put you out of your misery. I'm a house…"

Before he could finish the sentence, the man cut over him:

"I knew it! House manager for a private investment company. Why you chaps cream off all the best deals! Pick and choose at your own leisure. No shareholders badgering away at you all the time to prove your worth and demanding transparency."

"I'm a house-sitter for a London agency. We look after large private residencies for the sort of people you're talking about. I suppose you could also call me a caretaker."

"Eh?!" gasped the man, now looking down his nose at Bartholomew as if he were an unwanted speck of dust on his jacket sleeve that needed to be flicked off immediately. "You're what? Oh

God!" he snorted, and without another word moved rapidly off towards the nearest crowd of champagne quaffing hearties.

Finishing his own glass, he decided he'd just about had enough too and began to make his way towards the foyer. Just before he reached the entrance, he felt a small tug at his sleeve and turned to find Leonora Rissborough, dressed again in another Queen Elizabeth tweed ensemble.

"Off already?" she enquired, at the same time looking altogether unsurprised at his staying power.

"Oh, hello," he replied, shaking her hand. "Look, I'm sorry, I have to be somewhere. So, many thanks for the party. It's been a blast."

"Oh, really," she said, not at all sarcastically, just matter of fact. "I've been watching you. Five minutes each with old Lukas Hollander and SFF is enough to make anyone run for the door."

"Yes," he laughed back. God, he thought: so nice to talk to another human being again.

"At least you came. Hopefully it has given you a bit of a break from Minsham Court." She looked at him with the same concern as in the kitchen yesterday. "Everything still alright over there?"

"All in good order. Last time I looked, that is."

"Very pleased to hear it. By the way, a word of caution – best to avoid raising the topic of Minsham Court with Gerald. Because of my past connection with the estate Gerald seems to think it gives us some sort of hold over the place. I don't agree. As I said yesterday, it's all in the past – as far as I'm concerned."

Turning to survey the noisy gathering, Leonora continued. "Mind you, sometimes I really believe the past should shape the present. Take how these New Year gatherings used to be," she reminisced. "This hall would have been full of a cross-section of the local community. Lords, ladies and jelly babies, as they say. Why, you could have Lord Allerton over there mixing with a local tenant farmer. The farmer would be dressed in his best bib and tucker of course, minding his manners carefully, but he would drink from the same barrel of beer or decanter of claret as the peer."

"Now look at it," she sighed, gazing around at the heaving throng with an expression that was almost contemptuous. "There's only one theme that's common in here now and that's money. Gerald likes to feel the wealth around him. It gives him a sense of achievement I think, a permanent reminder to himself that he really has succeeded."

She stopped there as if she just wanted to forget about it all. Eventually, she resumed: "Keep to your house-sitting job, Bartholomew," she told him flatly, whilst continuing to look at him with those deep, sad eyes. "Money – it's a killer. You know, the…"

"The root of all evil," he finished the sentence for her.

"Yes, that's right. Look, I've said enough. I don't want to hold you up. How are you getting back?"

"I'm on foot. Through the woods, over the hill and straight back to my warm caretaker's flat."

She still held his gaze with what he could only interpret as a worried expression. He wasn't sure why. "Well, take care then.

You'd better go quickly as it will start to get dark by four. Goodbye."

Bartholomew bade her farewell, and, after collecting his overcoat, hat and staff from a stand just behind the dozing butler, stepped out into the cold.

Chapter 17 The Spread Eagle

Cold it certainly was, with the frigid wind roaring brutally away around Bartholomew's ears as he pulled the huge double doors firmly shut behind him. After buttoning the overcoat right up to his neck, he briskly crunched off down the drive, back past the assembly of luxury cars.

The champagne had given him an inner warmth and he felt marginally cosy wrapped up in his long overcoat, as he crossed the parkland and strode up to the edge of the wood. It was nearing four o'clock and there was already a hint of the oncoming twilight in the atmosphere.

Bartholomew retraced his steps along the familiar path through the woods, as the wind battered and bowed the trees all around. He thought anything half rotten stood a very good chance of coming down tonight. It was best to move on as quickly as he could. As the path neared the edge of the crater, some need, or subconscious urge that he couldn't quite explain, lured him off the track and he found himself once more skirting the rim of the old pit. He told himself this is a little foolish given the fact he could possibly get twenty tons of ancient oak crashing around his ears at any moment. It was, however, as if he knew, or more perhaps sensed, that there was something waiting for him.

He reached the point at the lip of the crater where he'd spotted the frozen mushrooms, just before he'd got his first real sighting of Olivia. It was a different voice though this time, that spoke to him from the shadows, from just inside the tree line.

"That'll do just nicely, Bartholomew. Stay right there."

The reality was – he'd been half expecting it. He turned very slowly to face the direction the voice had come from.

Gerald Rissborough stood looking at him, wrapped up warmly in his padded jacket, a cashmere scarf arranged smartly around the neck and a tweed flat cap pulled down low. Not low enough, though, for Bartholomew to ignore the smug satisfaction that shone from his hooded, calculating eyes. More pertinently, and with no attempt at concealment, was the double-barrel shotgun he held in his hands, aimed directly at the centre of Bartholomew's chest.

"Hello, Jerome," he replied quietly. "You took your time. I've been expecting you, but I think the shotgun is a little excessive. Don't you?"

"Ah, so you've worked it out," Rissborough laughed back, humourlessly. "May I ask how?"

"Let's call it intuition, shall we," Bartholomew replied, with a sad face. "Plus coming over to your little drinks party today for final confirmation. What do you want Jerome? I know it's been around thirty years, but I'm not really sure we've got that much in common for us to be bothered with each other – from what I've seen of you so far. So put that gun away, get whatever it is you want to say off your chest and then I can be on my way."

"Like these woods, do you, Bartholomew?" Jerome asked, maintaining the steely eye contact. "I've always loved it here, ever since I first came to Rissborough as a young teenager. I've always thought it would be a great place to die. With all that wonderful green canopy overhead."

"I think you're being a little melodramatic, Jerome. Can you get to the point? I'm freezing my bollocks off here. What do you want?"

"That's just it, Bartholomew. Don't you understand? This is where you are going to die. From the moment I saw you in the wood last week, you were a dead man. If that's an accurate description for you – a man, that is. To be totally frank, I wasn't entirely sure if it was you or not. Just a gut feel telling me deep down, somehow, that it was. After all, I hadn't seen you for decades, and back then of course you were only a boy. But I had it planned out in an instant, as soon as I guessed it might be you. It's always best to make a plan. Don't you think?"

The first icy sliver of fear crept into Bartholomew's consciousness, as he took in Jerome's words. The shotgun hadn't wavered an inch either.

"What exactly are you talking about, Jerome?" he shot back, trying his utmost to maintain a calm front. "Look, I can understand I may not be your favourite person, even after all these years. Nor, I imagine, would any of the others be from our little gang – bearing in mind how it all ended. But I have always been very sorry about Michael. After all, we all know it was an accident."

"An accident!" Jerome snorted, and Bartholomew saw all that emotion coruscate again, just as he'd witnessed on his first encounter with the landowner. It was like watching a volcano about to spew in all its glory. "It was no accident," Jerome went on, venomously. "You killed him. Simple fact. And for that, in the next few minutes – once I'm through with you that is – you are going to die in this wood."

"I didn't kill him!" Bartholomew blurted out. "It was the stupid balance game, for Christ's sake. Looking back now I can still see it was all madness. It was you – with your constant insistence we played it each day. The fissure was a bottomless pit. It was crazy. An accident waiting to happen! We both tried to grab each other and our arms just collided. Why, it could easily have been me instead of Michael!"

"You just don't get it, do you?" Jerome snarled back, shouting now in order to be heard over the shrieking wind. "It was you who was supposed to die that day! We planned it. We were sick to death of your daily bleating that the bundu runs were too tough. You just weren't up to it. So Michael and I decided to teach you a lesson. A permanent lesson, we had hoped."

"What? You actually planned to kill *me*? You're out of your mind, Jerome. We were just children! Children fight and give each other a bloody nose, at worse. Not murder each other."

Jerome laughed again, manically, with a twisted look on his face.

"Maybe in your world, Bartholomew, but not in mine. Why, I've crushed quite a few individuals who've crossed me over the years and some who'd committed far lesser offences than you. Not quite murder, no, but I'm sure a number had wished they were dead by the time I was finished. You had something in common with them all though. They didn't want to be part of the gang either – or follow the rules. It can be a very costly mistake."

The fear in Bartholomew's gut was now deeply rooted and he could feel his whole body beginning to shiver convulsively in the harsh, freezing conditions. He'd guessed Rissborough was a cold-blooded businessman, who would stop at nothing if something got in his way. But this man – Jerome in a former life – was something else entirely. A psychopath, who dealt brutally with people who got in his way. By whatever means it took.

"You see," Jerome continued: "You really hacked Michael and I off. So we hatched a plan to get rid of you. We knew our father's squadron flew over the peninsula on at least two or three afternoons a week. It didn't take much for us to creep into his study one night and check the flight plans for the next few days. We knew, on that day, exactly what time the Lightnings would practice landing and take-off procedures. We could time it virtually to the minute. We'd make sure we were all nicely lined up along the fissure edge, in the correct order, with Michael right next to you. Because, as it happens, Michael actually loathed you even more deeply than I did, and it was he who wanted to be the one to do it. When we were all balancing, the plan was he would whack you hard on the chest, just as the aircraft were screeching overhead. Down you'd go and we'd all be very sad and sorry at the terrible accident – the one where you'd somehow recklessly lost your own balance and fallen to your death."

Jerome's eyes hadn't budged an inch from his own, but Bartholomew could now see a strange and wistful look emanate from within. As if he was still there, back in the past, out in the hot bundu, right next to the fissure.

"Why, d'you know, we were even looking forward to attending your funeral? Instead, something went wrong and you managed to use Michael as a prop to stop yourself falling in. Killing him instead. Taking my brother away from me. You know how it affected my father? He never really spoke to me again. Not in any real sense, that is, and I'm sure it sped up his own death three years later – even though he was diagnosed with cancer. So, you could say you killed two members of my family."

Bartholomew now understood: whatever way he explained the facts to this madman, Jerome would never accept a word he said. He knew, without a doubt, standing there in the dark freezing wood with this dysfunctional monster, that he was very close to reaching the end of his own fairly short existence on earth.

"I could have tracked you down years ago," continued Jerome, the smile returning to his crazy lips once more. "Easily, through one of the private investigation agencies I use. But I chose not to. You want to know why? Because I came to realise that when I eventually met you, the pleasure of killing you would be all over far too quickly. The pleasure of anticipation, however, of ending your pathetic life, would be far greater if it could be drawn out over many, many, years. I knew we'd bump into each other again at some point – and when you fell into my lap, why, it couldn't have been more perfect. In the end you came to me. Right onto my own home patch. How wonderful, I thought to myself. You see, part of my plan was to ask you a couple of pertinent questions at the drinks party. Just to verify what I thought I already knew. After all, we wouldn't have wanted any innocent bystanders getting hurt, eh? But my dear wife managed to save me the trouble. Yesterday at tea, amongst the usual wittering, a couple of little gems surfaced about Cyprus and pilot fathers. I could have leapt for joy!

Leonora and the flapjacks. How ironic, he thought – without the tiniest grain of humour – they could be the death of him.

At the risk of enraging Jerome even further, Bartholomew just couldn't help himself: "You're mad, Jerome. Stark, raving, mad. How the hell do you think you're going to bump me off and get away with it? They'll catch you, and somehow I don't think spending the rest of your life in prison will suit a man of your standing, used to all the trappings."

"Oh, they won't catch me. You can be sure of that, Bartholomew; but we'll get onto that in a moment. You've interrupted my little thought pattern. Where was I? Ah, yes. The anticipation. That was it. I've had many a pleasant year looking forward to us meeting again, and a real sense of heightened gratification over the last week hoping it really was you. Why, I wasn't going to let anything get in the way of my plan. Even the misguided antics of that stupid bitch Roxy weren't going to spoil it for me."

"Roxy... Roxy Halsall? What's she got to do with it?"

"Oh, come on now, Bartholomew. Haven't you figured it out? Why on earth do you think Roxy and her band of merry men have been carrying out their campaign of intimidation at Minsham Court over the last few months? For me, you half-wit! That bastard Eves had to be put in his place – stealing the property from under my nose. Minsham Court had been in Leonora's family for generations. It was supposed to be a sure-fire thing when it came up for auction, that we would merge it into the Rissborough

Estate. But that jumped-up peasant Eves, or his representatives, just kept on going up and up at the auction. I wasn't prepared to pay way over the odds, so I decided to let him have it. For the time being, that is. I wasn't worried. I knew we'd eventually own Minsham again. We just had to find a way to get it back on the market – so we could buy the place at a sensible price."

"So you hired Roxy and those two local lads to harass the new owner of Minsham Court? Well, it worked out really well, Jerome, didn't it? I mean, they're banged up now. All for nothing."

"Oh, I don't think so, Bartholomew. There are plenty more from where they came from, all willing to do some dirty work for a few measly quid. And as for Roxy, she just happened to be around at the time and fit the bill. I thought I'd have some fun with her at first, but, as it turned out, I found her a little one dimensional in bed."

What you really mean is she wore you out, but your own inflated ego couldn't cope with the truth, thought Bartholomew scathingly.

"So I flipped her to Jeavons. He got her up in the flat, above the stable block. Reckoned it took him a whole day, but he assured me he had gained the upper hand by the end of it.

Christ almighty, speculated Bartholomew: That must have been one hell of a clash of the titans.

"Once Jeavons had had his fun and tamed her, she came crawling up to me asking if I could let her use some of the stabling at Rissborough. It seems the girl has aspirations to run her own livery yard. So instead, I offered her the loose boxes at Minsham Court, at a competitive price of course. But only on the proviso that the whole place was made vacant and available to me again."

Jerome shook his head frustratingly. "The stupid thing was they were only supposed to engage in a campaign of harassment. Not carry out a burglary and get themselves arrested – which, I gather was partly down to your own pathetic efforts. At the end of the day, it didn't worry me. Roxy knew on which side her bread was buttered and wouldn't go and squeal to the police about her real motives. And, of course, when I heard through my sources that she was pointing the finger at you – 'Mr Big' – for orchestrating the break in, well, I quickly passed the word she needed to retract the accusation immediately. I mean, I couldn't have you being banged up too, could I? What – and spoil our little planned outing here today?"

So that was the real reason for the sudden turnaround with Roxy and the gang. So much for Baxter's superior police methods, Bartholomew sardonically reflected, his teeth now beginning to chatter violently in the cold.

"Getting a bit apprehensive now, are we, Bartholomew? Ah, I could almost feel a little sorry for you. Don't worry though, we're nearly through. Or you are, to be precise. Do you want to know the specifics of how you are going to die? Well, I'm going to give you two choices. The first is I move a little closer to you, until I'm about two to three feet away, say, and then I'll give you both barrels directly in the face. It will rip it to shreds, so it'll look like a bright red, bloody stump. If you're not dead from that, well, I'll just re-load and give you another couple of shells in the same place – until your lights are fully extinguished."

"What's the other?" Bartholomew heard himself hoarsely utter, just about loud enough for Jerome to catch.

"Same tool of execution. But a little more humane. You lie down on the ground, just here, and spread your arms out wide so I can see everything. I'm then going to walk around you, so that I'm above your head. When I give you the nod, you tilt your head right back and open your mouth. I'll just slip the barrels in and – bang! You won't feel a thing. No mess made of your pretty face. Only a bloody great hole at the back of your head, but, hey-ho, who said dying was ever tidy!"

"I've already told you, Jerome," Bartholomew replied desperately, all the energy just about gone from his shivering form. "You're never going to get away with this. They'll hear you from the house."

"Oh no they won't. What, in this wind? No way. I've lived here for a long time now and I know exactly how sound travels around the place. In this weather you could hold a rock concert up here and no one would be any the wiser."

"When they find me, then."

"Find you? How will anyone find you, if you're not here? What do you think, Bartholomew? That I'm some kind of amateur floundering around! Jeavons is waiting in the house for my return. Once I'm back he'll be straight up here to get you nicely rolled up in a bit of old tarpaulin. I've got business interests all over the county and one of them includes an industrial incinerator plant, located about fifty miles from here. Jeavons will be over there within a couple of hours and have you discreetly fed into one of the big burners. They really are something, you know. Even used to generate electricity on the grid. Why, just think of it… all those people watching the *Ten O'Clock News* on the *BBC* tonight. All powered from a source using your body fat for fuel!"

"They'll search for me if I'm missing. They'll keep on looking until they get an answer."

"Negative, Bartholomew. You see, to prolong the thrill of not knowing for sure it was actually you, I instructed my private investigator to look into the background of the caretaker at Minsham Court, but to hold off sending me the report. Of course, after Leonora so obligingly filled me in, I called for it immediately. I know all about your shoddy property career in London. About how you really fucked it all up. You are a naïve fool, Bartholomew. And look at you now. Working for a woman no less. God! – how could you stoop so low? Sitting in successful people's houses, twiddling your thumbs on a poor man's wage. Oh, and I understand you think you can cook a little too and like to quaff a bit of vintage wine. Don't you understand? You have to be successful to earn the right to enjoy the finer things in life. No, you're a loser. That's the bottom line. Leading a transient life, moving unhappily from one assignment to the next."

Jerome continued on, sneering triumphantly:

"When you disappear, there will be a few enquiries, of course. As far as we at Rissborough are concerned, the last we saw of you was when Reddings the Butler watched you heading off up into the woods, towards Minsham Court. Why, we'd felt sorry for you, the one time we met you, and thought it neighbourly to invite you over to our New Year's Day drinks party. You seemed alright, perhaps a little down around the edges, although we did notice you had had quite a lot to drink. And, as concerns me, well – I think you saw a few of my business associates in the hall – they will all confirm I was with them the whole time. Not that the authorities would have any reason to link me particularly to you in any event. Past or present.

"They will find the few personal items of clothing you've left behind at Minsham Court. But you will have just disappeared. In view of your transient existence, I think they'll come to the fairly swift conclusion you'd had enough working for – what is it again? – *The Kennedy Agency?* – and have just taken off. Certainly that is what the police will conclude, knowing the way they operate and in view of their limited resources. No-one's going to really miss you anyway. You're a loner. Even Ms Kennedy herself won't be surprised. After all, it hasn't exactly been a routine job at Minsham Court and I'm sure you've already threatened to leave her employment in the light of the difficult environment you've had to endure there. Besides, in my experience, the likes of Ms Kennedy don't spend a lot of time worrying about the personnel side of things. She'll just be thinking about the next job and what other poor unfortunate she can fill it with."

It was the first statement Jerome had made all afternoon that Bartholomew had to begrudgingly agree with.

"So, it's getting nicely dark now. What's it going to be Bartholomew?"

"What's what going to be?" he shot back, trying anything he could to buy a little more time.

"Option one or option two? By the way, if you don't make up your mind in the next ten seconds then the automatic default is option one. As I've outlined though – it's a lot more painful."

Jerome stepped a little closer. Bartholomew knew he was now within what you could call proper killing range. The end of the shotgun barrels were no more than three feet from his ashen, rigid face.

After what he deemed in the circumstances to be the longest ten seconds he could possibly chance his luck to, Bartholomew eventually forced his shivering form down, positioning his legs flat out in front of him on the mossy floor, so that they nearly touched the lip of crater. Above, it seemed as if the wind's strength had gone up even a further notch. It was now really screaming through the treetops. Jerome moved in a little closer still, whilst maintaining an unwaveringly steady grip on the lethal weapon out in front.

"Good choice. Now lie back," he ordered, the tip of his tongue continually flicking across his lips in gory anticipation, like a komodo dragon about to devour a defenceless, tethered goat.

Bartholomew lay back and stretched his arms out wide. As his head touched the floor, the fedora gently fell off and was immediately whipped away by the gale – as if to underline the fact that the wearer really didn't have any further use for it.

"Very sensible," chortled Jerome, as he began to move upwards, around Bartholomew's left foot, still maintaining the direction of the shotgun plum onto Bartholomew's prone, white face.

A tiny, elemental part of him, from somewhere within his deeply frightened state, just about managed to judge that it was now or never. Over the preceding minutes, he'd tried as hard as possible to ignore the vicious, ever-invasive cold that seeped in through his overcoat and under his clothes, almost turning his body into a fixed, rigid block. In his utter desperation, he recalled he'd read somewhere that if you are trapped, but are able to fully focus all your possible thought energy into just one part of your body, to give it massive strength, you can still muster a decisive action. For the last couple of minutes he'd put every single iota of mental focus he had into his left arm. For the staff, the only weapon available to him, still lay at an angle by his side, and to use it effectively he needed some serious leverage.

He closed his fingers as tightly as he could around the smooth, wooden end. Raising the staff just a couple of inches off the ground, his arm outstretched, he swung it forward, with all the savagery he could muster. In a low, neat arc, just off the floor, he brought it to bear across Jerome's shins with an almighty crack.

The result was spectacular. Even in his terrified, frozen state, Bartholomew couldn't help but notice how vaguely comic it was. Jerome produced a shocking, high pitched shriek, as the swipe caught him totally by surprise. Hardly befitting a man of his stature, the whining continued as Jerome, precious indignation plastered all over his face, took a step back to avoid another potential blow. It was a grave mistake. His foot landed on the edge of the pit with just the front of it making contact, the heel meeting nothing but thin air.

Bartholomew sat up, all thought of the cold gone for the moment, transfixed by the spectacle. Jerome teetered on the lip, both legs splayed out now to try and recover his balance. His arms were spread wide, one hand still tightly gripping the shotgun, the other windmilling around furiously, in a desperate attempt to tip himself forward out of danger.

It was no use. In one, long, frantic moment of arm action, Jerome almost regained a stable position, but it wasn't quite enough. With a fearful cry, he keeled over backwards, head first. Bartholomew craned his neck forward to watch. As Jerome plunged down, his back and shoulders hit the steeply inclined side of the pit, hard. His body did a curiously neat backflip, with feet together, through the air, before landing heavily and rolling, arms and legs akimbo, all the way down to the scraggy bottom.

It was then that Bartholomew ducked. Holding onto the shotgun had proved to be another monumental error. Just as Jerome came to a halt, there was an almighty bang as the weapon went off. Bartholomew kept his head down low. He knew he didn't want to witness what damage had been wreaked at such close range. It was hard enough already, as he wretchedly tried to drag himself away, towards the trees, to have to listen to the agonising screams.

With Jerome still continuing to shriek obscenely, Bartholomew finally got to his knees. By sheer force of will alone, he began a clumsy, frozen limbed crawl into the trees. His breath threw out large clouds of vapour, but it was the noise his ragged breathing made that frightened him the most – even with the pitiful din from below.

He knew he had to make as much distance between himself and the crater as possible, and that his life still depended on it. It was only a matter of time before Jeavons set out in search of his master.

It seemed only a moment later, still coping with heaving the cumbersome blocks of ice that were his arms and legs, that he heard the deep, strangely accented voice of the power lifter gamekeeper soothing his master and calling on a mobile phone for assistance. Bartholomew tried to increase the speed of his torturous, tortoise-like crawl, once again in hunted mode, nerves screaming. He had absolutely no doubt about what was coming next: how he was about to realise the full brunt of Jeavon's fury.

All too soon he detected movement up the side of the crater and a moment later Jeavon's head appeared, with a grim, purposeful look on his face. As his chest came into view, Bartholomew realised he was carrying a hunting rifle in his left hand. No shotgun this time. No, something far more versatile.

One last burst of adrenalin, one last fear driven surge saw Bartholomew finally manage to stagger to his feet in the vain hope of shielding himself behind an old oak - at least for a minute or two.

It was futile.

"You fucking stop now!" Jeavons barked.

"You knew this coming housekeeper boy." Bartholomew slowly turned to face Jeavons, as the hulk moved closer in still, the rifle now mounted at shoulder height, his cruel eyes narrowed for the kill. "You shoot Mr Rissborough in the legs" he continued, with a hissing, raging fury. "He get better. But you don't, ever. First, I start with your knees, you motherfucker. Just like in movies."

Then, Bartholomew heard another, calmer, voice in the wood. It was Leonora Rissborough. Ordering Jeavons to put down the rifle, get back down in the pit and stay with Jerome. It was the voice of authority and decency, telling him clearly, with a stern finality, that enough was enough. There was to be no more violence on the estate today.

Chapter 18   The Reality

He had returned to Evensthorpe. Bartholomew parked the pickup, got out and walked briskly to the front door. Exactly as he had done on numerous occasions over the past few days. Strange how you can go through the same physical motions, in identical fashion, he reflected darkly, and mentally you might as well be a million light years away. It was like being in a different world.

He didn't bother with the bell. The rap of his knuckles on the door gave out enough of a harsh, insistent message. It didn't take long to provoke a reaction either. The front door was quickly wrenched open. Olivia stood there, an uncertain greeting playing around her mouth. One which quickly slid away, as she took in his emotionless facade.

"You'd better come in," she said in a low voice.

Bartholomew followed her into the kitchen. It was as warm, tidy and chic as ever, but somehow, it didn't seem to hold the same attraction for him this time around.

Olivia moved over to the far counter and leant against it, her arms tucked behind her back. She seemed to be having trouble looking at him directly, but then she lifted her head, her cheeks a little flushed, and stared at him defiantly in the eyes.

He waited a few moments more – maliciously he knew – but he just couldn't help himself. After the events of the last twenty-four hours he'd lost whatever sympathy he might otherwise have had for anyone else's feelings.

"So, when were you going to tell me, Olivia?" he began, in what was almost a low growl.

"Tell you what?" she answered, her voice quavering a little, although still able to maintain the hard eye contact.

"Tell me that you are Gerald Rissborough's mistress. Or, should I say – Jerome's?"

The colour in Olivia's cheeks deepened and her head fell forward, breaking the eye contact. Bartholomew looked around the kitchen and made an angry, sweeping gesture with his arm.

"Why, this isn't even your cottage – is it? It's his. He owns it. Bought it to cater for you. Discreetly tucked away a couple of convenient miles from Rissborough Hall. Pretty handy – for a quickie!"

Olivia was about to say something, but decided against it, her eyes dropping down once more onto the quarry tiled floor.

"How were you planning to make it work going forward? That's what I'd like to know, Olivia. Rotate us? Keep the bed warm; whilst one disappears down the village high street, the other arrives from the opposite end?"

She finally answered. "He hasn't slept with me in over three years. You don't understand. That's not what it's all about."

He thought he understood clearly enough. From what he'd heard, directly from the monster's mouth up in the dark, evil wood over the hill, Jerome was always onto new horizons. For such a man, one bite of the cherry was never going to be enough. He was sure Leonora Rissborough understood that far better than all of them.

"How did you find out?" she asked, her voice so low he almost failed to hear the question.

"My sub-conscious finally catching up with events," he answered, wearily now, as if he was stumbling wretchedly across a dark, inhospitable plain, with no hope of sunrise on the far side.

"I heard you say one word: in *Casper's*. I was in the bookshop trying to find an edition of something I hadn't seen in years. Strangely enough, it was a trilogy I'd read a long time ago – as a boy. Actually, at around about the same time as Michael's death." He paused and looked at her, for a reaction. A shadow crossed her face and her head seemed to fall forward a little more.

"You see, there I was with this cranky old shop assistant, tucked down low behind some bookshelves scouring around for a copy. All I could hear on the other side was a couple having a row, but it was so low I couldn't make out a word or recognise who they might be. That is, not until the one time you raised your voice and used his name."

Olivia frowned. "But even if you might have thought you recognised my voice, and the name, how could you know it actually was me, or that Jerome was Gerald?

"It was the perfume. Even the cranky old shop assistant got a waft of it. You see, Olivia, you don't normally wear perfume, do you? Well, you haven't around me. It's only for him. I knew I'd recognised it from somewhere before and eventually I twigged. On the first night I met you, I left this house in the small hours. I was half asleep and basically exhausted. As I grabbed my overcoat from the rack in the porch, I got a whiff of it. I was so fuzzy from conking out on the sofa half the night I didn't really think any further about it, but deep down, it struck a chord."

A look of resignation crept over Olivia's face, her eyes wide and tearful.

"It was you on the train, wasn't it?" he continued. "That first day I arrived in Brilcrister. You barged past me into the carriage, just before we left Waterloo. I didn't get a good look at you, other than your expensively clad back – but it was the same perfume. The same perfume in the porch. The same perfume in *Casper's*. It was too much of a coincidence."

"And Jerome? How did you know it was Jerome? Or Gerald?" Olivia whispered in a hushed, depressed tone.

"When I first met him in the woods with Jeavons something about his manner jarred – when he got riled. Something I'd seen before – but an age ago. I should have thought about it harder at the time but it just didn't seem to be important. But really, it was the final link: yesterday, that is. Up at Jerome or Gerald's – or whatever that psycho calls himself. I went to his self-satisfied freak show of a drinks party. I was praying I wasn't right. Hoping beyond hope that I'd got it all mixed up, that I'd got a bit paranoid myself. But there it was, parked in pride of place right in front of Rissborough Hall. A big, black, luxury 4X4. And there can only be one number plate like that – MICHA9. Only a psycho would drive a car around with his dead brother's name and age emblazoned on it. Especially, since he was personally responsible for his death."

The blood in Olivia's face seemed to drain away, leaving a white ghost staring at him. Even in his monologue of a rant, he felt momentarily perplexed by her reaction.

"You see, I'd caught a glimpse of that car twice before. Again – at Brilcrister Station, just as I was looking for a taxi in the car park. Didn't see the plate, just the outline. That was him, though, picking you up, wasn't it? Taking you back here to your cosy little love nest. Then again, at *Casper's*. Just as I was going into the bookshop. You were in the car with him too. Yes? Of course you were. From the quick glimpse I got of it in the distance, it looked like the owner was verbally abusing the driver of a council refuse lorry. Just his style I'd have thought, putting a smelly peasant in his place. I'm surprised he didn't get his shotgun out and actually put him down!"

Bartholomew stopped, chest heaving, some of the spite now gone from him, but none of the sadness.

"I never planned it this way," she began, in a low, deflated voice.

"So how did you plan it then?" he replied, head down now himself, sapped of emotional energy.

She began slowly.

"I just couldn't believe it might be you, when I swept past you on the train. Jesus, I hadn't seen you in nearly thirty years. We were children after all, when we last saw each other. As I sat in the carriage trying to persuade myself it really couldn't be you, I just knew I was wrong. I rationalised it by telling myself there are at least twelve stations beyond Waterloo. The chances of you getting off at Brilcrister were twelve to one. I had nothing to worry about. Even if you did, why, you were probably heading in a direction many miles away from the Haddlewell valley. So when the train pulled into Brilcrister, I dashed off and got out of the station as fast as I could. I just wanted to forget about what I might have seen. To put it out of my mind."

She shifted uncomfortably on her feet, wringing her hands frenetically in front.

"Imagine my horror therefore, when the next day, collecting my dry cleaning in Brilcrister, I saw you going into *Casper's*. There was no denying it, despite the passage of time. It was you. I sat in the car and wept at what I could see ahead. It was my worst nightmare coming true. I stayed in the car and waited for you to come out of the bookshop. And from there on the nightmare got steadily worse, as I followed your pickup out of Brilcrister and along the road to Haddlewell. After you left the Spar, you drove out on the road to Evensthorpe. It was as if a magnet was drawing you closer and closer to Rissborough Hall. To Jerome. Then you turned off into Minsham Court. Right next door."

She paused for a moment, eyes brimming with tears. With a breaking, distraught voice, she continued.

"I drove home in despair. I couldn't settle, or sleep. I didn't know what to do. Finally, the next morning I was putting the recycling out – anything to keep me occupied – when I bumped into Mrs Carson, my next-door–but-one neighbour. I could barely manage a pleasant good morning, but with Mrs Carson you don't really need to do much talking. She does it all for you. Out of all the usual local gossip, I gleaned one vital piece of information. A glimmer of light. Mrs Carson gabbled on that the postmistress Sheila had told her there was a new caretaker at Minsham Court. A dark-haired man in his forties, by the name of Bartholomew. And the best news was that she had been led to believe it was a very temporary appointment. For a month, at most."

Bartholomew grimaced. Good old Sheila, happily linking the community together. As they say, gossip is currency.

"I devised a plan from then on – to keep you away from Rissborough. I only needed to do it for a month and then you would be gone. It was a fair assumption to make that a house-sitter, or caretaker, would probably keep himself to himself on the estate. But the job would entail a regular patrol of the gardens and grounds. I run anyway, across all the local estates' land – that part was true. I don't care if they like it or not. So, I knew the terrain like the back of my hand. I could run in the woods above Minsham every day. Keep an eye on you and stalk you, scare you, make you want to avoid the place. Keep you away from Rissborough. Ensure that you'd want to return to London as soon as possible."

How laughable, he cursed. The pair of them, vying unwittingly to keep each other safe from a mad Jerome in the woods.

He paused and then replied. "God, I bet you even know about the boundary dispute, about Jerome's ridiculous claim on Minsham Court."

"All I knew was that he was very sensitive about people walking on his land. Yes, he mentioned he walked the woods with his gamekeeper. It terrified me to think what would happen – if he bumped into you and recognised your face. Even after all these years. Why, after all – I did at Waterloo Station."

He couldn't bear it, the way she looked at him imploringly, begging him almost to understand. A harder, more removed, bitter voice from another part of him asked a direct question instead. One he already knew the answer to:

"Why did you want to keep me away from Gerald Rissborough, Olivia?"

She dropped her eyes, her face once again closed and shameful.

"Because I knew he would probably want to kill you on sight," she eventually replied.

He didn't answer for a long while. A motorbike ratcheted up through the gears along the high street outside, the driver revving the engine for all it was worth.

"Why do you stay with him, Olivia? I don't understand."

"I don't know."

"You must do. It's been many years now, hasn't it?"

"Yes."

"Why then? Why stay with this man?"

"You really want to know?"

"Yes I do."

"Are you absolutely sure?"

"Yes."

Olivia, ever so slowly, raised her head and looked into his eyes with a desolate, pitiful stare.

"It's my penance, Bartholomew. My punishment. For what I knew and for what I did nothing about."

The shock of it seemed to make him lose the power of speech altogether. After a good minute, he finally recovered a little of his composure to reply in a strangled voice: "What... you knew they planned to kill me that day out by the fissure?"

"Yes."

Still in a kind of numbed paralysis, he struggled again to find any suitable words.

Eventually, he blurted out: "Why didn't you stop them, for God's sake? We were all children, after all. Innocents! Playing games out on a bit of wild scrubland."

"I didn't think they were serious! Jerome and Michael hatched it up together. I only overhead them a day or so before and I didn't think they ever really intended to carry it out. I was young, naïve. You know yourself, you didn't challenge Jerome lightly either."

"But after the accident! Why didn't you come clean! You could have told our parents and the military police about what they wanted to do. How it all turned out so grotesquely wrong. Someone still died! I carried part of the blame for that too."

He didn't mention the nightmares. He didn't have the energy. It was too painful.

"I wanted to!" Olivia was crying freely again now. She dabbed her eyes with the sleeve of her cotton top.

"I told Jerome I was going to tell the truth. What they'd planned. Somehow, he got me to swear to secrecy. Said it would just make matters worse. Michael was dead and that really it was all your fault that it had happened, but everyone thought it was just an accident. I… stupidly let him persuade me it was the right thing to do."

She wiped her eyes again and stared fixedly at the ground.

"Then I was off to boarding school, like everyone else. Until I was twenty I was able to push it out of my mind. The guilt, that is. Until I started working in London, when I found I couldn't ignore it any longer. But I was trapped. It was too late to change anything. The past was the past. So I searched for Jerome, who I hadn't seen since that time in Cyprus."

"Searched for him? You must have been crazy. Why?"

"I'm not sure. It was just something I had to do. To confront it somehow. That's how it started."

"Started?"

"My peacekeeping role. You see, Jerome is fine most of the time. Totally driven, yes, but he just about operates within the bounds of acceptable behaviour. Until he gets mad that is, or feels someone is not towing the line. We saw a lot of each other in London at first, until he got married when he was thirty and moved up to Rissborough Hall, when his stepfather passed away.

"How did Jerome become Gerald?"

"When his father died, he and his mother moved back to the UK. Both of them were in a bit of a bad way. They settled here locally – his mother had grown up in the county. Later, she re-married – an older man, a widower called Gerald Rissborough, owner of a great estate. He took Jerome under his wing and became like a real father to him. Almost more than the real father. He was a fearsome man, a bruiser in business, always wanting his own way. Jerome was like a chip off the old block."

She looked at Bartholomew again, with the same expression of dull resignation.

"When Jerome was in his early twenties, Gerald Rissborough finally registered him formally as his son and heir. Jerome decided to change his name by deed poll, out of respect for the family name and continuity. The forename wasn't so very different from his own, and in a way it allowed him to bury the past, and the shame. It didn't mean, however, he could forget about Michael."

She paused, her face distant.

"You see, my penance is to be there when the fireworks go off. Most of the time, I don't know the detail. I don't want to. He calls me, rants and raves, and slowly he gets it off his chest. In the main, I can calm him down and feel I've been at least partly absolved for my own particular sin, all those years ago. Stop him hurting some other poor unfortunate, hopefully. I don't know. I feel it helps."

"It was him – calling the night I first came back here. We were eating supper."

"Yes. That was him." Olivia managed a small, harsh, rueful laugh. "I've spent the last twenty years counselling him. It varies: At times I might get three calls in a day. Or I might not hear from him for a whole month."

He looked up at the ceiling and then replied, the sarcasm pathetically coming from somewhere deep within,

"So when I caught you in the wood, it was pretty handy. Lost your bed partner. Me turning up was just dreamy. Counsel Jerome all you liked, whilst I cooked and serviced you on the side."

She looked at him squarely.

"It wasn't like that Bartholomew. Well, not at first. Once I'd got over the initial shock of being caught by you, I was happy that I could monitor your whereabouts even more closely. I could influence where you went, and – after all – I nearly got there."

"Got there?"

"Got you back home, Bartholomew. Safe from Jerome."

He didn't want to answer that.

"The real truth is, as soon as I'd met you in the wood I knew it was a mistake. I tried to keep it to the one time, but you wouldn't let go. You wanted to see me too much."

"You should have refused – if what you are saying is true."

"I couldn't because… because I wanted you as much as I've ever wanted anyone in my whole life."

She almost snorted the last words, crying now desperately, the tears rolling freely.

"Why don't you understand? Can't you see? I've had other casual lovers over the years but with Jerome around it's not been possible to live a normal life. Long ago, I accepted I would never find happiness. Not in the normal way that other people do. And then, in the act of playing out my millstone of a penance, you come into my kitchen, talk to me like a human being, care for me, cook for me, make me feel natural again. Make kind love to me, not like you want me to act out some sort of personal fantasy for you."

He looked at her, holding himself back with everything it took. Everything it took to stop him taking her in his arms, to inhale the warmth of her skin and hair, to tell her it was going to be alright.

"I need you, Bartholomew," she choked, trying to reach out for him.

A voice that he felt wasn't really his own, answered:

"Do you know the detail of what happened in the woods above Rissborough Hall yesterday?"

Olivia stopped, moved away, her eyes sliding back to the floor. He didn't get a reply.

"You know some of it, don't you? Not because Sheila the postie has gossiped it to Mrs Carson, or because someone at the police station has already leaked it to the Press. It's because you've spoken to him, on the phone. He's already called. From hospital, or wherever he is. With his latest bombshell. Called you, demanding you counsel him. To tell him it's going to be ok, to calm down, that it'll sort itself out. And I know you've spoken to him. Olivia, do you realise this man has hurt many people over the years? I mean really hurt them. If they got in his way. He told me so yesterday up in the woods, with great relish. You may not have wanted to know all the detail, but the truth is there. That's what he does."

Head down now, in bitter despair, he rubbed his eyes with a thumb and forefinger, wishing he could just wipe all the hurt away.

"I want you too, Olivia. With all my heart. Forever, if I could. But you see, I can never have all of you. For every time I look at you I will be wondering where he is. Because you can never be free. He will pursue you for all time. Even when he's in prison, which is where he is going to go for a very long time. And the most truly dreadful thing is, I don't think you can ever really cut away from him either. Because the warped reality is he does something for you - doesn't he? Whether it's the dynamism, or later the money and the prestige, I'm not sure. Perhaps all three. It's not just about the penance. Sure, that might assuage your conscience a little. But you share an awful secret and the truth is you've been freely under his spell for thirty years.

He couldn't take anymore and turned to the door, waiting for the flood of tears which a small part of him knew would never come.

Chapter 19 The Lure

The Strand was cast in strong sunshine, taking a little of the chill off the otherwise bitter mid-January morning. Bartholomew strode down it at a pace from the Charing Cross end, heading for *The Savoy*. He was feeling chipper, after a few days back in the flat and having finally shed the last vestiges of his emotional hangover from the preceding couple of weeks.

After some wrangling, he'd managed to scrape enough money together from his bonus to settle the outstanding energy bills. He now had the gas back on – which had been abruptly cut off in his absence. It had seemed like a new beginning. The mood that had accompanied him back from Minsham Court, which had hung there like a cloying black shroud, had suddenly lifted, as his bones were warmed by the first hot bath he'd had in over four days and the luxury of round-the-clock gas central heating.

He'd walked every day from Earl's Court, down to the river and past Battersea Bridge, sometimes going along the Embankment as far as Vauxhall, and beyond to Westminster. It had served a number of purposes: he'd found the exercise helped his flat, heavy mood; it was the only way of keeping warm; and, frankly, it occupied a decent wedge of the day – which he might otherwise have spent wasting in the flat. Whereas previously doing nothing at all had seemed to come easily to him – that is, as long as there was something interesting to cook and drink – now he was back in the flat, he couldn't settle, he was fidgety, pacing around. Bizarrely, though, his sleep had improved. One night he'd actually managed eight solid hours and White and Solville had only come to haunt him on one, spiteful occasion.

He had yet to meet Kennedy face to face. They'd spent a good thirty minutes on the phone on the first day of his return to town. Some of it had been to ensure that the Scottish couple – who'd replaced him at Minsham Court – received the correct handover. Kennedy wasn't going to let him off the administration hook on the mere petty excuse that someone had tried to murder him on the job. No, sir. It was business as usual with the caring Kennedy. Once those details of utmost importance had been confirmed, he was allowed to spend the rest of the call updating her on the latest news following his one-on-one with Gerald Rissborough, up in the never-to-be-forgotten woods.

He'd even managed to smarten himself up for the bonus lunch. Well, it was *The Savoy* after all. He'd shaved, had his hair trimmed at the barbers and donned a reasonably smart, beige-coloured corduroy jacket over a white shirt, jeans and the slightly pinching brogues he'd bought in Brilcrister.

She'd also paid his overtime bonus, although that was nearly gone already. So here he was, loping down the Strand before taking a right into the little private side road known as Savoy Court, ready to collect the final instalment. After that, it was adieu to The Kennedy Agency for once and for all – and onto a new life and whatever that would bring.

The American Bar, where they'd agreed to meet for an aperitif, was fairly empty. It was midday on a January Monday after all, but he was surprised, given the year-round propensity to London for visiting tourists. Kennedy was seated to the right of the bar, in one of a pair of little leather armchairs, decked out in one of her trademark pinstripe suits. The hair wasn't gelled today. It fell in a wave across her forehead and, *sans* spectacles, it almost gave her a softer look. Blimey, thought Bartholomew, mildly disconcerted. Perhaps, as this was the last time they'd ever meet, she'd made an extra effort to look like something other than the usual, well-attired Rottweiler.

"Very kind of you to wait for me to order," he jibed, after nodding a brief hello.

"Well, Bartholomew. It's your lunch, after all. It would be rude of me not to."

Crikey, he laughed inwardly. Did I actually clock the hint of a welcoming smile accompanying those warm words?

As he sat, the barman casually – but ever-so politely – wandered over and asked them what they would like to drink. Kennedy was about to answer, when Bartholomew held up his hand.

"Remember the deal? I choose."

He ordered a dry martini and a White Lady. His and hers. For a little while they both just sat there, enjoying a couple of the best cocktails London had to offer.

"So how are you?" Kennedy finally asked, looking at him inquisitively over the rim of her glass.

"Oh, pretty good actually. Managed to get my flat warm again and heh… it's the New Year, there's hope in the air. How about you – managed to cook those curry puffs yet?"

She pulled a face. "No – too busy. I need to write the recipe down. It seems a little involved."

He was about to throw a sarcastic reply back, but then decided to hold his tongue. Anyway, she'd never looked the type to him to spend a lot of time in the kitchen.

"No, I mean after all the goings-on at the end of your stay," she continued. "At Minsham Court."

"Ah, yes. I think I've just about recovered now. Can't say though the night I spent in Brilcrister nick was anything I'll want to remember in a hurry. Especially the wooden pillows in the cells."

"What is Detective Sergeant Baxter saying now about the charges being made against Gerald Rissborough, or whatever he's called – Jerome is it?"

"He's up for attempted murder. That's the charge for what he tried to do to me, in that hideous wood of his. There's going to be more though, once they piece together some of the history that's coming out. Leonora Rissborough is doing what she can to corroborate any evidence that's unearthed. Although, of course, she herself is nothing to do with it all. He never included her in anything. It's just what she was able to observe, over the years. A woman scorned, as they say…"

"Yes," agreed Kennedy, slowly nodding her head, looking at him thoughtfully. "You were lucky there, that's for sure."

He recalled with a shiver, the freezing wood, the naked evil on Jerome's face. Over a sip of the dry martini he reflected a little further and with a bitter expression looked at Kennedy.

"Baxter was less accommodating, though. He had me shoved into the back of police car without any wish to hear my side of the story at all. I'd been in the cells for hours, it seemed, before he'd even talk to me. Then all he would say was that Gerald Rissborough wanted me charged for attempted murder. That I'd come to his party, got drunk, taken one of his shotguns from the gun room and disappeared off up into the woods. On being told by Jeavons what I'd done, he'd pursued me alone, thinking that as the owner of the estate he would be able to persuade me to hand back the gun. But instead, I'd lost my head and given him both barrels in the legs up by the old pit."

"Well, Bartholomew," she countered. "He's hardly going to come clean – is he? Men like him, with money coming out of their ears; they just don't operate that way. With their standing and the powerful lawyers they can engage, they will always feel they can wriggle out of anything. It's all part of their arrogant ruthlessness – a big game, at the end of the day."

Kennedy would know, he thought, scathingly. Wonder if it's a coterie in which she included herself?

"Even when I told Baxter what had really happened, he was pretty sceptical. Then, abruptly, he let me go. At first dawn. Once Leonora Rissborough had been interviewed. She'd obviously reached a decision point that had been building up within her for many years. She confirmed I'd left as I'd described. That she'd seen her husband follow me up into the woods and it was he who was carrying the shotgun. She told the police a lot more too, apparently, about things she has seen and heard over the years. Deeply unsavoury matters, from what I understand. Baxter thinks it will tie up a lot of loose ends for the police about certain unsolved crimes. He could eventually be up on a number of different charges. He'll be ruined. His reputation destroyed."

He didn't feel the need to tell Kennedy that Olivia would have to answer some questions from the police too, about what she knew.

"What about the other evidence?"

"Well, at least Baxter did help me in the end, by further corroborating my story. He re-interviewed Roxy Halsall and her two side-kicks. After further pressure about how it would help with her sentencing and that she wouldn't have to worry about any repercussions from Gerald Rissborough – as he wasn't going be around for many years – she finally came clean and confirmed what I told Baxter. That Gerald Rissborough had been sponsoring their activities all along – he was overall responsible for the campaign of intimidation at Minsham Court.

"Will you have to go to court?"

"There'll be a trial of course. As you say, he'll never plead guilty and it will go all the way if there is the tiniest chance he could be acquitted. But it looks pretty damning. Yes, I'll have to give evidence. Something to look forward to."

At this point, he decided he'd had enough reminders about the merciless wood above Rissborough Hall and suggested they decamp to the Grill Room.

They were seated in a far corner. Both facing into the restaurant with its chandeliered ceiling, the lights dazzling off the mirror-clad pillars spanning the floor. Bartholomew proceeded to ask the waiter for an *à la carte* menu and wine list for each of them.

He gave Kennedy enough time to digest the contents of both, before ordering baked Hereford snails in garlic butter for her, and for him the lobster bisque. Torn by the various temptations on offer, he finally settled on beef wellington for two, with horseradish and red wine sauce, accompanied by mashed potatoes and honey glazed carrots. Simple, but classic.

The wine selection was next. He was really starting to enjoy himself now. Thinking it fun to drink some champagne with the first course, he decided they'd try a bottle of *Pol Roger White Foil*. In true Churchillian style. Rubbing his chin thoughtfully, whilst keeping half a discreet eye on Kennedy's facial expression, he took his time selecting something special to go with the beef. Finally, after huffing and puffing a bit, moving his head from side to side, and raising his eyebrows theatrically, at least three times, he settled on a *Margaux*, a *Chateau Palmer 1996*.

Handing the menu and wine list back to the waiter, he scrutinised Kennedy's face with some amusement. The price of the *Margaux* was well on its way to four figures. Strangely though, to his slight annoyance, she didn't seem to bat an eyelid. He knew she'd perused the wine list and must realise now she was in for some serious damage.

It wasn't the only surprise. Kennedy swigged the *Pol Roger* back like it was going out of fashion and attacked the snails with a gusto he hadn't seen since watching a friend's two young children do with similar fare, in a riverside brasserie on the outskirts of Cognac many years before.

Between mouthfuls of fizz and the chewy, fiddly crustaceans, she ventured:

"A last question relating to Minsham Court: What's going to happen about that other business, the one out in Cyprus?"

He winced slightly at the thought of Olivia and the final moments in her cottage kitchen.

"I don't know. It's all so long ago. The other individual involved is prepared to make a statement and tell it how it was. The problem is, it's in a different legal jurisdiction – but involves the UK military, as they are still on the base. I think it's going to take a long time to unravel. And, after all, they were children and their plan to all intents and purposes… failed."

Bartholomew drained his glass of champagne as the waiter began to clear the plates away. He just wanted to think about the future now, nothing more. The beef arrived and was grandly served. The *Margaux* was exquisite. He seriously thought he might have to order another bottle.

"Well," Kennedy continued, eyeing him clinically, after a lull during which both of them had silently immersed themselves in the food and wine of the gods. "You have to look on the bright side. I admit it was a tough assignment, but you came out the other side having helped clear up the mysterious goings-on at Minsham Court – and resolving some old questions you may have had from your own past."

He thought, furiously – clear up the mysterious goings-on at Minsham Court! What she really meant was put his own life on the line and act as a sort of sitting duck – or punch bag – for a variety of lunatics to work out their various agendas on. He was definitely now thinking about calling the waiter for another bottle of the *Margaux*.

"You were never straight with me on this one, Kennedy, were you? I accept that you knew nothing of the motives of Gerald Rissborough. Sending me down there, however, in the full knowledge there were prowlers on the loose at night, that was completely out of order!"

"Come on, Bartholomew… the previous incumbent had mentioned a few bumps and noises in the night, but I thought she was sensationalising to be honest. Just to secure a change of assignment, or get back up home to Yorkshire. You don't get it, do you? I told you at the outset. You were the man for the job. You moan like merry hell, but you're more robust than you think."

He couldn't even be bothered to answer. In the past, he'd never really felt inclined to let on to Kennedy about his army experiences, about what being 'robust' really entailed. She'd have just twisted the facts into her own particular version of the truth. Besides, he knew he'd never get to the bottom of what she knew before engaging his services for Minsham Court. Even if he hung her upside down by her dainty ankles from one of the Grill's fancy chandeliers. Indeed, on further reflection, the thought of that was mighty tempting. Perhaps he wouldn't waste his time on the questions first, either.

The pudding had arrived. Pineapple soufflé for him and a smart looking vanilla crème brulée for Kennedy. He decided he'd had enough of the *Margaux* and ordered a cold, Australian *Muscat*. Sipping the icy desert wine, letting the sweet flavours roll around his tongue, he instead asked a question that had been bugging him ever since he'd arrived at Minsham Court.

"So, Kennedy – who is the elusive Mr Eves? You can tell me now. I'm never going back there again, or ever likely to meet him."

She gave him that clever, superior look that always worried him. Finally, she answered:

"Look, Bartholomew, I don't see any reason why you shouldn't know now. You see, there isn't a Mr Eves. Or should I say... there are a lot of Mr Eveses."

"Eh?" replied Bartholomew, now really confused.

"You see, Minsham Court is owned by a consortium, not by one man. They operate all over the world, acquiring mainly property investments – both commercial and residential. They buy, improve and sell on – at a decent profit, of course. The consortium is worth many billions of pounds."

"So why do you call many men Mr Eves?"

"They like to remain anonymous. In their game and with the amount of money involved they want to remain as low profile as possible. For reasons of security – and, especially when their rivals will do anything to scupper them. Most of all though, with all the banker hate still going around, it's to keep out of the press – for obvious reasons."

Kennedy took a small gulp of the Muscat, and expanded further.

"The house doubled up as an investment, and – how can I put it? – *a convenient retreat,* which was within easy reach of London. Some of the consortium liked to take their wives there for a quiet, private break. A few, well, you know… took other women… or even other men… away from prying eyes. It worked well. They took it in turns, could all call themselves the same name, and it kept their real identities a secret. The locals probably wouldn't have noticed anyway, as the visits were sporadic and often only for a couple of days at a time. If the contract staff asked, or got a bit confused with the multiple Mr Eves, well, the consortium members would just say they were a guest of the owner."

So, he thought, it would have been business as usual for OCD to clear up after his romp with Roxy in the mirrored master suite. Jesus, she must have had the blue bed cover on permanent wash.

Bartholomew queried, "You said: It worked well. As if it was in the past?" She looked at him again, with something akin to smugness. He got the feeling he was playing in a metaphorical game of cards, with Kennedy about to play her trump.

"Well, Bartholomew. Now that the problems on the estate have been resolved, Minsham Court has a clean bill of health, so to speak. There will be no fire sale, as Gerald Rissborough had planned. Indeed, in the year the consortium has owned the property, prices have spiralled. It all fits in very nicely with their usual cycle of investment. So, they've decided to sell and the latest valuation is showing a handsome profit. Additionally, they are very pleased – or should I say impressed – with the Kennedy Agency, for sorting out all the niggling issues."

At this point Kennedy paused for a moment. She observed Bartholomew's face intently, almost voyeuristically, before smoothly adding:

"Actually, so much so that they've asked me to handle the sale for them."

The conniving b…! No wonder she hadn't blanched at the cost of the lunch, he realised, almost reeling back in the chair at the sleight of hand. Why, it would be a drop in the ocean compared to the commission she was going to earn for managing the disposal of Minsham Court. Over and above the fees charged for the house-sitting services. Or more accurately, the extremely dangerous, life threatening house-sitting services.

Bartholomew looked around furiously for a waiter, to see if he could get hold of the wine list again. Surely, they must have an ancient Napoleonic brandy in there somewhere. One of those rare 150 year-old cognacs that cost many thousands of pounds. Christ, he'd order them a bottle each.

Instead, he decided to leave. That was it. The straw that broke the camel's back. He pulled the napkin off his lap and slung it onto the table.

"Well, Kennedy, in the interests of good manners, thank you very much for the lunch. I can't say my employment with you has always been a pleasure. Frankly, we both know that would be a misrepresentation of the truth. But there is one good thing that's come out of it. It's at an end. Goodbye."

As he got to his feet, she looked up at him, almost amused.

"That's a shame, Bartholomew. And I thought we were getting along so famously. So much so that I'd already got another little assignment lined up for you. One that I thought would suit you down to the ground."

"No way, Kennedy," he replied, pushing his chair in under the table. "This is where we finally part. Adios."

He started to turn away. She shrugged her shoulders – and casually added:

"You went to Cambridge Poly, didn't you?"

He stopped and looked back at her, with a perplexed expression. "Yes. And?"

"Oh, nothing really. Never mind. Ok. Well, good luck for the future, Bartholomew. See you around sometime, maybe."

Kennedy picked up her glass of Muscat, sipped at it and looked blandly around the room.

"Why do you want to know whether I went to Cambridge Poly?" he asked again, not liking the question one bit, but somehow compelled to ask.

"Oh… sorry… you still here? Gosh, I'd thought you'd gone. Oh well, I suppose it's not important now as it's not going to happen anyway – but I've got a little job that needs doing up in Cambridge. Actually, it's in central Cambridge. It's a townhouse a client wants sitting for three months."

Cambridge Poly – bloody hell. He hadn't thought about the place in years. Of Pete, Cam, Roddy and all the others. Especially those euphoric drunken weeks in the first term when they'd all arrived and gone wild – for many of them their first time properly away from home. Rugby training on Parker's Piece, crazy nights in the Student Union bar, cavorting along the streets at midnight in stolen supermarket trolleys…

But then, the dark shadow of Bill crossed his mind. Bill, who they had all loved intensely. His free spirit acting like a shining beacon. His ancient, tiny car and the lifts to inter-college rugby matches, all of them jammed into the vehicle, singing at the tops of their voices. Then, suddenly, no more Bill. As if he had just gone up in a puff of smoke. There one day, gone the next. Not a problem at first, but when his parents turned up a week later asking where their son was, a big problem. An unsolved mystery, which, although they had all managed to move on, was one that hung over their crowd like a sad, guilty nag, deep at the back of their minds.

"Yes, I went to Cambridge Poly, Kennedy. But that was a long time ago. All in the past. Where it belongs."

He walked away, heading for the restaurant exit. He caught sight of Kennedy, back at the table, observing him in the mirrored façade of one of pillars. She was captivated – entranced almost – by the human experiment she was conducting. Watching to see if the puppet strings she had so adroitly pulled would result in the ending she desired.

Bartholomew shrugged his shoulders contemptuously, left the hotel and walked up to The Strand. He looked around for a minute or two and wondered about a stroll into Covent Garden, or perhaps down through Whitehall, to the river, and then back along the Embankment to the flat.

The flat. Empty, lifeless and soon to be an icebox again, once the money ran out. He wasn't going to go on benefits. He'd made that solemn promise to himself a long time ago.

It was almost as if he could physically sense his head go one way and his heart another. A moment later, he felt himself being carried along, slowly re-tracing his steps and then, dazedly, re-acknowledging the door man, before being ushered back into *The Savoy*.

Watch out for... the next in the 'The Reluctant House-Sitter Mysteries'

A smart Cambridge townhouse – occasional home to a distinguished French professor – sounds like a tailor-made assignment for *'bon viv'* Bartholomew, particularly as Cambridge Poly is his *alma mater*. But when his scheming boss Kennedy is involved it is always anything but straightforward. Cash-strapped as ever, Bartholomew must accept the job.

Life is quickly disrupted by visitors from old student days and the resurfacing of guilt surrounding the disappearance of their close friend, Bill. In typical style, Bartholomew retreats to the kitchen to lose himself in the concoction of his favourite gourmet dishes. With a raft of bolshy, eccentric and elusive neighbours to deal with plus the intrigue surrounding a valuable piece of garden art, it's set to be the usual rollercoaster of a ride for our reluctant house-sitter…

T.A.P. Woodard is the author of fictional novels and short stories. The Carob And Other Short Stories was published in 2015 followed by Balance, the first in 'The Reluctant House-Sitter Mysteries' featuring down-at-heel *bon viveur* Bartholomew.

The author spent much of his early childhood in Malaysia, Malta and Cyprus as the son of a serving RAF pilot prior to attending boarding school back in the UK. Before he finally settled down, he spent time backpacking in India and South East Asia. A career in the property business selling the houses of the rich, spoilt and sometimes famous in central London was followed by a stint in a rural surveying practice in Devon and latterly with various big guns in the telecoms industry.

More about the author and his works can be found on:

www.facebook.com/TAPWoodard

https://mobile.twitter.com/TAPWoodard1

Printed in Great Britain
by Amazon